P9-BZV-381

Late City

ALSO BY ROBERT OLEN BUTLER

The Alleys of Eden

Sun Dogs

Countrymen of Bones

On Distant Ground

Wabash

The Deuce

A Good Scent from a Strange Mountain

They Whisper

Tabloid Dreams

The Deep Green Sea

Mr. Spaceman

Fair Warning

Had a Good Time

From Where You Dream: The Process of Writing Fiction
(Janet Burroway, editor)

Severance

Intercourse

Hell

Weegee Stories

A Small Hotel

The Hot Country

The Star of Istanbul

The Empire of Night

Perfume River

Paris in the Dark

Late City

A Novel

Robert Olen Butler

Atlantic Monthly Press
New York

FIRST EDITION

Published simultaneously in Canada
Printed in the United States of America

First Grove Atlantic hardcover edition: September 2021

Library of Congress Cataloging-in-Publication data is available for this title.

ISBN 978-0-8021-5882-6
eISBN 978-0-8021-5883-3

Atlantic Monthly Press
an imprint of Grove Atlantic
154 West 14th Street
New York, NY 10011

Distributed by Publishers Group West

groveatlantic.com

21 22 23 24 10 9 8 7 6 5 4 3 2 1

For Spencer Wise

Late City

There's a copydesk in my brain, with a gooseneck lamp and a pot of rubber cement and a coffee mug full of Dixon pencils.

Let's edit this at once: Not precisely my brain. I am separated even from that, it seems. Ironically so, as I feel a clarity inside me now that I haven't felt for a long time.

The copy chief is at the desk as well, hunched there, composing a headline for the story that now is unfolding not in my brain but somewhere else. He hands it to me. Triple deck:

Mountebank Wins,
Editor-in-Chief
Begins to Die

I've been watching. For years I've been watching the television screen floating near the ceiling, beyond the foot of my bed. Tonight they thought I was asleep for good. Accompanied by a solitary figure in the darkened room, vague to me, sitting on a chair at my bedside. The screen lit before both of us has also just gone dark.

Where I lie, the time is a quarter to two in the morning on November 9, 2016.

But at this moment I am somewhere else.

My copydesk editor is having his little joke. Walter Mandel. From the *Chicago Independent*. Dead long ago, I know. Both man and newspaper. Though somehow I am not surprised that it's Walter who has turned his mare-gray eyes and his ocean-wave mustache toward me, the latter masking beneath its surface what I take to be a sly smile.

I look at the first sentence of the story: "Ten minutes after Donald J. Trump was declared president of the United States, the last living veteran of World War I began to die in a nursing home in Chicago, Illinois."

This I take to be true. The event on the television and the last living veteran of the Great War in his nursing home, certainly. That's me, or so I've been told, the last one. That's where I am. And that's what the United States of America has suddenly become. I have to believe the news hook as well. It's high time I began to die.

And another thing I believe is that I am about to hear the voice of God. I believe it with an instinctive assurance that is no doubt straight from Him.

"Samuel," He says in a mellifluous tenor voice.

For a moment I try to convince myself it's Walter. But it clearly is not. Walter has vanished. The voice has come from the dark.

But God apparently has taken Walter's chair at the copydesk. He edits that last thought of mine: "From the *dark matter*," He says.

This recent scoop about infinitesimal stuff teeming in the void has been lingering in the news, and in my mind. I say to God, "Does all that have something to do with you?"

"I have no comment," He says.

"I have no newspaper," I say.

He humphs. Gently. "I'm the interviewer for now," He says. "I want you to talk to me, Samuel. About your life. On the record."

"Can I ask another question first? Off the record?"

"Yes, you can."

"What the hell just happened?"

"You have begun to die," He says.

"I don't mean that," I say.

"Oh, you mean *him*," God says. "You tell me."

"Tell you what? I have no idea."

"Neither do I," He says. "But that's how I chose to make you humans. Full of surprises."

I feel a sudden draft from the dark. A sigh, I assume.

And then He says, "So talk to me, Sam. Who are you?"

This gives me pause. I've been expecting to die for quite a while. Since I turned a hundred, certainly. I was pushing 116 till a couple of minutes ago, which has for some time been daily surprising the hell out of me. But I haven't been particularly religious for many decades, in spite of spending plenty of this-nation-under-God time in pews as a boy, reading and retaining verses. But that passed soon enough. So at no time have I been expecting a Judgment Day, if that's what this is. "May I ask one more question?"

"Yes." This time the sigh is in His tone.

I pause ever so slightly.

"Yes, I'm omniscient," He says.

Which, indeed, is the answer to my most current question, the one that arose in me in that pause as soon as I asked the question about asking a question.

He says, "Now you can ask the previous one. The important one."

"Do I need to speak it?"

"Yes, you need to speak it. Not that it's strictly necessary. But it's part of the process. Trust me."

I feel the urge to chuckle.

"Go ahead and let it out," He says. "I'll share the irony with you."

I chuckle. *In God we trust.* Now the Man Himself feels He has to solicit my trust so I can tell Him my American story.

The Man Himself.

Man.

Another digressive question comes to mind.

"I'm gender fluid," He answers.

For a guy born in 1901, this was another difficult concept that had lately floated from the screen at the end of my bed. One I have struggled to understand.

"Look," God says, "don't concern yourself with pronouns. Think of me the way you need to think of me. Now ask your real question so we can get on with this."

"All right," I say. "Are there consequences?"

"To the telling of your life? No."

I wait for more. Nothing is forthcoming. No consequences to the *telling*. But how about to the life itself?

He reads my mind.

"Ambiguous?" He says. "Yes, I admit it. But you'll find I've always been ambiguous with humanity. You surprise *me*. I surprise *you*."

"It's your surprises I'm worried about," I say.

"I want you to tell me your own story. As it comes to you. Like brainstorming." God pauses. He edits Himself. "No, that will lead you astray. Think of it as *dream*storming."

That sounds like what I used to do as a young crime reporter in Chicago. Out by the lake or in a tenement or on a back path in Grant Park. At the crime scene. Before figuring out the lede and putting it all in logical sequence for the bulldog edition, I'd fill my notebooks with the bloodstains or the weeping in the corner or the oblivious wind in the trees. The stuff that felt like how it all really was, and like the story I was going to write was true enough but artificial somehow.

"You were a good newsman," God says. "Just tell it to me straight from your notebook. But I will give you this much guidance. A commandment, if you will, which you all are always so eager to get from me. I want you to live your stories just as they felt in their own moment, with the next day's news yet to happen. Given that, don't be surprised if your memory consistently fails you about how things turn out. You will inhabit your past as you lived it, without knowing the future that will come of it. And until you and I are nearly finished, you may not recall the outcomes even as you lie here having already lived it all. So I'm giving you a commandment to be patient."

God falls silent.

I accept all that. It sounds familiar. God runs the show. His creatures set their own agendas. Especially under the present circumstances, however, I hanker for a little direction from Him.

And God says, "You want a commencing direction, Sam? Okay. See your *earthly* father . . . Start with *him*."

So I try.

I find a time gone by. A century gone.

But I'm not looking at Papa's face, though I'm walking beside him, right enough. We've just stepped out of the general store and turned north on the wood-plank sidewalk that runs along the main street parallel to the river. He has made it a point to take me for what he calls a sweets run, him being under instructions from Mama, who is doing up jams and running out of sugar and needing cane, not beet, for land's sake. So we each have a kraft bag, he with ten pounds of cane sugar, and I with Necco wafers and sorghum drops.

This is the town of Lake Providence, the parish of East Carroll, the state of Louisiana. I'm not looking up at Papa but at a chestnut horse hitched at a post along the way. He's fluttering his nostrils in my direction, making the sound of a whopping-big cat purring like he knows me, which he does.

The sun is halfway down from noon and it's hot, and on this particular day the farthest I've been from Lake Providence is the forests of oak and gum and pecan west of town along the St. Louis, Iron Mountain & Southern Railway track, and sometimes I've been with Papa on the oxbow lake, also called Providence, the place full of cypress stumps that I always fancy to be steeple caps of wizards waiting to rise from the water one of these days. Rise and do what, I'm never sure. And sometimes I have climbed to the crown of the levee and stood to watch the Mississippi flowing wide and muddy from way up north and on past to New Orleans and into the Gulf, and already I'm starting to think about leaving.

I turn my eyes from the river to the dark where God is lurking.

"You're not looking at him," God says.

He's right.

I return to Lake Providence.

We're still treading the planks and I give my father an upward glance, past his shoulder, ready to find his eyes. But he seems intent on something up ahead. So I turn to the horse who knows me, and he stops his purring as I pass and gives me a snort. I think to address him, to ask him if he's God standing there in this memory of more than a hundred years ago trying to keep me on track.

But it's Papa who does that now—keeps me on track—by slowing and letting his free hand fall gently on my shoulder to hold me fully beside him, and I look ahead to see what he sees.

A man and a boy are walking toward us, filling the navigable center of the sidewalk. They're still a little ways away, but I know why it's an issue. It's Louisiana and it's 1908 and they are colored. A father and son in patched-all-over overalls. The boy is about my age, about my size, a milk jug for filling in his hand. His eyes are fixed on the spot on the sidewalk where he will step next, and I look to his papa. He's got a brace of mink skins over a shoulder and his eyes are just now moving from my father's to mine, very briefly, and then back to Papa's.

The colored man and his son keep on coming this way.

Papa stops and I stop.

I look up at him. He's focused straight ahead, but I can imagine the double crease that has just appeared on his brow, between his eyes. That crease, when directed at me, always gets my full and fearful attention. And it is about to have the same effect on this man and his boy. Or so I assume at the time, that it's my papa's severe expression that commands what happens next.

The father also slows and his restraining hand falls to his son's shoulder, gently, and even at the time when this is all going on, long ago, I am struck by how these two papas have done that same gentle thing to their sons, just the same. His father's touch brings the colored boy's eyes up and straight to mine.

I give him a look and he gives me a look and it's like we recognize what creatures we each are and what our fathers need to negotiate, but also that there is nothing he and I could ever put into this look between us other than: *Well, I do recognize you, generally speaking, and sure enough, there you are.* Only that.

We all four of us are dead stopped now.

My papa lets this be for one breath, and another, and the colored papa is doing the same.

Then mine says, "You're a trapper, I see."

"That I am, boss," the colored papa says, and that last word does not come out of him like he's being submissive. But not sneering either. More like familiar, casual.

My father says, "You a new fellow in Lake Providence?"

"New to your eyes, maybe," he says. "I don't of a usual walk this street, but I am just looking to make a simple trade at the store for some basics."

"That's it then. You're new to the street." And with a serious, slow dip in his voice, he somehow makes it clear he's *not* saying, *That's why you're new to my eyes*, but rather he's saying, *Then to get through this situation without a big fuss, let's just assume you don't yet realize that you and your boy are to yield the way to the whites in Lake Providence, Louisiana.*

I can tell the colored father knows what Papa is really saying because he turns his face from us and looks down at his son, and he does this slow and keeping quiet, and you know he's sad for his son to be facing this situation and he's wondering how to teach him the rules of Lake Providence, Louisiana, in 1908 without losing his own dignity or putting a crack in his son's spirit, choices that colored fathers might rightly have expected to cease being necessary forty-some years ago. Before this particular colored father was even ever born.

But the boy is looking at me and seems oblivious. And I'm looking at him and probably seeming just as oblivious. Which is probably what I am. At the time, I didn't know all this nuance was going on. I guess that's a thing God is letting me understand now in the retelling of it as I die.

And the colored father says, "Boy, slide off this here planking so these folks can find their way on by."

I feel my father tense up just a little. How this man put it to his son is the reason. What was clear underneath those words.

Boundaries being set to the spirit of what they were doing. Boundaries set by a colored man. That is evident to me now. So Papa is tensed up. He's got cane sugar and I've got a bag of penny candy and he's got his views, but for whatever else I'm picking up about my father, I see those views of his have their own boundaries. He doesn't make a fuss. He just stays tense while he waits for the colored man and the colored boy to slide on off the sidewalk.

Which they do.

And they collect themselves out in the street.

And they spectate as we move on by.

My papa waits till we are out of earshot to break the silence between us. "These ones born since all the trouble are incubator chickens. Raised without a mama to tell them who or where they are. Specially these trapper boys. All they have to measure themselves by are trees and animals."

And he says no more till we are approaching our house and the road beneath our feet is dirt and he stops us. He nods for me to hold my ground as he takes my bag of penny candy and steps away, and he puts it over on the verge of grass and sets his bag of sugar next to it. Then he takes up a water oak switch off the ground and heads for me and I worry.

But no. Surely no. The thing in his hand is stiffer than a switch. A thing meant for a true beating. Beatings that have persuaded me in the past. Persuaded me that I earned them because I came to accurately know when to expect them. And I know that today, so far, I have not earned a stiff-wood beating.

He stops before me.

He says, "Now, boy, listen close. First let me make something clear. Have you ever heard me speak of those breed of folks by using a slang word?"

"No, sir, I have not." Though it is also true I clearly know what breed of folks he's referring to.

"Nor will you ever. Nor have I allowed *you* to use slang words about them."

This is true. I nod in affirmation.

"They are *coloreds*," my papa says. "This is a simple fact. Like we are whites. All of us are made by God in these bodies, as Henry is made in his body, as Whimsy is made in hers, as a mountain lion is in his and a deer buck in his and a wolf. You understand?"

"Yessir," I say. Henry being our dog. Whimsy our sometimes cat, feral but ours at her whim. I have heard all this before from my father. But this is his way. What someday, as a cub reporter in Chicago, I will learn to put at the bottom of stories—the background from previous stories—my father has a habit of putting before the lede.

For which I wait.

He lifts the stick.

I struggle not to flinch.

He turns his back to me.

I am, as I suspected, off the hook.

I can see he is stretching out his stick hand before him and touching it down. And then he moves his whole body to the right, starting to walk around me, drawing in the dirt as he goes.

He returns to where he began and stands at my side.

My papa and I are in the center of a circle.

"We got no choice in this life," he says. "We are here to figure out one thing. Who are we? Where do we belong? There has to be a circle around us. Because we ain't everywhere. And we ain't everybody. We all understand that, deep down. Sometimes who's in that circle with you is clearly for the best. Sometimes it's regrettable. But you have to figure out where it must be drawn."

And he stops talking. He tosses the stick outside of the circle.

We just stand there. I'm expected to ponder.

I do ponder. But at the time, as a boy, I'm just calculating: once that circle became what it was, the stick went out. So what about my bag of penny candy sitting over on the grass? It ain't where I am. It ain't me. Have I lost it?

And Papa asks, "You understand?"

I feel him looking down at me.

I do not look up.

Whatever I've been picking up on through this whole thing and whatever I've not, whatever I'm not understanding then and whatever I will not fully understand—if at all—even all these years later, I do recognize what I need to say at that moment. So I say it. "Yessir. Yes, sir. I understand."

But I say it with my eyes averted from him, as if speaking to the circle in the dirt.

I was a stupid boy.

I may be a stupid old man.

I have still not looked into my father's face. A realization that turns me to the dark.

I wait for a rebuke from God. I almost say, *Am I reading* your *mind now?* Almost. I do not.

But God replies nevertheless. "There've been legions who believed they could do that." He pauses. Makes a vocalized snicking sound—weary disapproval. Then: "But at least in this case . . ."

"You've told me twice already," I say.

". . . you read my mind," He says, oozing the words to make their sarcasm clear.

I turn to my father.

We stand at the edge of a clearing in the woods south of the lake. I am lowering my boyhood rifle from my shoulder, a Winchester '90. Twenty-two caliber, for me to kill anything small we happen upon. My father is beside me. I sense him there. But all I see of him, out of the corner of my eye, is the barrel of his own Winchester, dipped downward. A Model 1894 Special. Thirty-two caliber, to kill anything big. We have the killing covered. A fine circle around the two of us, to my boy's mind.

I will look into his eyes now, as I have indeed just killed something. Of course I will look. Their gaze in this moment is what I have killed for.

I turn to him.

He turns to me.

I have my father's eyes, my mother says. The same dark blue. Gun-barrel blue.

Those eyes of his hold fast upon mine.

And I find myself seeing something in them. And I find myself believing it. A fierceness. But a tenderness as well. How do I see those contradictory things? Things that are abstract to speak of but are, in fact, minutely, complexly of the senses? Somehow. Somehow I do. There is something in the shaping of them or the casting outward of an internal light or a latent weltering in their depths, things manifest to see but unnamable, that say, *You are my son and you have done good.* That say, *You have encountered a small living thing of flesh and bone and blood and fur or feather, a small thing unable to do you or me any harm, and perhaps we will eat it but that isn't really necessary; you have encountered this creature and because you understand that you are stronger than it is and that you have this weapon, you therefore have mortal dominion over it; and so you have shattered its body and taken away its life, which affirms who you are, and I am proud of you for that, my son, for that I love you.*

"Oh, fuck."

I say this aloud.

But not to my papa, who vanishes with those two words.

"'Oh, fuck' you say?" God's voice.

I look in His direction.

"Sorry," I say, diverted now to the matter of my profanity before the Creator, curse words being a habit I acquired in my seventies.

"Oh please," God says. "Who do you take me for? Profanity has nothing to do with words. Talk to me about your fucking heart."

And I am standing on the levee. I am still a boy.

The river flows before me, familiar as my coonhound.

I must have come here to cast my mind once more upon the current and glide away.

And I realize someone is nearby.

I turn. He is turning to me as well.

The colored boy from the sidewalk.

He rolls his shoulders. Like the levee has no rules of race.

I agree.

I nod at him to say so.

He hesitates.

He nods in return.

"You got a name?" I ask.

"Course I do," he says.

We let that be for a few moments.

"So do I," I say.

He humphs.

The boy has his daddy's spirit, I think. My own daddy would not like that. Papa would expect me to walk on away from this boy. Or maybe more likely expect me to tell him to go.

But I say, "Ain't seen you here."

"Likewise," he says.

I may even have gone hunting with Papa since me and this boy confronted each other with our fathers. Maybe even gone hunting and Papa gave me that look I will remember someday as I'm dying. Anyway, I think to say to this colored boy, "You go hunting with your pa, do you?"

The colored boy says, "If you mean them skins, he trap 'em."

"I know you don't shoot a mink," I say. "Hurts the pelt."

The boy nods.

We fall silent.

Then he asks, "You go trapping with your pappy, do you?"

"We just shoot things," I say.

We don't speak for another few moments. The boy seems to be contemplating me and the situation. He reminds me of how his papa was, in town. In the way of thinking carefully about what's next while standing at the edge of a circle drawn around white people.

Then this boy says, "Cyrus Dobbs."

He has done some thinking that I didn't rightly expect, and it takes me a moment to catch up. His name.

"Cyrus Dobbs," I say.

"Cyrus been given me, but Dobbs was a name we got from the man owned my granddaddy. Not rightly our name, seems to me."

"Then what is?"

"Don't have a clue."

"Sam," I say. "That's mine. Sam Cunningham."

Another silence, and I am thinking how no one owned my granddaddy. This boy Cyrus is probably thinking the same thing about me. Which makes the silence drag on out. Makes it hard to have anything else to say, seeing as how things are.

Hard to tell how I'm picking up on what we've both been mulling over. Same way I read my daddy's face in the woods, maybe. But I know. And I know Cyrus Dobbs knows.

We both turn back to the river. Then I am on to my own thoughts. How my granddaddy was sure enough owned by somebody, for a few years at least. The Confederate army owned him body, brain, and soul.

Eventually my mind comes back to the colored boy. I wonder if he is up here on the levee thinking like me on one other matter: getting away someday from Lake Providence. So I turn to look at him again and his back is to me and he is already fifty yards or so on along the levee, heading off with a firm stride.

The light on the levee fades now with that colored boy's leaving and it vanishes and I am in the dark again, though God doesn't pipe up right away. And I think, more than a century later: *They owned him for more than a few years. The Confederate army owned my granddaddy from the war onward, to his dying day.*

"Do you remember my granddaddy?" I ask in the direction of God.

No answer.

I keep asking. "When he stood or lay or stomped around before you, pissed as hell about the act of dying not being what he expected?"

Nothing.

"Do you remember him? Ezra Theophilus Cunningham?"

"I remember them all," God says in a weary voice.

"Dare I ask?" Meaning Heaven or Hell for Granddaddy.

"No," God says.

"I'm not surprised," I say, taking this to be an answer.

"Don't jump to any conclusions," God says. "Has any of this so far gone the way you thought it would?"

Then a cloud. A seething cloud. My mother's form dark within. With light pouring from a window. Our kitchen in Lake

Providence. Her back to me. Steam, I suppose, from pots on the cast-iron stove, where she stands. I think of the sugar Papa and I sought, the jams she was making, but that's simply me trying to impose my sense of order on these visions, a continuity, and I know that's a mistake. There seems to be so much steam and she is large within its cloud. I am very small. This is another time. Earlier. Through my child's eyes.

I watch her. I wait. She does not turn. She seems unaware of me. Her shoulders move at her work. Her hands are out of my sight, before her.

And a rushing now. From behind me and past me, a vast dark form striding into the cloud. My father. His back eclipses hers and his voice bellows. I can't make out the words, but I know their meaning. My mother has offended.

And now it is night.

I am alone in my room and his voice again, down the hall. And my mother's voice beneath, making a sound I sometimes hear from my own mouth. And I wonder, *Does he have a stiff-wood branch in his hand? For her as well?* I sit up in my bed. I think to rise, to go to see. At least to my doorway. To what end? He has rightful dominion over us both. Instead I lie back, I shroud my head with the sheet.

And I am in this bed another time and my head is uncovered and it is fiercely full of fire, and the muscles, the sinews, the very bones of my body, are minced fine with pain and my mother's hand is on my cheek and then on my forehead, and now her hand is upon my chest and spreads a quickly expanding chill there, and the chill rises into my nose—menthol and eucalyptus—my head fills with the cold flame of Vick's Croup and Pneumonia Salve.

"There," she says, low, almost a whisper, leaning close, a secret. "Good Doctor Vick goes across the ocean to Japan just for you, for a special mint leaf. Does it feel nice?"

"Yes, Mama," I whisper in return.

"It will help you," she says.

"Am I going to die?" I ask her.

Her hand ceases its rubbing. But it stays where it has ceased, in the center of my chest. She is collecting herself. She is waiting until she can answer without weeping, without letting even a hint of tears taint her words. And finally she says, "No, my darling. You will live to be an old, old man."

Even as a child I quailed at her hesitation. I knew she was afraid for me. Perhaps that hand on my chest was feeling my heart, was waiting for it to stop.

What am I looking at through all this? Not her face. Vaguely the room, a low lamp she has placed on a dresser, lighting a patch of the far wall, a corner of the ceiling. I try now to turn my eyes to see hers. But I cannot move my eyes away from a meaningless patch of light.

Still I try. In vain. Until what I see is only darkness.

"Help me," I say into the dark, assuming God is there.

He does not answer.

The darkness persists.

I say, "I want to see my mother's eyes."

Nothing from God.

"Hey," I say. "You were pushing me about Papa's eyes."

And God says, "You creatures there below never were very good at figuring out divine plans. Even small ones."

I feel myself dumbly staring into the dark.

"This you want for yourself," He says, like He's telling me something I should already know.

I'm still feeling dumb.

He says, "So?"

Okay. Okay. It's up to me.

I close my eyes.

I open them.

I'm standing at the kitchen window. She's crouched on the ground outside, beside a cast-iron kettle. She's facing me but her kerchiefed head is down. She's dry-plucking mallards. Her hands are moving quick but gentle. The feathers are going into the kettle. The dead birds, adorned as they were in life, are piled on one side of her. The plucked birds are on the other. The air around her is filling with woolly down and she is focused on this work of her hands, her assigned role in our hunt.

Lift your head, Mama. Look up, Mama. See me at the window.

She does not.

I wait.

And the fog is thickening and Mama fades within it and I still have not seen her eyes.

It's been a hundred years. More. But it's my mama. I can't have forgotten them.

"It's you holding her away from me," I say to God, even though the fog of feather down is still before me, too dense now even to make out her shape.

I turn my face from the window, to my mother's stove again, in this little dream. Surely all of this is a dream. But no. It's just me dying. And it's Mama's stove. Cold now. Empty. She's in the yard plucking fucking ducks and I can't see her.

Of course not. Of course not. I was a little boy. I loved my mother and she did her work. A mother's work. She pressed away my fever with her hand. She put her hand on my chest to save my life. She whispered to me when that's what I needed. But that was all temporary. Surely I had to become a man. I became a man. Surely that line was already drawn around me.

I look back through the window.

And my father is standing there.

My mother is gone.

My father's eyes are upon me.

But they are not fierce.

It is my papa, waiting calmly for me to come join him.

Which is what I want. In this boy's body, standing in our kitchen a century ago, this is what I want. I want a papa. And this man is my papa. My only papa. I want to be his boy, want to be his big boy, want to be his son. I want to be loved by my papa, want to be a good boy in his eyes, want to be a fine young man. I want to be fit to be his son. I want to earn another day without a beating. Because the beatings when they come are my own fault. That much I have learned even if I haven't learned how to avoid them.

And now Papa is gone.

The yard is empty.

Then the yard is gone.

And the room is dark. My room at the nursing home. But the door is open, and the night corridor lighting has moved in like ground fog, bearing loud talk from down the hall. The voices of people I am familiar with.

I sit up in my bed.

Have I stopped dying?

I find myself standing in the open doorway. Suddenly. Unsupported. I'm still dying, I suppose.

A reasonable supposition, as I am now standing in the corridor a couple of steps short of the front desk. The clock on the wall behind the desk says it's nearing 2:00. I have not focused on the words roiling before me, but I hear enough to know the subject. The new president of the United States has lately been declared. It is once again—or perhaps still—the moment, according to the story in the *Chicago Independent*, that I first began to die.

Behind the desk is Nurse Bocage, a tall Black Creole woman, an immigrant from my once home state, her hair lately done into cornrows with a bun at the back. At this moment she is taller seeming than usual, as she has drawn herself fiercely upright.

Facing off with her, at the other side of the desk but staying beyond her reach, is Duke, the guy from maintenance, a welterweight white man with cauliflower ears.

I do not understand his being here at this hour. Perhaps something has broken down. From Nurse Bocage's point of view, of course, something has. From Duke's point of view, the Maintenance Man in Chief has arrived.

These two are slugging it out with combos and flurries of words, slippings and bobbings and clinchings of words. *Swamps* and *great agains*; *morons* and *racists*. I do not allow the words to shape into actual sentences in my head. The voices pound on as mere sound, a thing I find I can manage as I stand unseen among them. A privilege of dying, I assume.

And a nurse assistant called Peaches, of her own special in-between color, is leaning on the desk just beyond Nurse Bocage. She always has a soothing voice for an old man's ear but carries it in a body with a man's wide shoulders and thick arms, looking like she could go ten rounds with Duke and give him all he can handle.

And there's one other figure. A tall, slender man standing in the center of the common room beyond the desk. I see him in profile as he watches the muted television. He has a sizable bun of hair at the back of his head, like a woman, like Nurse Bocage. A man clearly of color, though somewhat mutedly so, someone the likes of whom my mother preferred to call "high tan." He's dressed in the home's pale blue scrubs. Nurse Bocage's new licensed practical nurse, no doubt, her last LPN a woman having gone off to take care of children at the Shriners Hospital.

Abruptly the words cease.

But I'm still standing near these people.

Head nurse and maintenance man—Black woman and white man—are staring at each other as if waiting for one of them to step off the sidewalk and let the other pass.

And Nurse Bocage says, low, almost to herself, "I suppose I shouldn't be surprised. But Mother of God. How did we come to this?"

Duke opens his mouth, but before a sound can emerge, she says, "Do *not* attempt to answer that question."

Duke snaps his head in my direction, as if it were me who'd told him to shut up. I think for a moment that he sees me. But his eyes don't register my presence. I am invisible to him, to all of them. Duke's mouth has crimped tight. He's looking inward, where he's fuming.

And I am in my bed, in the dark.

I ask, aloud, "So am I dead now? Am I a ghost? Returned to the crypt after a little foray into the flow of time I'm no longer part of?"

"No. No. And no," God says. "Respectively. You floated off on your own."

"On my own?"

"It's what's next in the tale of your life, is it not? Striking off on your own? Away from the papa whose worthy boy you ached in vain to be?"

"Yes," I say. "And yes." Then I snag on that last one for a moment. But: "Yes," I say. "Respectively."

Then we wait, God and I. He for what is next, no doubt. I to pause for the passing wish that I could just die and get it over with. But that is the wish of either a man who expects streets of gold or a man who expects final comfort in simple oblivion. I am neither such man.

I am a newsman. Even now. Though I am having trouble recovering my surest newsman instincts when it comes to the story of my American life. But I was a nascent newsman even when I was first ready to strike out on my own. And Papa was a banker. The Planters & Merchants Bank of Lake Providence. He was a smart banker and he recognized the need for news. So we always had a newspaper on subscription through our postmaster, a real daily up from New Orleans. I spent a childhood reading the daily newspaper as if it were my Brothers Grimm or tales from Oz.

I am sprawled on the front-room floor with a newspaper before me and it's all mine now, Papa having read it and folded it in half and placed it in my hands with a nod. It's the *Times-Picayune* and I'm thirteen years old and it's April 1914 and I've read it all, every story, every advertisement, every want ad, not yet dreaming that this would become my life, the making of a daily newspaper, but I'm seeing it all through those young eyes, between childhood and manhood, seeing both ways at the same time, as a recent boy, as a nascent man.

And now I become self-conscious as I inhabit that boy-man lying on his father's hardwood floor, still three months away from the start of the Great War. I know I will dote on headlines throughout my boyhood, and so the pages of the *Times-Picayune* riffle forward and back and forward again.

Army of Invasion Sails To-Day for Mexico *Funston Commands Infantry Brigade Sent to Vera Cruz*, and the American oil fields of Mexico are made secure and **Colquitt Orders Militia to Border** but the anti-American Mexican president, General Huerta—how unlike our Princeton professor of a president he is!—is quaking in his boots, and Jeff has the comic strip to himself and has cast off his top hat and is dressing up as a bluejacket to go off to war, till Mutt shouts in from the other room that the Mexican sharpshooters are picking off the American troops from the housetops of Vera Cruz and Jeff dumps his uniform in the trash, and **President Resents Negro's Criticism** *Refuses to Be Cross-Questioned About Racial Segregation in Government Offices*, Wilson enforcing anew the policy of segregation in the Capitol "for the comfort and best interests of both races" and my papa is pleased with his man Wilson on both actions, and **Hair Fell Out by Handfuls** but after the prolonged, sleepless, scalp-itchy assault of baldness *Cuticura Soap Healed All*—I will discreetly fold the paper to highlight this ad for Papa to cure the horse's hoof-print of hair on the top of his head—and Christy Mathewson twirls a two-hitter to beat the Brooklyn Superbas, and appearing at the Orpheum Theater are the **Dancing Girls of Delhi** who will dance in my head, vague but alluring, for days, and **Wilson Refuses Women's Plea for Aid in Struggle** asserting that his refusal was final as the issue had not been addressed in the Democratic Party platform when he was nominated two years ago, and on the Latest Shipping and River News page is the ad for **Cunard Fastest Steamers in the World** with a photo of the S.S. *Lusitania*, its four stacks pluming coal smoke, and for months the ship will race through my head, precise and thrilling, and **3,000,000 Have Left Russia to Come Here** most of them in the last seven years, and **Many Mexican Refugees Visited the Maison Blanche Yesterday** the Canal Street department store stressing in a newsy advertisement that it *welcomed the refugees gladly* and would provide *clothing or other things* and the ad headlines its way immediately onward with the declaration that *Of No Less Interest Is the Display of Summer Dresses* with an accompanying line drawing of a beautiful woman standing in profile, hair in a pompadour, wearing a summer dress of frills and ruffles and insertions, a woman who would also provide fuel for heated thought for a long while, and down Canal Street is the chance to **Show Your Colors** *a Large Stock and Complete Assortment of United States Flags Sold at Reasonable Prices*, and a Mississippi man retrieves his fourteen-year-old bride who ran away with a traveling carnival show and a Mexican refugee is murdered in the Quarter and a Negro is lynched and another is lashed as **Friends of Postal Clerk Use Force to Instill Respect for White Woman**, and Mutt in the final panel of the day's cartoon punches Jeff in the eye—in a frequent running gag of a climax—leaving his friend on the floor with stars circling his head, and this episode of Mutt and Jeff brings me back to the recent episode from which I now extract another thing to dwell on, which I do, off and on, for many months, the news of Mexican sharpshooters attacking our American invaders from housetops, and I have already won my papa's rare and precious praise for my shooting skills, and I begin to imagine myself wearing the bluejacket of an American marine and rushing up to a rooftop in Vera Cruz with my Winchester Model 1894 Special and one by one methodically killing all the Mexican sharpshooters who would oppose our country's fighting men.

And that nurtured fantasy begins to inform my solitary climbs to the top of the levee to think my usual thoughts up there, until three years later, almost to the day, these headlines: **Wilson Calls Country to Arms by Signing War Bill**. After keeping us out of the Great War for all that time, President

Woodrow Wilson and the U.S. Congress finally declare war on the Imperial German Government. And elsewhere on the front page: **First Call to Be for 500,000 Men Between 19 and 25**.

On the day we decide to go after the Huns, I am sixteen years, two months, and five days old. But I have lately grown to be a strapping young man and I am mostly aware of it—even as my mama strokes my brow the next morning at the breakfast table and calls me her baby—but strapping enough. That very afternoon my papa has gotten him a whipping switch for some damn reason and he is coming up to me out under the water oak in the front yard, and though my back is turned I can hear him rushing my way and cursing and I turn and I stand straight, as I have done for a year or so now when this still occasionally happens, and he stops and we are staring at each other, eyes to eyes, him not looking down and me not looking up. And it's like that moment early every spring when you realize, at the end of the day, that the sun is still up while your winter mind expects it to be dark already, and though the sunlight has been lingering a few seconds longer each day for months, you realize the change all at once. It's the same with this. After our whole life together so far, on this particular occasion of our being father and son in this particular way, we look each other in the eyes and pause. For a moment. For a thought. And he throws down the switch. And he says, "I've done all I can do for you, boy. You are what you are."

And in response I stand taller. And I keep an impassive face. Not because I've been ready on my own to stay his hand and fistfight my father under the water oak. But because what I am is his young man. What I am is fit to be his son.

That's what I tell myself.

Even though a part of my mind hears the exasperated, terminal disgust beneath his words.

Be that as it may, he also recognizes that I am becoming a man. And that's something considerable from him, it seems to me at the moment.

So a couple of weeks later, when I know what I want to do, I think for a little while about sneaking around and putting a few things together in Granddaddy's knapsack from his war, which is tucked up in a corner of our attic. They're sending recruiters out to the parish seats and I figure they aren't looking too close at the men standing before them, since they need half a million right away and a million in a year. I can't get away with anything in Lake Providence, but I can walk six hours to Oak Grove in West Carroll Parish and maybe I can lie my way in.

School is out and it's a Monday morning. Papa has gone off to the bank and Mama is doing laundry and I am sitting on the overstuffed chair in the dimmest corner of our front room, planning. I can pull things together and spend some time with Mama and still be in Oak Grove by nightfall. The weather has turned warm and clear, and I can find a place in the woods to sleep a few hours and be in the army by noon tomorrow.

A list of what I need starts assembling itself in my head, and it's not that much. A change of shirt and pants. A light camping blanket. My toothbrush, which occurs to me in order to please Mama, and maybe that's what leads me to an ignorant thought: *They'll have a uniform for me, but do I need to bring my Winchester?*

No.

That's the thought of a boy. The American army will have a swell rifle for its sons. And I curse the naive boy lingering in me. Which leads me to Papa and our recent confrontation in the front yard: I'm becoming a *man* now. I'm clearheaded enough to realize he didn't put it that way. But I still pause and say to myself, *He meant as much. He just wasn't going to give me the pleasure of the word.*

And I put a stop on my list-making for the moment. There's another thing to decide: Should I tell Papa beforehand? I just won't tell him my plan. I'll just tell him right out that I'm going to do it. Something makes me want that. Makes me want to see his face. He can't stop me going. Even if he forbids me. Even if he tries to whip me for thinking of it. I can fight him then. Or take the beating one last time. Either way. Because from then on he can't watch me every day, every night. If I have to walk away from Lake Providence in the middle of the night with only the clothes on my back, I'll do that. I'll just vanish.

So I stay where I am.

I let myself climb a tree in France and look out over a battlefield with my rifle and methodically kill all the German sharpshooters across no-man's-land, one by one.

All morning long I kill them, and all afternoon, and I am waiting in the overstuffed chair when Papa comes home from the bank.

He opens the door and steps in, and I stand up in the shadows and I say, firm and clear, "Papa."

He starts. Just a little. But enough in the shoulders that I can see it. Not expecting me to be waiting. Not expecting a man's tone in my voice, maybe.

He turns to me.

"Papa," I say. "Sit with me for a time. I have something to say."

He does not make a move. Not to go on. Not to come to me. Not even to square around to face me from the pose he has struck at my calling him out.

This is not going to be easy.

"Please, sir," I say, the *sir* a thing he often expects.

Something releases in him. He turns to me. He crosses to me. He places his business satchel on the nearby divan. But he isn't going to sit at my beckoning while I'm still standing. I want this to seem merely to be a little chat. It's better we sit. So I sit first, on the chair.

He lingers above me, just to clarify things between us. Then he sits on the divan.

But he does not settle in. This is no little chat for him. He is sitting stiff-backed at the front edge of the seat.

I need to be straight with myself about this. I try: In the couple of weeks since our final whipping-switch confrontation he has said nothing to undo his declaration. That I am fit now to be his adult son.

But no. Straighter still: He's said nothing to undo *my interpretation* of his declaration. What he openly, verifiably said was far less than that.

So I find myself ready for him to take it all back.

I tell myself again: *It makes no difference. I can still walk away.*

"Papa," I say, in a tone that surprises even me as I hear it. Surprises and dismays. A small voice. A beseeching voice. I am a boy again. I am still a boy.

I clear my throat.

"Papa," I say once more. Quietly. But as if I have a deep conviction. "I want to go to war."

That needs revision. I say, "I *intend* to go to war." And then, so there's no misunderstanding: "Right away."

We look at each other in silence for a few moments.

His back is to the window. The twilight is upon us. He is in shadow. I cannot read his face.

I am braced for a declaration: *You're just a boy.*

But he says, "And how do you propose to do that?"

His tone is not that I am young but that I am stupidly without a viable plan.

I say, "They need a lot of men fast. They need men who can shoot. I may not be what they're calling a man—not by my years—but I can shoot. And maybe I can pass for a man with a confident lie."

I say that and I wait.

Let him get it over with: *You are no kind of man. Not yet. You may not properly ever be. But you are surely no man at all by any of the standards of the United States Army. Just go off and help your mama in the kitchen.*

But he's not saying this or anything else. He's just looking at me.

I wish mightily that I could read his face right now. Read his eyes.

God knows I do.

But I can't. He makes me wait a little longer for what I know is coming.

And then he says, "What possible kind of lie? They know you in this town."

"I am fixing to walk to Oak Grove." I make sure to say this before he can get the how-stupid-can-you-be objection out of his mouth.

And he nods. Once. A nod of assent.

I say, "If I wait to be nineteen, the war will be over. If my country needs its boys to go do some hunting, you taught me how to do that and I don't want to waste the lessons."

My papa laughs. One syllable's worth. A single bark of a laugh. And he says, "Damn right I taught you. You don't need to go walking to Oak Grove. I know the man they've sent to us. I'll make sure he lets you in."

And that is that.

My papa rises and picks up his satchel.

But before he continues on into his Monday evening, he squares around and stands over me and he says, "These animals shoot back."

"It's about time," I say.

"They'll have their hands full," he says, and he turns and moves off.

And I am left with tears welling in my eyes as if I were a pathetically grateful little boy.

Which brings me back to the dark, where one of those tears—just one of them—presses onward and then down my cheek.

"Do I still have tears to shed?" I ask.

"He was your father," God says.

"Which one of him?"

"All of him," God says.

"Don't be fooled," I say, lifting my hand to wipe the tear away and finding my cheek to be dry. "I was still glad to go."

"Were you glad that you went?"

"Away?"

"To war."

I hear a trap of a question, given the present circumstances. It pisses me off. I say, "You personally sanctioned a lot of those."

"So I've heard," God says.

"Didn't you? Come on. The peoples of where? I knew the list once. Proudly. Jericho and Makkedah. Libnah and Hebron. Bashan and Midian. To name a few. Fuel for a fine little American boy's under-God imagination. Your boys Moses and Joshua and David did a thorough job of those folks. How'd the verse go in Joshua's book? 'And they utterly destroyed all that was in the city, both man and woman, young and old, and ox, and sheep, and ass, with the edge of the sword.' But wait. Midian went off your plan. Didn't your man Moses get pissed with his captains at Midian for sparing the women and children? He dutifully fixed that. Mostly. He just had them kill the kids and the mothers. He showed his compassion for his captains by sparing the virgins for their own use. Were you proud of him for that? Or peeved?"

With that I find myself empty of words.

I'm getting only silence from the dark.

Maybe this is the end of the whole process for me. It's time for Hell or oblivion.

So I take a long, slow breath—if it's even still breathing that I'm doing—and I try to shape an apology in my head for God to pick up on, but I get stuck on the King James. Not as the Word of God. As a book. As stories. As the written word, which has been my life from a childhood of ravenous reading onward, where the Bible became for me simply the fifty-second volume of Papa's Five-Foot Shelf of Harvard Classics.

I think, *So be it. Hell it will be.*

Then in a tone of voice that reminds me of Papa's when he complimented me off to war, God says, "You always knew how to hear when your news sources were lying to you."

"Moses?"

"It was his book. But let's just say he had it wrong. About the mandate. What is it you never failed to tell your reporters?"

"Verify."

"Listen, Sam. A lot of stuff that tries to pass for my voice is just humans tweeting in all caps in the middle of the night."

"You know about tweeting, do you?" I say, admittedly just a pout of a comeback.

"I do," God says. "Just be careful. Thou canst not look upon my Twitter handle and live."

I'm not quite sure what to do with that. I'm looking into the dark where God is presumably keeping His face hidden from view. He's taking another little dig at His man Moses.

I want to laugh.

"Go ahead," God says.

So I do. Moderately.

A silence settles between us.

Then God says, quite gently, "So it's about time for you to go to war."

"Yes," I say.

"But aren't you inclined to revisit one more event before you go?"

"Yes."

"Trust your impulse, Sam. It's a needful one."

So I am in the East Carroll Parish Courthouse in Lake Providence on Hood Street in the second-floor meeting room with a portrait of Woodrow Wilson on the wall and, beneath it, a slick-shaven and bejowled U.S. Army captain sitting behind a table with an empty slat-backed chair across from him. And I find myself approaching that chair.

What I am here for should involve only me and this army officer, so he can sign me up to help my country go wage a war in Europe.

But my father is beside me, walking with me step for step.

Because Papa has arranged all this. He feels entitled to be here with me. He feels it is essential for him to be here. The front doors of the courthouse have not yet been unlocked for the day. This will be private, arranged by him. The captain will not question the veracity of the information I am required to provide, will not question my age.

But as my father and I approach the captain, I want desperately to halt, to take a step back, to turn, to bolt out the door and take off alone for the courthouse in Oak Grove. I want to do this the way I had planned.

Granted, the plan my father has intervened to create is more certain to put me in uniform. But I am paying a price.

I realize this even as I arrive at the slat-backed chair and look this army recruiting officer in the eyes. Though everything has already been arranged, I am struggling to stay focused on why I am here, what brought me here, who I am trying to be. And so I make sure I am standing straight and tall, and I say to the captain, "Sir. My deep impulse at this moment is to salute you. But I feel I've not yet earned that right. May I ask you for guidance, sir."

An act of my own.

My father is standing quite close to me on my left side, and I am aware that his right arm can rise without the captain seeing, which it apparently has done as I've made my request, for his hand now punctuates my words with a sharp little pinch in the middle of my back.

To bring me back in line.

I do not show the sting of it in my posture or my demeanor.

The captain's face, meanwhile, after a brief freeze to absorb what is no doubt an unusual request, blooms into a full-fledged smile.

"Young man," he says, "you have just now richly earned the dispensation of this morning. I may not see you again. I would regret not receiving your salute."

So I shoot him one, which I've been practicing, and I sustain it, and he smiles and reciprocates, and we release our salutes together.

"Have a seat," the captain says.

I arrange myself before the chair and I begin to descend.

In objective time my physical passage will be only a few moments. But in fact I travel a great distance in the descent: I begin to realize exactly what the price is that I'm paying. What price I've always paid. My becoming a man, my fighting for my country, is no longer about me. My father has made all that about himself. Even now he is standing with me at the chair, close beside me but just a little bit behind. And as I descend, his hand is suddenly upon my shoulder, a gesture I recognize from our life together, an assertive grip there upon me but encouragingly so, almost gentle, really, as I've always understood it. My papa's touch. Rarely but strategically employed, so it has been even more precious. Seemingly a fit-to-be-my-son gesture that could readily draw tears from me over a felt love and connection. But now I think, *What has always made me weep exists only in the gesture itself. Not in the man who is making it. For him, it is a gesture of control. Of ownership.*

And now a subtle variation of the grip. I feel in the last moments of my descent an unmistakable downward pressure in his hand. This is new. He is *placing* me here. Placing me in the chair before the army recruiter. The act is his.

I understand.

I settle into the chair and I think, *I will shed no tears about you and me.*

Nor do I.

This has to end.

It will.

I go to war.

And I'm folded on the duckboard flooring of a forward trench near Albert, France, my back pressed against the earthen revetment, my knees tented in the narrow space. A trench occupied by the French army. Full of *poilus.* Literally the "hairy ones." The French infantrymen. My uniform is presently more or less clean. I do not yet stink. I do not have lice or trench foot or rat bites. This is my first day at the real war, as I am among the first Americans to leave our training trenches. General Pershing has made a goodwill show of sending some select troops to help the Allies defend against the shockingly effective German breakthrough offensive begun barely more than a week ago, on the first day of spring. The goodwill was reluctant on Pershing's part. He has held the million of us from battle till we are ready to cohere as a purely American army. No military mixed marriage for us, by God. But this thrust by the Huns was serious. This very trench was a rear reserve trench on the last day of winter. Now it's half a dozen kilometers from the front.

Though I am with the French, a man with an American voice begins to speak beside me to my right, an American who is already rat gnawed and mud begrimed and sharing the unwashed, latrine-hole-vapored, offal-tainted stink of the other men.

He offers a hand. I take it.

"Johnny Moon, Buffalo, New York," he says.

"Sam Cunningham, Lake Providence, Louisiana."

At once he starts in. "My *capitaine* sent me over to you. Me being your fellow American to welcome you to Hell's Bells, France. So *bone jury*, Sam Cunningham. Been with my frog pals for two years. Sniping. It's what I do. A hundred and fifty kills: Boche machine gunners, line officers, stupid-ass trench soldiers sticking their heads up, fellow snipers. With the war on and Wilson with his thumb up his ass, I got on out of New York as a trimmer in the engine room of a French tramp steamer. Docked in Bordeaux and said thank you very much and joined their Foreign Legion to fight. They were happy to have me. Specially when they found out I could shoot straight. No pledge of allegiance. Still an American. But I did pledge to fight the Huns to the death for them. So I've been carrying the flag for our country till our professor in the White House wised up and extracted his thumb. Heard the popping sound of that gesture last spring and I went, *Hooray.* Glad you're finally here. You're young. Did you lie? You don't have to say, though it don't make a louse bite's worth of difference now that you're here. Good for you. That's a fine rifle you're carrying. Looks to be almost an Enfield but it's not."

Here he actually pauses for a moment.

I nod at my rifle, which sits upright in my left hand, its butt on the duckboard, its scope attached. I say, "It's the red, white, and blue version. An Enfield of our very own, made in Pennsylvania."

"Heard of it. Glad to see it in an American's hands. Looks to be better than the Springfield. Especially for our line of work. Myself, I do like my French kiss of a Berthier." He nods at his scoped rifle of red-tinged walnut, upright in his right hand. "They must have tagged you as a pretty damn good shot from the jump-off. Like me. Did you go study sniping with the Brits?"

"We had our own school," I say. "Camp Perry in Ohio."

"Glad to hear it. And furthermore, my underage liar friend, that's a second lieutenant's bar I espy on your still-starched tunic. A looey who forgives the bold talk of an American noncom trench rat fighting for the French. For which I am happy and grateful. They give you that after Camp Perry to keep the noncoms off your back to fight your solitary war?"

"Only reason I could figure," I say.

And then Johnny and I both stop speaking.

Distant thunder.

At our backs. Out to the east. But instead of the cascading sound of thunder and rain, a traversing ripple of thunder from the German field artillery starting their fire sequence.

Johnny's hand rises by reflex, touches his helmet with its metal coxcomb and flaming bomb insignia, touches it as if it's the only way he can know for sure it's on his head. I am new enough to this that I'm always all too aware of my washbasin of a doughboy helmet.

Beyond him, down the dim corridor of the trench, there's a weary scrambling of bodies. But Johnny casually angles his face a bit upward, lifts his eyes, waits, and now overhead a shrill rushing, a whistling hiss, and another and another and more still, some directly above us and plenty of others down the trench in both directions.

And then we begin to hear a wide-field flurry of gouging crumps a few hundred meters to the west.

High explosives. Trench killers.

Johnny says, "They'll walk them back now. Too bad they didn't get you and me forward in time to pick off their spotters."

Then we wait.

And indeed, the crump and the crump and the crump are getting near.

Johnny says, "They'd let you into a dugout with your looey stripe. But it's a long stumble to get to, along the trench and over the huddled poilus."

I say, "If a shell's got my name on it, it'll get me wherever I am."

Johnny flashes me a smile. "They teach you that at Camp Perry?"

And now a basso thump off to the right, not quite upon our line but nearly, and another to the left, and from that one I feel the earth ripple in my butt.

I lower my head a little, close my eyes, and somewhere to the right a shell explodes, but past the trench, to the east, and another out there, and I have a small surge of hope that the gunners missed the interval by fifty yards, that the shells have passed us by and will walk on away toward Albert now.

But from our left, in slow simultaneity, a shattery crash and a great thump of air against my face even as I'm turning my head away and a scuttering sound rushing at me, the footfall of rats if they'd all donned armor.

I pull my legs tighter against my chest.

I expect a bite of metal.

But none comes.

The sounds cease.

More crumping now, distant, easterly.

And then silence.

A silence that persists for a breath. Another.

The shelling seems to have stopped.

I turn my face to Johnny.

He's looking past me, down the trench in the direction of the abated swarm of shrapnel.

I do not follow his gaze.

He stands, steps over me.

I hesitate.

And I return to the dark.

"Back so soon?" God says.

I am.

He waits for me to explain why I'm not following Johnny down the trench.

Oddly, I don't have a reason to offer. I eagerly went off to be a soldier, after all, and I've not yet personally encountered the carnage. In that first hour at the front I had no more reason to fear the sight of the wounds of war than I did with the recruiter in Lake Providence. And it even seems the detailed hindsight I've been experiencing in my dying is not yet upon me. I don't see what's immediately to come. But there's one thing I broadly know. There's that. And I try to speak to it.

I say to God, "I'm seventeen. I can shoot the head off a squirrel at a hundred yards with iron sights. My right hand, my right eye—they are ready to fight this war. But only those. Just hand and eye. Only those. And for the most part they're all I'll need, as things will go. I'm a sniper. A scout some. But the killing part is sniping. It's going to be less personal for me hunting in France than hunting the woods along Lake Providence. In the war I'll rarely see anything more of the critter I'm killing than an ear or a temple, a forehead or a cap badge, usually at three or four hundred yards. The stricken bodies I will leave behind are as simplified and sanitized and denatured as the words of a thousand war headlines and the thousand stories beneath them that I will preside over for decades to come. My boyhood skills are far more personal. I don't even have to handle the Huns I kill. Don't have to bag them. Don't have to dress them and eat them. But my boyhood skills don't match what awaits me down that trench."

I stop.

The dark stays silent.

I say, "I don't want to follow him down the trench. Not now. Not then."

"Were you really so hesitant at that moment?" God asks.

I don't have an answer. He's right. I'm contradicting myself. I was fine with squirrels. I was too stupidly young to know to fear anything else.

"So what's holding you up?" He asks.

God's tone is surprisingly gentle, but I'm getting irritated with this whole process.

I grab some obvious words. "The animal you've just savaged on the hunt you don't have to shovel and scrape off the duckboards and trench faces and your shoes. And it wasn't one of you. It wasn't a man."

I wait to see if that's what God wanted from me. But He's clammed up again.

My irritation is growing. I say, "I don't have to explain that to you, do I? You've got your own oblivious snipers doing your work. The cancer cell and the flu virus and the pneumonia bacterium. And they're not even looking at our cap badge, seeing we're from Bavaria or Württemberg or Saxony, before pulling the trigger. They're in the dark just trying to stay alive by killing us. Which is the life you gave them to lead."

"Look, Sam," He says. "When the universe finally expands into nothingness and *I'm* about to die, I'll summon you back to interrogate me. But right now just try to be the self that you were in your prime as a reporter. You were compromised by the times and the influences you lived through, but in your mind and in your heart, as a newsman and as a man, you at least tried not to look away, didn't you?"

I should be glad to hear this. The first approving thing I've gotten out of God. But this moment's reflection later, the praise begins to fester. I was compromised. Even as a man. Even in my humanity.

God eavesdrops. "I'm not being sarcastic with you, Sam. Just follow your story."

And I am huddled on the duckboards once more. Johnny has vanished down the trench. I rise to my feet. I follow.

As I move I stoop in deference to my German sniper counterparts perhaps waiting a few hundred yards away for heads to appear.

I navigate some bits of shrapnel.

Ahead are thin, selective sounds. No moaning. No wailing. Just a few strands of words emerging from an afterclap of surprising silence. Sounds like quiet conversation. I pass the stirring and rising of other men who are still whole, and then things get slick underfoot and I try not to see why.

Now I find Johnny on his knees, crouched beside a French soldier lying on the trench floor. Johnny slips one arm upward beneath the man's back to lift him and angles the other beneath him so he can cup the man's head in his hand. What I know, what I see but do not let myself fully see, is the poilu's missing leg, sheared off in a gaping smear of blood and tissue and a white bone end, the whiteness a shockingly clean-seeming thing, an inviolably essential thing in its color but severed into a shard as jagged as shrapnel.

Johnny brings his face close to the soldier's.

The dying man is looking him intently in the eyes.

Johnny holds the gaze.

The man says, but softly, "Maman." And again, "Maman." And then, "Je suis tombé."

Johnny says, just as softly, "Ça va. Ça va."

I don't follow. I am seventeen. I am as ignorant a boy as Lake Providence and my papa would have me be. I recognize the French language, but we are North Louisianans. What is south of us in our state is another country, as foreign to me as this trench.

The poilu says once more, "Maman."

And Johnny replies, more softly still, though I hear it clearly, "Je t'aime, mon fils."

And Johnny Moon bends to the dying soldier and kisses him on the forehead.

He pulls back just a little, and the poilu closes his eyes.

I lift mine away.

I do not understand a man kissing a man. Not at all. And insofar as one might infer simply a thoughtful assessment from *do not understand*, it is a drastically inadequate phrase. It's the sharp snagging of my breath, the quick, nauseated blooming in my chest and throat, that make up this consideration.

But my averted eyes see farther along the trench. Another man bends to another man, another wrecked man.

I retreat to the darkness of my own dying.

Like opening my eyes in the night to stop a disturbing dream.

But I quickly return to France.

I have at least changed the scene. It's several hours later. I am lying in a shallow, improvised trench—more trough than trench—just wide enough and deep enough to expose only head and hands and rifle at ground level. I'm part of an array of French sharpshooters in a hundred-meter line flanking National Route 29. We're less than a kilometer outside Albert, waiting for the Huns' advance infantry, waiting for the further German push intended to take Albert's rail center that would cut off the French forces from the British and open the way to Paris.

Highway 29 is lined with poplars adangle with catkins, and Johnny Moon is lying barely two arms' length away. We have just swabbed our rifle muzzles and gauged the wind and familiarized ourselves with our telescopic view of the highway and the flat fields before us.

Now, finally, we are settled in.

Johnny Moon and I have had very little chance to speak since the shelling of the trench. He's had his French comrades to attend to, and I have kept my distance.

I think, *Whatever I witnessed, this man and I are now the only two Americans in this field and we are, perhaps, about to die together.*

And, in truth, as I lie on the verge of real war, it feels as if Johnny Moon and I are the only two men in this field, in this country, in the whole wide world.

I look over to him.

He senses my glance and turns his face to me. "Ready?" he says.

"Yes," I say.

"It's been a tough day so far," he says.

"Yes."

Our gaze holds for a moment and I feel myself disconnecting from him. He suddenly seems stranger to me than the Huns down the road. I don't like the feeling.

"Was he your friend?" I ask.

For a flicker of a moment Johnny doesn't understand. He didn't realize I was witness to the kiss. But he figures it out now. "I didn't know him," he says.

My seventeen-year-old brain, trained killer though it be, is bewildered as hell. Johnny sees it. I just stare dumbly at him for the few intense moments while he works out exactly what's going on and figures out how to handle it.

Then he says, "Do you understand French?"

"No."

He nods thoughtfully, refining his decision about how to approach this.

He says, "A death blow like that can put a man in another place. He called me 'Mama.' Which is who he was seeing. He told me he fell down. Told his mama. I said it was going to be all right."

Johnny pauses. Studies my reaction so far. My face probably hasn't changed much.

He knows what's disturbing me.

Johnny says, "Then he spoke to me again as his mother. I knew he was about to die, whoever this poor bastard of a Frenchman was. So I said to him, 'I love you, my son.'"

I am still a blank.

"Like his mama would," Johnny says, and he looks away.

I think, *And then you kissed him.* And then I think of that other embrace going on down the trench.

Johnny turns back to me. He says, "Look, young looey, he didn't even have to take me for his mother. And it didn't have to be me that got to him first. It could have been most any other man in the trench who'd been spared for one more day from dying. And the dying man could know exactly who it was who'd taken him in his arms. It would all have gone the same way. But don't jump to conclusions about any one of us. This is about millions of men being forced to become somebody who has to dig a hole in the ground and then go down in it or jump up out of it and die a ferocious, savaging death when you just want to be a farmer or a teacher or a sales clerk or a guy stoking coal in a tramp steamer. And there ain't nobody else in the world but you and the rest of the fellas in the same fix, and you have good reason to believe that's how it's going to be till you're dead. Your mama doesn't even exist anymore. And never will. Nor your papa. Nor your girlfriend, nor your children, nor anybody else. We are all we have out here. Just us men. So when it's your turn to die and you need some mothering, you need some tender something like a mother would give you, then by fucking damn we give it to each other. Most of us—*most of us*—know that and live by that, my innocent young boy of a lieutenant, and so will you, I bet, after you get a good taste of what's coming at you from down that road. And if today's your day to die, at least maybe you'll have an American mama who can hold you when you go."

And Johnny Moon turns his face away from me and looks down Highway 29.

I turn my own face and I am in the dark.

God says, "You back from the war already?"

"Am I?"

"Did you get a story down that trench?"

"Not one for a family newspaper."

"So what now? I'm just a reader paying a penny for the late city edition of the *Cunningham Examiner.* You're the editor. With no advertisers hassling you and with a journalistic version of that little earthly thing called free will."

I suddenly think I know what God's looking for. I get it. It was a big thing for me.

I stand at the back wall of a second-floor room in a shell-wracked cottage in an abandoned village near the Moselle. I am invisible there in the early-morning shadows. Before me is a clearing that stretches not much more than fifty yards to a coppice of hornbeam and beech. A clear rifle shot through the empty window frame.

It's September 1918, and America is fully engaged now in the fighting. I am part of the First American Corps at the right flank of the Saint-Mihiel salient, the bulge in the front line that's been there from the second month of the war. We Americans are finally flattening back that bulge nearly to the German border.

It's a war of movement now, not trenches. No-man's-land is no longer mappable but always shifting, merely the fraught and flimsily temporary space where the world will clash next. But on this day, before we all do, I am on my own, hunting the German artillery spotters and scouts and snipers who are stealing along toward our line.

At first he is a flittering shadow behind the outer layers of the tree line. I am looking through my binoculars but switch at once to my rifle and its scope. My work is—even from this ridiculously close range—every bit as much about rapid execution as it is about precision.

Then he steps from the trees. A German in standard field gray with a soft cap. His rifle is also standard issue, no scope, and slung over his shoulder. Not a sniper. Likely a spotter.

He seems almost casual. He's been at it a long while. And I can see he's an older man, even before he does what he now does: he reaches up and takes off his cap while dipping his face a bit, displaying a horse's hoofprint of hair on the top of his head.

I draw in a sharp, needless breath. An ignorant, novice reaction for a fellow in my line of work.

But the head seems terribly familiar to me.

I have recovered myself. My breathing is under control. I can kill him now.

Except that I know such a head.

This is all going both very quickly and very slowly. The quick part is keeping me from identifying the familiarity.

The man turns his high-cheekboned face my way.

He looks at the cottage.

And a crease shoots up his brow, between his eyes.

He is a German soldier. Clearly that. I never lose track of that. He is in my sights.

But the crease confirms it. This is also the image of my father before me.

And for all that I more or less resolved in Lake Providence—less, it suddenly seems—for all that I left behind, there is one more thing to clarify.

This man before me is a fitting target in his own right. But because for me he is another man as well, I owe him this: I take a step forward from my invisibility at the back of the room. And another step. And another. I move all the way to the window.

I must let him see me first.

He lifts his face.

He has his chance.

So I lift my rifle and instantly steady it and, as is my skill in my sniper's suspension of time, I assess the fleeting and inextricable combination of wind and distance and humidity and trajectory and target.

And I squeeze the trigger.

And I put a .30-caliber bullet in the center of the crease in my father's brow.

He goes down dead.

I lower my rifle.

I retreat to the rear wall of the room, press my back against it, and I slide down to sit on the floor.

I lay my rifle beside me.

And I see him go down once more. Slowly.

And watching it, I think how it is that in a trench, behind a machine gun, across a field, in a window, down a street, emerging from the trees, the men I've killed rarely fall backward. The well-placed sniper round enters and leaves cleanly and swiftly in its narrow path, and I am put in mind of a phrase from one of the books of my youth. "Straightway his knees were loosened."

It is an apt description. This is how the men I kill fall down. Though in the book—I am well aware of the irony—it is not about a bullet-borne death. It is not about a death at all. It is from Homer. When Odysseus comes home from war a decade after it is over and reveals his identity to Laertes, the papa's knees are loosened, and he falls into his son's arms from love.

At this moment I have already selectively killed dozens of men like this. I remember very few faces. Almost none. No more than the faces of the squirrels and the birds and the raccoons. But on this day, the face of the man I killed for my own reasons, this face I can see. And even after the deed has been done and wind and distance and humidity have all changed, the face of what was a weary, careless German has become forever the face of my father.

And I return to the darkness.

I think once more, *Hell it will be.*

But instead, I am wearing my uniform and I am descending from a St. Louis, Iron Mountain & Southern Railway passenger car onto the platform in Lake Providence.

No one is waiting for me.

I did not telegraph ahead.

Indeed, I sit down on the platform bench and place my bag next to me. I become the one who waits, though I'm not sure for what, at this point. I have thought my plan through already a hundred times.

It is July 3, 1919, and it has taken eight months for the army to manage to get me back to America. Me and, so far, only somewhat over half of the two million of us.

I am ready to deploy myself forward. Technically speaking, I am eighteen years and six months old. But I am far older than that. I even look it now. Every man who went to war and is not a fool shows palpably upon his face what he saw and did. I have grown a stubble beard to boot. I will go away to a big city somewhere—I am leaning toward Chicago—and I will seek to begin to be the man I will be for the rest of my life.

But here I sit. Because of my mother. I cannot vanish from Lake Providence without seeing her once again. And so my moment of patricide in France has been exposed for what it was, a thing invented in my mind. The device of a would-be novelist, not the report of a nascent newsman.

Though it still feels true.

To me, my father is a dead man banking.

Presently at work in his office at the Planters & Merchants on Lake Street.

Which is to say not dead at all.

This moves me to grasp the handles of my kit and rise. My mother will be alone for a few more hours. So ten minutes later, I stand at the street edge of our yard. The only house I have ever known sits before me, its hipped roof and galleried porch and triplet gabled dormers, the oak-canopied fieldstone walk to its front door. And now it's *my* knees that are straightway loosened, though from a cause not nearly so simple as either a kill shot to the head or the fatherly love of an ancient king.

I clench my knees into service once more and move along the path and onto the porch. Behind the screen door the front door is open. I peer through the metal fog but my mother is not visible.

It's no longer my house. I lift my hand to knock.

I hesitate. It's still my house.

I lower my hand. I step in.

But I set my bag just inside the door.

I pass through the front room. I do not see her yet, but I hear water running in the kitchen. And though the house from the entry door onward is dense with July heat, I press now into a slow tsunami of even hotter air flowing from the kitchen door, carrying the smell of peaches.

Mama has been baking pies.

I stop in the doorway. Her back is to me as she hunches slightly over the sink. She's washing dishes. Her hair is bunned tight. As always, she has tied her bib apron's knot at the small of her back with as much beautiful correctness as my father's bow tie.

I am suddenly afraid to speak, I presume because I will startle her. I should have knocked.

But her arms stop moving and she straightens.

She knows I am here.

She turns without surprise, and she smiles, but as if about herself, how she knew.

I take a step.

"Wait," she says.

And I do.

She begins to dry her hands and forearms on the skirt of her apron, dipping her face to oversee the job, saying, "I don't want to get you wet."

When she lifts her face again, I see it clearly for the first time since I have begun to die. And though I am still in my mother's kitchen, I realize I am presently seeing her from my deathbed.

I think, *I know my eyes.* At least the eyes of the man I have come to be at the end. She always told me I have my father's eyes. I always believed that—assumed it—when I looked into his. They were close enough in color to persuade a boy yearning for connections to his father. But I have often looked into my eyes in the mirror after my hundredth year, just to wonder why they still have sight. They are not the blue of a gun barrel. *They are my mother's eyes.* They are, like hers, the blue of a forest shadow on snow.

They are the eyes I see now before me.

And she comes to me, embraces me tightly but carefully, because I am a man now, leaning to me from a little distance so it is all shoulders and arms and cheek.

She feels very fragile.

I hold her and linger in my mind with the afterimage of her face. Her squared chin, which is also mine. Her high forehead, centered at the hairline by a widow's peak. Her perpetual pallor.

"Sammy," she says softly. "Sammy, Sammy."

"Mama," I say.

She draws back from me, her gaze, at first, minutely restless as she considers my face, as if searching for something misplaced. Then she says, full of effort, trying to brighten her voice, "Look at you. So handsome in your uniform."

Her eyes are filling with tears.

"Mama," I say. "It's okay." I almost add, *I made it home.* But I cut off those words before I voice them. I can't get her hopes up. I am not home. I am here only to tell her goodbye.

"Did you stop at the bank?" she asks.

"No," I say. "I came straight to you."

She takes my hand and leads me to the front room and beyond, through the door and onto the porch. We sit in the twin oak rockers, turning them a little toward each other.

She says, "He may be home early today. Tomorrow being the Fourth. He's making a speech."

I sense what she's actually saying: *It's best we sit out here as if your coming to me first was so we could wait for him together.*

Not because I preferred her to him. She would pay for that.

I look to the street.

Empty for now.

I think of the lesson he taught me there, drawing a circle around us. To define who I am. Where I belong.

The father and the boy.

When last I saw him I finally emerged from that boyhood. Barely so. Unbeknownst to him. And I wait for him now a precipitated man. And along with my beard I've grown a stubble of irony: it feels, in this moment, that the circle around me contains simply my mother and me, and I had to become a man for this to be true.

True at least until I leave town.

I look back to her.

She says, "Should I ask how it was for you over there?"

I say, "It's enough simply for me to know."

"It's not too much to carry alone?"

"Do you want to feel my head, Mama? The fever has passed."

She smiles.

She leans forward in her chair.

As do I.

She lifts her hand and places it softly on my forehead.

She holds it there and closes her eyes for a moment. "You're right," she says, and leaves her hand upon me for one more breath and another, making it the restrained embrace I invited, and then she pulls it away.

She straightens around to me. As if there is a plan to what's next.

There is.

She says, "I want you to understand, my darling, that I have been all right. That I love your father, and now that you're safe, I am content in my life. Do you understand this?"

I realize that this is also what I came home for. Permission from Mama to go. I am in her life on this day in order to pass from it.

So yes. "I understand," I say.

"We don't have much time alone, is why I speak like this so abruptly."

"I understand that too," I say.

But I have made myself a child again. I hear the sounds down the hallway and explain them away, understand there is nothing for me to do. And maybe that's true even now. Maybe I could only make things worse. But from my deathbed I wish I had ignored her declaration of contentment. I wish I had asked, *Are you afraid of him? Is he a danger to you? Is that why we are sitting here?* I would make her tell me. And then, as her son, as a man, I would think of something to do about it.

But to my shame, I do not ask those questions.

I have nothing to say.

Instead, she says, "Do you have a plan for your life?"

"The beginning of one."

Her nod at this is minute, as if my answer was expected. She says, "*He* has a plan."

"Does it involve sending me away?"

"On the contrary."

I am, at that moment, incapable of reading her tone. It is more muted than I was expecting. It is darker.

She reads my face. "Does that surprise you?"

"Yes," I say.

"You've made him proud," she says.

I believe that. Instead of a brisk recap of fatherly beatings running through me in contradiction, I pull a trigger and loosen a set of German knees and sense the hundred or so such Germans to follow, so yes, I believe he is proud.

She says, "He wants you to join the bank now. He will commence your life there. Groom you."

This presses me back in my chair. I rock a little. I am silent from the complexity.

"You see?" she says. "He's proud."

I say, "Mama, I'm going to some distant city. Some big city. I will become someone."

"Good," she says. Instantly: it is a thing she wants for me, wants for herself as well. And softly: this understanding is just for the two of us.

Once again I am surprised. I feared I would hurt her.

She knows this. "That's good," she says once more. Firmly. I can believe her.

I do believe her, that she finds this good. But she does not as well. She wants me to remain in her life. This I also know, but I ignore it.

With all this out of the way now, she and I talk. Mostly I talk, and she listens. I tell her all that I have come to feel for *words*. Words I've devoured from our Harvard Classics and from the newspapers spread open on our front-room floor and from books I've read beyond our house. I tell her about the consequent weltering of my own words, words inspired by things I've witnessed and continue to witness around me in the world, things the likes of which teem forth in words from the pages of newspapers. I tell her how I want to live a life of words. Writing them. Editing them. Publishing them.

And I am back in the dark.

And I say to God, "How self-absorbed I was."

And God says, "That was how she wanted it for you. You pleased her by being a selfish young ass. You had to be, to save yourself. Which is what she wanted most of all."

"I still regret it," I say.

"Good."

"And what's up with you? Is that a whiff of forgiveness you're giving off?"

"Don't get cocky," God says.

And I'm back on the front porch and my father has just appeared out on the street, business satchel in hand, and he turns into our yard. I recognize the moment when he sees me. His chest lifts in surprise and his first few steps are brisk. But with those steps he thinks through my sudden appearance, my failure to inform him, and he slows and I do not need my rifle scope to see the crease shoot up the center of his brow. But I wish I had the rifle. If not to kill him, at least to scare him a little, to let him know I'm not the same Sam Cunningham he last knew.

As he nears, I'm glad I'm wearing my uniform and that I have the silver bar of a first lieutenant sitting on my shoulder loops. And I'm glad my pleasure at this is only very incidentally about his possible admiration or approval. I am mostly glad that my looeys tell him to back the hell off from me.

And then, with his final, exaggeratedly deliberate steps, I realize something from the next century: it took a while in this dying process for me to see his eyes in a memory, but I've still not seen a blow. I have recognized, have generally experienced, have invoked the *fact* of the beatings. But I have not felt again, in a specific moment, his angry hand upon me.

So now, as the memory of my father's gaze arrives within arm's reach of his transformed son, a moment returns in a flash. For all the variety of his assaults, as I stand before him in uniform on nearly the Fourth of July 1919, I remember this one.

I am lying on the front-room floor, the newspaper open before me. It is the day after my twelfth birthday and I am reading the paper as fully and piercingly as any adult in Lake Providence—or even in New Orleans, I would wager—and I am well aware of it. But the man who is least likely to credit me with anything but a good kill in the woods and an obsequious *yessir* has entered the room just as I am having what I feel is an adult, original, creditworthy thought.

So boldly I say, "Says here there were sixty-four lynchings this past year. How can this happen in America, Papa? And all but two of them were Negroes. What's wrong with us? Since they're the weaker race, dependent and credulous, shouldn't we protect them better under the law? This should be front-page kind of awful."

Though I'm telling my father, I'm addressing the page-eight, three-inch, below-the-fold story on the floor before me, improvising thoughts that are still rooted in my time and place and my own credulousness but also freethinkingly uprooting a thing or two as well. Did I really expect to please the man who nudges me in the thigh now with the toe of his shoe?

"Stand up," he says.

I do.

And as soon as I am on my feet and looking him in the eyes, his right hand flashes in my periphery and my left cheek and temple flare and my head jolts to the side.

I am twelve. But I have come along fast in my life. I no longer cry when this happens. I no longer try to run off, no longer curl up and try to cover my head. I grit my teeth at the pain and struggle to suppress any outward show of it. I am learning to collect myself—to identify myself—by standing my ground even if only in silence, if only to receive his blows and rebukes as impassively as I can.

But I understand this blow is different. It's the first one for an idea. An idea that feels like my own.

I straighten and wait.

"You will not indict America for this," he says. "You will not even indict the misguided white men who did this. These men are your people. They were hasty. They acted unlawfully. But they have grievances. They rely on you for understanding, not censure. Is that clear?"

In my head I am telling him what else is in the story. The listed reasons for all these lynchings. Murder and rape, yes. Though merely accused. Not tried and convicted. But also lynched for refusing to give evidence. For being impertinent. Not paying debts. Brushing against a girl on the street. For an insult.

I say none of this.

My father is ready to strike a second blow at a word of defense or explanation.

For being impertinent.

I resolve never again to make the mistake of speaking to him about any maverick thoughts. Not just to avoid a new class of beatings. I am suddenly, wisely afraid that he will withhold my daily newspaper.

"I am teaching you compassion," he says.

"Yessir," I say.

"You couldn't send us a wireless to let us know?" my father says, and I have returned to my homecoming scene, with him having not said a word until he came up the front steps to be on the same level with me.

"I couldn't," I say, squaring to face him.

He waits a moment, as if for a fuller explanation.

But I am clearly giving none, and I see a quick shift in him.

The crease vanishes from his brow. He glances at first to one shoulder loop on my tunic and then the other and then back to my face. He takes a chest-puffing breath and even unfurls a faint smile.

He offers his hand.

Okay.

I lift mine to shake, but he withdraws the hand before I can grasp it, saying, "Wait. Am I supposed to salute?" There is in his voice a bit of fatherly bravado, a faint you're-still-my-whelp sneer. But there's something else in his voice as well, an ever-so-slight, almost tremulous after-tone. But I hear it clearly. Right then. On the third of July 1919.

And I even have a maverick thought to explain it. My father's own papa, Granddaddy Cunningham, went off to war and never stopped fighting it, to his own highly vocal self-aggrandizement. My father's son went off to war, and I stand before him now with the signs clearly upon me of my trials and successes in that most severe test of manhood.

My father did not go to war. Did not have the opportunity. Not to fight. Not to fully or effectively find the identity he deeply sensed was his.

As he stands before me now, he is feeling keenly that a circle has been drawn around his father and his son and he finds himself outside of it. Forever. He is not one of our own. He is somebody else. And he doesn't fully know who that is.

I understand this in a flash as he waits for me to tell him, *Of course you don't salute me, you're my father, I should salute you.* He waits in the assurance that even if he has stopped his whippings, their lessons and their asserted chain of command will endure.

But maybe his lessons on compassion didn't stick. I say, flat-toned, "Yes. You're supposed to salute."

He stiffens very slightly. As if he were the son and I'd struck him across the face and he was already past the cry or run or curl-up stage. He is going to stand his ground, though he has felt the blow keenly.

Then he constructs a smile, as if we've just had a little manly joke between us.

And he offers me his hand again.

I take it. I shake it.

"I'm glad you made it back," he says.

"I am too," I say.

"You and your mother have things to say to each other, no doubt. I have to work on my speech for tomorrow. The mayor has yielded to me at the celebration of our country's birth. You had something to do with that, of course. We're all proud of what our boys did. I would like for you to wear that handsome uniform. You and I can catch up after bombs burst in the air tomorrow night."

My mother and I do have things to say, but they are constrained with my father in the house, and even after she and I have eventually found our way back to the front porch, as dark comes on, she leans to me and touches my hand and says, "You look tired, my darling."

And I say, "Yes."

And she says, "Sleep."

And I say, after hesitating, after wondering how to say this and when, but deciding simply and now: "I can't stay."

"I understand," she says.

She stands and I stand and she puts her arms around me and holds me close. She pats me on the back, as if I were small and full of fever and she'd picked me up to lay my head on her shoulder.

Then I go to my childhood room to rest for a while, lying in the dark on the bed, the dense heat of the night weighing on me as heavily as if I were six feet under, as if the vast chorus of crickets and katydids were keening me onward to the afterlife.

I have removed only my shoes and tunic. What remains of my uniform is my only protection against the draw of the past.

Then through the din of insects I hear my father's voice, distant but clearly enflamed.

I rise. I move to my door and crack it.

I am prepared to fight him. To kill him if he is abusing my mother.

But words emerge.

He is pleased to have this opportunity.

He is honored to stand before you on this holy day.

I look from my room and down the hall to a spill of light from a doorway that I know.

I step out. Quietly. I have the skill of quiet movement and I go forward and find a place in the verge of the hallway shadow to observe him. He is in his study. His back is to me. He stands before his desk in the light of an electric table lamp.

He's practicing his speech.

He says, "The United States of America won Europe's war. In four long and terrible years no other nation on earth could do what America did. And we did it in a matter of months. We have grown at last into our full identity. We as Americans have taken our rightful and righteous place as the leader of the world, the greatest nation on earth."

I draw back into the shadow. I turn. I move silently, quickly away.

I restore myself to my full uniform. I close my kit bag. I sit on the side of my bed.

And I wait. I wait like a sniper, with a focused but simplified mind, for whom the distinction between five minutes and five hours is irrelevant.

After I am certain my father is asleep, after I turn my face very slightly to the door and bid my mother a silent farewell, I rise and I pass out of our house and steal off into the night.

I hobo my way for the first fifty miles, traveling by foot, by dairy wagon, by Stanley Steamer automobile, by pig cart, and finally by skiff ferry, this last of which carries me across the river and deposits me in Vicksburg, Mississippi. There I catch an Alabama & Vicksburg train to Jackson, where I catch the Illinois Central's *Louisiane*, and the next morning, at last, we are decelerating into Chicago, Illinois.

I've been sleeping deep until nearly the last minute, when I awake to cheers from the folks in the Jim Crow car just behind mine.

I look out the window and see what has moved them so keenly, though it will take a few weeks for me to understand this. Up ahead, rising high over the roof of the arrival shed, is the thirteen-story Romanesque clock tower of Central Station. The colored people who have been traveling unseen behind me are immigrants, migrating from the American South to the American North. The Chicago train station's tower is their torch of Miss Liberty lifted high in promise, inspiring their cheers.

I am slow gathering myself and my kit bag, and then I find myself holding back from the press of other passengers along the aisle, find myself vaguely dissociated from them. I am a little surprised at this feeling, recognizing that it's been forming in me for a while. Eight months after the end of the war my military uniform evokes only a very occasional appreciative nod. I am okay with that. I am tired of wearing it. I wait now to be the last traveler to leave this coach.

And at last I do. I step down to the platform and I'm caught up with the immigrants who are flowing along with suitcases and valises and parcels but also with implements of a possible next life. A hoe. A bag of mason's tools. A rooster in a cage. One man carries a duffel and wears his leather blacksmith's apron.

These colored people, more than my own, nod at me, at my uniform, but no one makes way for me here. My father in my head leads me to expect deference from them. But unconditioned by him I also find myself content being among them now, just as they are. I realize they feel more immediately at home in Chicago, Illinois, than I. They are a community already.

I school with them along the platform and down into a connecting tunnel and up to the first floor of the station, and now it's time to leave them.

I stop at the foot of a wide marble staircase that leads to the main sitting room. The last of the colored people swim on past.

I stand there as the welter of their voices fades. I presume the others of their kind who have previously migrated are waiting for them.

I hesitate. I look up the stairs.

I climb.

And I step into a vast waiting room beneath a coffered vault of a ceiling.

I head for a newsstand and buy three things: a two-penny picture postcard, a one-penny stamp, and, for seven cents, a hundred-page, nine-section *Chicago Sunday Tribune*, with a bold claim under its front-page masthead: The World's Greatest Newspaper.

I go to one of the long oak benches and sit down with my first Chicago paper. But first I write the card, which carries the image of the building I'm sitting in, clock tower and all. I address it to my mother and father both and tell them I have come to Chicago to become a newsman. Simple as that. Not that I care to let my father know even that much about me. But I need to prevent any ruminative suspicion he might have from falling upon my mother in all of this. For good measure I end the message: *I know how this will shock you, Mama. I am so sorry not even to say goodbye.*

When this is done I turn my attention to the world's most self-confident newspaper. Bannered across the eight columns of the front page is a story about a crippled British airship trying to land safely in America after the first-ever east–west air crossing of the Atlantic. But painful though it is to me, conscious though I am that this might be the first time in my life it is so, I do not linger with the news in my newspaper. I unfold deep into the Sunday bundle, all the way to part nine, page nine, to *ROOMS TO RENT.*

And I soon find myself hopelessly lost in advertisements calling out terse combinations of common features of their rental rooms. Large or small, front or rear, sunny or private, quiet street or near shopping. An occasional access to a piano, a shower, a telephone. Rooms for rent to the north, to the south, to the west and the northwest.

I crumple the paper down to my lap for a few moments, grateful that at least to the east water is the only feature to choose from.

From all the other points of the compass I could not imagine making a choice.

But the sun is rising, the waiting room in Central Station is brightening, and all this implies the coming night. I return to the greatest newspaper in the world, and this time my eye falls on an ad for a room to the north that I overlooked before.

It reads: "WENDELL ST. 380—TO RENT—Small but vibrant furnished back room. Near Oak St. L."

One word now leaps into me. *Vibrant.* Unlike any other word in all these ads. A word I know from the Five-Foot Shelf. A sonnet by Elizabeth Browning, the context gone but the image still of "a sculptured porpoise, gills a-snort / And vibrant tail."

A rental on Wendell Street vibrating with something or other—its essence as a *room*, perhaps—awaiting a tenant.

I figure I have come to Chicago to make a life of words. Why not rent a room from someone who has a feel for them?

So I stand in a residential neighborhood full of Chicago worker cottages and bungalows. Before me is a subtle outlier of a brick house, a worker cottage but with a full second story under its street-facing gabled roof and with a wide front porch.

I go up the steps to an oaken door commanded by a brass lion-head door knocker.

The lion looks a little surprised and vaguely insulted by my presence.

It is Sunday morning. This fact should have impressed itself upon me before this. But it's late enough that if the occupants are not at church, at least no one is asleep.

I raise my hand. I knock.

The lion, I suppose, is why I am expecting a man to answer the door. The man of this house.

The door opens.

It is no man.

She stops my breath. From my life so far, the only point of reference I have for the insistence of this breathlessness is when I was about to pull a trigger to kill a man. Her hair is gathered and bunned, and for its chestnut hue my only reference is a nuzzlingly sweet-natured trashman's horse from my Lake Providence childhood. Her eyes are vast and gray, and for them I have Louisiana storm clouds rolling in on a boyhood Sunday afternoon. This is how unprepared I am for the woman standing before me.

However, I have not, in turn, stopped her breath. Or perhaps I have, just quite differently. Those lovely eyes take in my face and then my uniform and then return to my face—all of this in brisk comprehension of me—and they fix now on mine and she says, sharply, "No. I'm sorry. Not a man."

I murmur a benumbed "Sorry" and I turn.

But before I can move off she says, "No, wait. *I'm* sorry. Please."

I turn back to her.

She says, "I'm sorry for being rude." Her shoulders fall a little. Her eyes soften a little. "That wasn't like me. Really."

"I was the rude one," I say. "Just showing up on your porch on a Sunday morning."

"Not at all," she says, and as she elaborates, she reexamines my face and my uniform, though more slowly this time. "It was entirely my fault. This is the first morning for the advertisement and you're the first to answer, so when I opened the door I immediately realized what I must not have specified—gentleman or lady. The paper gives you little helpful boxes to check on a form. I think I neglected to check one of those."

And through this, I've also been taking her in more closely. She wears a white middy blouse with blue edging and a sailor collar and a bow at the bottom of her throat, as if she were a navy deckhand ready for inspection. It makes her look like a girl, and in some basic way it's the comparable boy in me—from before I went to war—who has been experiencing her so far. But she is a woman. Perhaps in some ways the Great War veteran who is standing before her is as old as she, but, in fact, she is at least four or five years senior to the eighteen-year-old still hiding inside the soldier.

The veteran now says, "Being a gentleman, I will take my leave."

"I didn't check one of those boxes," she says.

"I understand," I say.

"Perhaps in that moment I meant *not* to specify," she says.

She seems to be struggling with this. I try to help. "Perhaps not," I say. "But clearly now you wish you had."

"Not clearly," she says. "No. Not clear at all, really. Would you like to step in? We can talk about it. I do have a room for rent."

I nod.

She leads me into her living room at the front of the house and to an overstuffed davenport and chair portraying upon them a mustered battalion of hollyhocks and goldfinches. The davenport squarely faces a fireplace; the chair sits at a right angle beside it. I wait for her to place me.

But she has paused to stare at the chair, seeming to ponder a decision that should be easier than this to make.

And I notice the wedding ring on her finger.

She's looking at her husband's favorite chair and is hesitant to put me in it.

Though if she is hesitant about that, she no doubt is hesitant about my sitting with her on the davenport as well. Or even about my presence in the house. Her husband's feared response might have been her problem with me at first glance, why she had needed to check the ladies-only box for the *Tribune.* All of this observing and reasoning flits through me quite quickly, and even before she has made her decision I say, "I should go."

She looks at me. "Ah, it's to be like that. My fault, I'm afraid. I need to command you now, Lieutenant, but I am uncomfortable doing so without our at least exchanging names. Mine is Colleen Larsson."

I've been increasingly conscious that I have never spoken to any female—any person, actually—in the manner this woman and I have fallen into. A manner I cannot easily characterize. A manner that gives me no choice now but to say, "Sam Cunningham." And to stay standing where I am.

Chaotic perhaps.

"Fine," she says. "Sit in the chair."

I sit.

She remains standing. She says, "You served our country. Our world, in fact. You deserve consideration. At least a few minutes of conversation. And something to drink of a Sunday morning. Would you like coffee? Or do you drink tea?"

"I don't want to trouble you."

"Consider me to be at least a captain, Lieutenant Cunningham."

"My superior officer would order *me* to make the coffee."

Colleen Larsson faintly wags her head. "Holy Mary, Mother of God," she says. Her eyes do not leave me in this reaction, and they show neither a narrowing nor a dilating of disapproval. I look for a twinkle of tease, but I do not see that either.

I say, "I have no rank. I am no longer a soldier."

"Don't you have any proper clothes?"

"I'm only very recently discharged."

"Thus the room."

"Thus the room," I say.

"So I will serve you tea or coffee. Which is it to be?"

"Coffee," I say.

"Black?"

"Yes."

"Rightly so," she says, and she goes.

She very shortly returns with strong black coffee for each of us in heavy mugs. The coffee apparently was already brewed. She sits at the far end of the davenport, swinging her body around a bit to face me. The distance and the twin heavy mugs make me think again of her husband. He is probably not in the house or he'd be conducting this business. Nor is he at church, not alone, with a Colleen of a wife. And then, at last, the obvious thought: he's one of the more than half a million still in Europe, waiting to come home.

She asks, "Is it good, the coffee?"

"It's good," I say. It is. "I needed it, as a matter of fact."

"And you need a room."

"A room. Yes."

"I'll show you when we've finished our coffee. It's at the back of the house, just off the dining room. A small room, but I think it's very nice."

"Vibrant."

"Yes. Vibrant."

"From the nearby elevated train?"

"Ah, no. Not actually *vibrating.* If we decide you shall live in the back of this house, you won't expect me always to be *literal*, will you?"

I say, "No, not at all," gesturing with my free hand but perilously sloshing with the other. I calm the coffee and add, "I intended a joke. I was actually drawn here by that word."

Her free hand lightly waves away my explanation. She says, "I meant the room has an oddly intense sort of *life* to it. In spite of—no, *because* of its cozy, quiet isolation. I once was known to go in there now and then and shut the door and sit for the pleasant sake of that."

"I'd hate to deprive you of the space," I say.

"It's time," she says. "Besides, I can use the money."

The declaration and its pronoun surprise me, begin to disarrange my understanding of her.

"And yes," she says. "I got your joke about the L train. I laughed on the inside."

How does this last remark suggest the truth about her situation? By the way she has delivered it with a ragged sadness in her tone. By that laughter being buried in her. And if laughter, then grief perhaps buried as well. Her free way of speaking—that touch of chaos about it—which has been charming me, now also informs me. It is her way of courage.

He's dead.

I am inclined once again to offer to go.

But she would not understand why, and I do not know how to verify what I suspect.

So I sit there looking at her. Saying nothing. My coffee mug hangs suspended before me.

And she has stopped too. She lifts her free hand. My eyes move to it. I watch her slip the hand beneath the cup, formalizing the pause.

It is her left hand. Her wedding ring has vanished from my sight.

Perhaps she is reading my reading of her.

But she says, softly, "You doubtless have no job and only a bit of final pay from the army."

"I do have plans."

"Plans," she says. "Of course. Would four dollars a week be possible?"

"Only until I find a job. At which point I would expect you to raise my rent."

We fall silent.

Then she lifts the coffee mug to her mouth and sips, keeping her left hand at the bottom but it rotates upward a little. I can see her ring. I look at it.

She has watched me.

She has finished her sip and lowers the mug and she says, "He was a lieutenant like you. He died at Belleau Wood. I meant to take it off a couple of weeks ago, at the anniversary of his dying. Not with the intention of forgetting, you understand. I would take it off to begin the life to come. But not yet." She looks down at her coffee mug. "Except it's time to rent a room."

"Don't you still need to shut its door and sit?"

"I've not done that since he died."

She rises.

"Come along," she says.

And so that night I lie on a narrow bed in a narrow room with a window and washstand, closet and dressing table. And with a vibrant darkness that holds me awake and returns me to a street in Albert.

We snipers have held our place on Highway 29 and the French army has held its own, and the Germans have begun to retreat. The war is moving from the trenches, and in a mobile war, a sniper sometimes becomes a scout as well.

Johnny Moon and I are among those who have been sent forward to locate and begin to deal with the German rear guard. The machine gunners. The enemy snipers. On this day we are the ones exposed, emerging into our counterparts' settled crosshairs, our own sniping to be improvised.

Our contingent spreads out in pairs from Highway 29 before we enter the town. Johnny and I make off to the northwest, through a wooded area of hornbeam and beech and past a rock quarry, and then we find ourselves seriously exposed crossing what was once a brickfield, a chalky barrens along the Albert–Bouzincourt road, where the topsoil has been stripped away for the brick-making clay beneath.

The field makes it clear that the Huns bivouacked here and that, yes, their retreat has begun. But the refuse and stench are fresh, and as we approach the road the dangers increase from across it, with a brickworks drying shed up the way and, nearer, directly before us, less than a hundred yards off, a row of half a dozen beehive kilns.

Johnny and I instantly recognize the allure of these for the Hun snipers—the vantage behind the chimneys or within the dark of the arched doorways—and we both slow and crouch as we go forward. He says, "I'll watch the three on the left."

He drops out of the periphery of my vision and we move forward, safeties off, rifles ready, and I am intent on the dark of the doorways of the three kilns to the right, and as if materializing from the very darkness itself, in the center kiln, a rifle barrel appears, and I drop to a knee while raising my rifle as I say, "Shooter," and I scope the dark above the barrel, and even as my brain whisks the command to my forefinger, the muzzle flashes from the kiln and I am not hit and I squeeze my trigger and feel the sweet thump of the stock against my shoulder and the muzzle in the kiln wavers and quakes and vanishes downward, and I wait, and I look for movement, and I wait for more shots, scanning the central doors on my three kilns. Nothing. The shooter in number two is hit. From my angle to him he is probably dead. The other two kilns seem clear.

I look to Johnny.

He has fallen back. His elbows are thrown behind him, struggling to hold himself up.

At the base of his neck, just off-center, just above his collarbone, his shirt is quickly blooming red.

I step to him, lay my rifle down, kneel beside him, try to think how to stop the blood, my hand even rising to the button of my tunic, and for these first few moments things are a blur in my head.

Then I feel his eyes on me.

They clear my head, make me see him in return.

He says, "I'm done."

And he's right. The blood is bright. Arterial. The very beat of his heart is killing him now.

Johnny closes his eyes. His arms tremble and he is about to fall completely to the ground.

I lean to him, run my arm behind him, just below his shoulders.

I ease him down flat.

I gently remove my arm from beneath him and pull away.

Johnny opens his eyes. He is looking at the sky.

He knows I am beside him. Or at least someone is. He turns his face a little in my direction.

I lean over him.

His eyes find mine. He says, "Fast. The dark. Hold me now."

I cannot move.

"Take me up," he says.

I cannot draw a breath.

"Please," he says.

I cannot move.

He opens his mouth but this time no words come out.

I know what he's asking.

But he is a man and I am a man.

I understand this world he and I are in. As he explained it to me. I know what more he wants. But I cannot move my arms.

His gaze drifts away.

I think, *Good. He needs to find his mother elsewhere.*

But this I do: I pick up his near hand with both of mine and I hold it.

That much.

He returns his eyes to me, clearly to me, and he says, "Please."

He waits.

I cannot do more.

And something shifts in him, his gaze now lays hold on me as focused and calm as if I were a Hun in a machine-gun nest and he has settled his scope on the center of my forehead.

And then the gaze fades, and his eyes go blank.

I know he is gone.

I struggle to take a breath.

I look at my hands holding his.

And I think, *He saw me for what I am.*

I sit up gasping in my narrow bed in my narrow room.

I sit up gasping in the dark on my deathbed.

I failed him and he saw I could do nothing else, and my failure was too great and he was prepared to squeeze the trigger.

I look into the dark.

Is God there? At the back wall of an upper floor of Heaven? Am I now in the crosshairs of *His* scope?

"I am so sorry for failing him," I say to God.

He does not answer.

"Okay," I say. "Pull the trigger."

Nothing.

"Go on," I say.

"Easy, Sam," God says. "I'm glad Johnny Moon endures among your regrets. That's important. But it's just one story in the late city edition of the *Cunningham Examiner*, which is like any late city, a last-hour chaos of fragments from an arbitrary bracket of time. No matter it's a single day and night or it's a hundred years. Everything won't get in, but the chaos of what does is part of the bigger story. Wasn't the late city always your favorite?"

"Yes," I say. "Yes. At two in the morning, the smell of newsprint and ink and the thumping rush of the rotary press. Better than booze."

"Then move on, Sam," God says.

And I sit up gasping in my narrow bed in my narrow room.

I turn and put my feet on the floor.

It is still my first morning.

What did she say, the widow in this house? She would seek this room for its vibrance and close its door. But she has not done so since her husband died.

It's not a room for mourning or regret.

I let go of Johnny Moon.

I dress and step into the kitchen.

Colleen Larsson is there and she puts minced ham and eggs before me.

"Here's a bit of a welcome to Chicago," she says. "For four dollars a week rent money, I'm sorry it has to be just this once."

"Thank you," I say. "But I do plan to have breakfast each day. May I pay you instead of a local eatery?"

"That would be fine," she says.

"And would that include coffee?"

"It would."

"That you might drink with me? At least on this first morning?"

She nods and she pours for us both and she sits across the table and she says, "So where do your plans carry you off to after your eggs and ham?"

I tell her—concisely, with confident dispassion—of my regard from childhood for newspapers and of my intention to write for them. I admit my current ignorance of how to go about securing such a job, and with an outburst of unguarded intensity I tell her that I am ardent to find a way.

The next morning I sit down to breakfast and my mood is troubled, but Colleen Larsson lays a *Chicago Daily Tribune*, neatly folded, beside my plate.

"No extra charge," she says. "A boy throws it to my door every morning. It wasn't just for Paul."

This is the first time she's spoken his name.

"My husband," she says, tenderly enough but with a dying fall of a tone, and I imagine I hear a faint something beneath it. Maybe it's: *Yes, he was my husband and I loved him, but he's gone forever and I accept the fact.*

Yes, maybe that, because then, with an almost brightness, she says, "The world interests me. What was your word yesterday? It interests me *ardently*."

She pours coffee for both of us and sits at the table, saying even as she descends, "How'd the job search go?"

I glance down to the folded newspaper, where I partially see the banner headline, which says **Kills French**, and I see the full headlines on the columns seven and eight stories, though their smaller font helps me stop myself from compulsively reading them.

The glance is a reflex, actually an implicit answer of sorts to Colleen, but it registers wrong. She says, though with sweet cheerfulness, "Sorry. I know you're focused on what you must do."

I look back to her.

I find myself wanting to talk to her. About how the search is going, for starters.

Which must show in my face but register in a misleading way: She says, "I like a man reading his newspaper with his breakfast. Just ignore me."

"No," I say. "It's not that."

I've known Colleen Larsson for less than forty-eight hours. Her dead husband first appeared to me in this house by name just a couple of minutes ago. But I want to talk to her.

Fully talk to her.

There is no one else.

I lay my hand on the newspaper. I say, "This was my search yesterday."

She cocks her head at this.

And so I begin. "I spent the day in the third-floor reading room at the Chicago Public Library. Poring over the big papers. The *Tribune* and the *American* and the *Herald-Examiner.* The *News* and the *Post* and the *Independent*. Weeks' worth. Months' worth."

I pause.

That's enough to say, I realize. It's all she expects.

But I go on. "And it finally dawned on me. I have nothing to show for myself. To any possible employer. Nothing to qualify me even to be a cub reporter. Yes, I'm ardent. But a pup at a fire hydrant with a full bladder is that much. How oblivious have I been? You know the only skill I can show? The only thing I can verifiably do? I can kill men. From three hundred yards. And beyond. I can kill from five hundred. With nuance and precision. With delicacy. I know how to do that. I know how to nurture the breath that I hold even more than the breath that I take. I know to encourage the trigger with the pad of the tip of my forefinger. I know—and I learned it for myself—I know to keep that fingertip where it belongs by pointing with the knuckle at the man I'm going to kill."

I hold up my right hand and I bend my forefinger to show her the aiming knuckle.

I watch her eyes move to it.

I do not know how to read the look on her face.

I regret the demonstration.

I whip the hand away.

I regret my words as well.

And I realize the next words shaping in my head will be even worse to say: *I learned all this, I became an expert at this, I did all this, from age sixteen to eighteen.*

Worse because technically I am still eighteen and she will suddenly see me as that. But I am actually older. Far older. Old enough that, achingly, I fear becoming this woman's little brother. She must never feel I am anything but a man. Because I *am* a man. Fully as old as her husband. He and I are the same age. Were. As old as Belleau Wood. As old as the Albert–Bouzincourt road.

So I do not speak those next words. Instead, I say, "What I did yesterday was finally look at myself with my sniper's precision. I saw before me a blunderingly naive, oblivious young man. And I shot him. In the forehead, square between the eyes."

And square in the forehead between Colleen's eyes her brow furrows sharply at this.

I look away.

I keep my gaze averted from her for a long moment.

She stays silent.

I look back to her, and her brow is smooth again.

"Can you write?" she asks.

"Can I?"

"You apparently think you can."

"Of course. Every night as a boy, after reading that day's New Orleans *Times-Picayune*, I'd write my own stories in my head. Just for me. And I wrote from the war. Letters to my mother. Reporting. For me it's like talking. I figure I just need to talk to the page. It was always voices I was hearing in the newspaper stories, talking to me."

And Colleen says, "So that's what you have to show for yourself. Your voice on a page. Write something."

I flop back in my chair from the force of her logic and the shame of my chuckleheadedness.

"You're right," I say.

"You need a new weapon for a newspaper. Do you know how to work a typewriter?"

"No."

"Isn't that . . ."

"Necessary," I say. "No doubt, nowadays."

"Even if they're ready to teach their cubs," she says, "it could be a foot in the door."

I am suddenly an eighteen-year-old boy sitting before this worldly woman.

I do not know why I feel so desolate about that.

We are looking each other in the eyes and staying silent for a long moment.

Then Colleen Larsson says, "I have been thinking about the same machine. I receive thirty-eight dollars a month from the U.S. government in return for my husband having given them his life. Even with a boarder, I need to work. So what's a woman to do? I know the Gregg system. That's for stenography. A foot in a door. But I need to perfect the nuance and precision of my typewriting to find and succeed at a job of my own. You can give me the four dollars for this week's rent, and this morning we can go to the Oliver Typewriter Building on Dearborn Street and I can begin to pay three dollars a month to buy the Oliver Model 9. I can practice and you can learn and then you can write. The machine weighs thirty pounds, which is why you're needed this morning. Now finish your eggs and ham before they go stone cold."

And all of this she and I do.

I put aside the question of boy or man. Of big sister or woman. I learn to work an Oliver. Meanwhile I start to thrash about for something to write that will win me a job. I buy a map of the streets of Chicago and I see where the courts are and the police stations and city hall, but I figure I could never steal a beat on a veteran reporter. I have to do a human-interest piece, which would give me a chance to write a story in something closer to my real voice anyway.

So a plan is shaping up in my head, though I still need a story.

And then a Monday morning *Tribune* arrives. The eight-column banner headline is about the murder of a six-year-old girl by a child offender, whose smirking face under a natty boater dominates the center of the page as he signs his confession. But across six columns just beneath: **Report Two Killed, Fifty Hurt, in Race Riots**, where a story commences that will roil the city and its front pages for a week to come. A colored bather at the Twenty-Ninth Street beach was stoned unto drowning by a white man for crossing an unofficial color line on the lakefront beaches. Before what will become the legendary Chicago Race Riot is all over, thirty-eight will be dead, more than five hundred will be injured, many blocks of the city's Black Belt will be burned, and a thousand colored people will be driven onto the Illinois Central and back south again.

And that late Monday night, as I lie in the dark in my rented room—lie there neither boy nor man—I find my father in my head. Alive there. Part of me. Not just part. He seems to be as much me as I am. Thinking: *Didn't that dead colored man understand? It was for his benefit as well, the system. No slang. Just a man of a color that we are not. And why would we want to be? How then would we recognize ourselves apart from them?*

Yes. That's my father. Being reasonable. Seeming to be reasonable.

But I adjust it some, for myself. *Why would that colored man even want to swim near a man who could take up stones and kill him for a thing like that? The killer an inferior sort of man. Identifiable by his color. So go ahead and draw the line around your own color. There's plenty of lake and a place where the colored man could peacefully find his own.*

But I hear myself.

And I ask, *Is the man who taught me this pattern of logic really one of my own? Inextricably my own no matter what that makes me? Even if it's by more than color? Even if it's by blood? But haven't I already answered that question? Am I not here in this room in Chicago expecting never to go home? Though perhaps my being here is for a simpler reason. A more personal one. About that one man's rigorous judgment of me. About his violence against me. But are those things not part of all the rest of what he is, what he believes? Inextricably?*

Then abruptly these night thoughts—the posturing logic of them, the very diction of them—these thoughts stop sounding like any voice of my own. I want to be a newsman. I want to speak to a page in the way of a newsman. So my city editor looms over my desk and says, *Cunningham, we've got plenty of our boys covering the streets. Find me a human-interest angle.*

So I become keenly aware of the body of water in today's front-page story and the colored man who died in the water and the circumscribed world surrounding him that he had been expected to live in. These things draw me back down the Illinois Central line and into Vicksburg and back across another great body of water and into a skiff ferry on a landing on the west bank of the Mississippi River.

I rise from my bed and I dress and I go to the corner of the dining room where the Oliver awaits on a typewriter desk. I switch on the electric lamp and I begin.

Colleen gives me breakfast and gives me room to write and gives me fleeting small hourly pats on the shoulder, and by the evening I have a voice. And a foot to put in the door.

I have written:

> I sounded a tin horn that hung on a post on the west bank of the Mississippi River. I had on my best suit of clothes, a fresh khaki field uniform with a silver bar on each shoulder. I'd been mustered out of the army ten days ago, and I was on my way to Chicago from Lake

Providence, Louisiana, to secure a new suit of clothes and a new life, replacing .30-caliber rounds from an Enfield rifle with words from an Oliver typewriter.

The horn summoned a colored man from the tar-paper house up the bank. He was wiry with hair the gray of the troop ship that had brought me home. He sized me up as he approached and saluted me briskly.

"I'm Jonah," he said as I offered my hand for shaking.

"I'm Sam," I said, and he nodded in the direction of Vicksburg across the river, asking the obvious question with a corresponding lift of his eyebrows.

I answered, "Yessir."

"You going on up the line?" he asked.

"To Chicago."

"Seventy-five cents," he said. "I'll carry you across the Big Muddy and up the Yazoo to the train depot just over the levee. Two rivers for the price of one."

"Done," I said.

He extended his arm, offering for me and my kit bag to step into his fourteen-foot skiff of weathered oak.

I climbed aboard, and he followed. As we were settling in, he said, "My son gone up Chicago way some years ago. Had him a boy too, who done volunteered to fight the war you fought. In the Ninety-Third Division, 370th Infantry."

I'd heard tell of a couple of colored divisions in the war, but just sidelong comments from boys who didn't like the whole idea.

"A volunteer?" I said. "I was too."

"Before the draft even began," Jonah said. "He wanted to fight for his country."

"Who'd your grandson serve under?" I asked, thinking maybe Black Jack Pershing.

"They give the whole division to the French," Jonah said.

From the place I was coming from, I understood what he did not say. That the Americans did not want to fight next to their coloreds.

He turned his attention to the skiff's Evinrude outboard. It took him half a dozen cranks to finally bring the engine to life. We slipped out into the river.

Jonah immediately angled our bow sharply upriver, toward mid-channel but away from our destination, and we began to creep against the current, the motor protesting all the way.

I turned my head toward Vicksburg, which was slowly receding.

I looked back to Jonah.

He was watching me. He leaned in my direction. "Got to do it like this," he said. "The river always tries to have its way with you, tries to carry you off to where you can never get back. Got to push against it. But at an angle. Let it think it's carrying you away but you end up where you need to be."

And so Jonah curved our way to the mouth of the Yazoo River. Then for a mile we hugged its shore along the Vicksburg levee, and he dropped me and my bag at a landing near the Cherry Street Depot.

As I paid him I asked, "Has your grandson been mustered out of the army yet?"

Jonah replied, "My grandson died in the Argonne Forest. Fighting for France."

The next morning, on the Illinois Central Railway, I woke in my seat to cheers. The train was slowing down, and the uproar came from the Jim Crow car behind mine. The colored men and women had caught glimpse of Chicago Central Station and they cheered the new life they sought.

Now, three weeks later, as Chicago's Dark Town burns and whites and coloreds fight in the streets, I wonder if the colored man whose death began it all was one of those newcomers cheering on the train. A colored man seeking a new life who had not yet learned that even in Lake Michigan there was a current you had to account for or it would sweep you away.

I roll the last sheet of the clean-typed final version from the typewriter, tap the three pages on the desktop to square them together, rise, and turn to go in search of Colleen. She is immediately in view, across the dining room, through the opening to the living room, sitting with her profile to me at the near end of the overstuffed davenport before the fireplace. She need only turn her head a little to see me.

Which she now does, as if she senses my looking at her. The evening has come on and she has a book in her hand. The book disappears into her lap.

Any confidence I have in my story vanishes. But I make myself move.

When I arrive before her, I look down at the typescript. I am still holding it with both hands, one on each side, clutching it tightly, and my bearing seems that of a child.

I drop one hand to my side.

"Are you finished writing?" she asks, quite softly.

"Yes," I say.

She nods me to the companion chair before the fireplace.

I sit.

She slides to this end of the davenport. "Read it to me," she says.

I do. Keeping my eyes strictly on the text. Not giving her even a glance.

And I finish.

And I lift my face to hers.

Her eyes fix on mine. A smile begins, close-lipped but in a compressingly prideful way.

"What?" I ask.

"I am so relieved," she says.

I am in the darkness once more.

I am weeping.

But I hear nothing. Perhaps I'm only remembering tears, as I am remembering all these other things, outside of time. As at our first meeting, she ordered me into a chair that had once been her husband's. But this time, I did not give him a thought. It was just the two of us, sitting near to each other as we began the rest of our life. Nearly a hundred years ago. I would go on to have half a century with her. And there has been almost a half a century since.

A stirring in the dark.

"Are you there?" I ask.

"It's just me," God says.

He's right. I was thinking of her.

"You gave me a little peek forward," I say.

"Yes," He says. "An awareness of time."

I say to Him, "Can't you take me now and put me where you must and get this over with?"

"No."

"There's too much ahead," I say.

God says, "It's the late city you're putting together, Sam. Forget I'm listening for a while. Just read the ticker and let the pieces gather as they will."

I sit before Colleen and her approving smile resumes and she is relieved, and it is the long but not long enough bracket of our years together that brings my timeless tears as I hear her full meaning from the vantage of the coming century, a meaning which, at the time, neither of us can fully hear.

She is of course relieved that I am not rotten at this thing I want to do. Relieved for this boarder of hers who she may even sense is younger than he seems, who is certainly naive in his lack of preparation for his job search. Poor kid. But at least he can write okay.

And she is relieved as well for what she can hear as his nascent sympathies for colored people, against early twentieth-century America, against his white southern blood and roots, for she has the same thing stirring in her against this time and place, against her Irish blood and roots.

And these combine in a deeper relief in her, the one that sourced my tears. She is relieved that she is thus free to fall in love with me.

As I am—still largely unawares—falling in love with her.

The pieces begin to gather. These are all about her. Human-interest stories. Feature narratives. In the separate Colleen Larsson news, feature, and rotogravure Sunday supplement.

That very night, after I read her my story, I hear her humming. I am lying sleepless in my back room and I rise and gently open the door a crack, just wide enough to place my eye and see her sitting at the dining room table. She is wearing her nightgown and she has unbunned her hair and she is brushing its chestnut billows. I am struck by the tune and I try to place it. But she turns it over and over and gently pulls it apart, and I think she has no song at all in mind but only the impulse to hum. I ease the door shut again.

Then it is not until the middle of the night, as I wake to throw off the sheet from the July heat, that it strikes me she went not to her dressing table in her bedroom upstairs to brush her hair but to the dining room table—near the place where I wrote my story, near the place where I was sleeping. I try to find some mundane explanation for that and am pleased that I cannot.

The next day we are ready and we each go out into the city to find work and we return the first night to share news of the quest, and the billows of her hair have vanished. She has had her hair bobbed and fluffed into a helmet of soft curls. She has made a thoroughly modern, forward-thinking, independent working girl of herself and, not incidentally, dramatized the bloom of her lips and the great gray depths of her eyes.

She quickly gets a job. In the typing pool at the home office of the Mutual Life Insurance Company of Chicago. And I have barely begun to make the rounds. We've been eating our breakfast together each morning and I have never refilled my own coffee cup from the stove. She has always done this for me. On this morning I stand up to do it for myself and I am passing her where she sits across the table from me. I have caught her in mid-sip and she hurriedly lowers her cup. I sense she is about to rise to serve me. My hand goes out in reflex and touches her lightly on the shoulder to keep her in her chair.

She recoils from my touch.

It is slight. But to me it is manifestly a recoil.

Too sudden, that touch. Too soon. Too surprising. Surprising to me as well. And meaning no more than *Please stay seated. I can serve myself.*

Well, perhaps more.

A little more, but known only to my fingertips at that moment. But very little more, and not the primary intent. Not the presumptive intent that her shoulder has reacted to.

I go on and refill my cup and I make my voice say, "Would you like some more coffee?" and she makes her voice say, "No thanks."

As I pass back by her, she says, "I've had enough coffee."

As I sit, she says, "Too much makes me jumpy."

She is sweet to offer this. But I know it is not the explanation. She has had no more coffee than usual this morning—somewhat less, in fact—and she has never before shown the slightest taint of coffee jitters.

It strikes me hard: she senses a wrong thing latent in that touch. Wrong because I truly am to her the little brother I have feared I would become. Which is how I then interpret her arranging a lunch for us shortly thereafter with her lifelong girlfriend, Miss Hettie Harper. Colleen wants to introduce her two platonic pals.

She dubs it a working girl's splurge, with me as the honored guest. Eleven is the commencing hour for the two girls' respective lunch breaks, and that's when we are to rendezvous at a Wells Street eatery that features half a dozen small tables in addition to its counter and a special twenty-five-cent lunch including dessert.

I arrive first and take a table seat facing the door.

I am instantly aware of my two selves. Sam in this moment in 1919, the Sam whose long life has barely begun. And Sam whose long life is presently ending, with this farewell late city edition making its way to press in the twenty-first century. If everything's not going to get in and yet the chaos is still going to be meaningful, I'm not sure I understand the news angle of the story of this lunch.

But it's not a news story. It's a human-interest story. Even if the interest of it has been lost on me for many decades and I am now surprised to find myself in the middle of it.

So here I sit, restlessly waiting in my lunchroom chair, and the two girls walk in. The friend has a bobbed haircut that twins Colleen's in fluff and curl and, precisely, in mid-cheek length.

I rise.

They approach.

There is no hesitation in the two of them. Colleen moves to the chair to my left and sits. Her friend arrives behind the chair that faces me, but before she sits, she reaches across the table and offers her hand for shaking.

I take it.

Her grip is firm, and as we shake, she does not offer her name but acknowledges she knows mine. "Sam Cunningham," she says.

"Hettie Harper," I say.

She prolongs the shake for another few pumps, and she prolongs as well her comparably firm gaze.

She is a complement to Colleen. By any first glance Colleen is clearly pretty. Hettie is not. And yet, to my eye she's not entirely plain, though probably so to most men. But her unyielding dark eyes are arresting, her squared jaw is right for those eyes and her high brow. Still, she is clearly contrasted, though fittingly, to her sleekly featured friend. And I feel in her handshake what I know about her from Colleen. Instead of both friends making marriages when they graduated from Holy Family Academy on the Near West Side, Hettie Harper launched into the world, wanting to manage her life in an independent way that the tumult of this new century was beginning to suggest might be possible.

I fear that I am instantly disappointing the lifelong friend. Her smile accompanying the shake is wan. Damning, already, with faint praise. Particularly in contrast to the no doubt characteristic firmness of her grip.

She releases my hand and sits.

I sit.

She has not taken her gaze off me.

But all I see in the persistence of her eyes is something that seems like sadness. Perhaps because even the weak smile is now gone. And there seems to be a process going on behind those eyes. A resigned sort of searching. A reading of me, as if I am a Dickens novel and little Nell is on her deathbed.

"So," I say. "Did the two of you sit side by side at the barber?"

This animates Hettie's face a bit, but not for the better. She doesn't know what the hell I'm talking about.

I glance at Colleen. Neither does she.

"Your identical bob cuts," I say.

"Ah," says Colleen. An exuberantly exaggerated *ah* of recognition, sweetly offered to suggest I'm not actually making a fool of myself.

And then, one breath later, she says, "No." Though soothingly. "Hettie has had her bob for a couple of years."

"Ever since Edna," Hettie says.

I look to her.

She is watching me carefully, saying no more. A little test. I am supposed to understand the reference.

I don't.

Colleen quickly jumps in. "Edna St. Vincent Millay. A wonderful poet."

"She was all the rage in France," I instantly say to Hettie. An impulse. For her testing me.

We both put on poker faces and continue to hold each other's gaze.

Then she says, "In Paris?"

"At the front," I say.

"Remarkable," she says, clearly not believing a word of it. That's okay. She's getting my message, though I have a flutter of a worry that I'll irritate Colleen for not letting that test simply pass after she has already saved me.

Hettie counterpunches. "What's one of your favorite Millay poems?"

"We thought of her as the Ty Cobb of poets."

If Ty is to her as Edna is to me, Hettie isn't showing it. There's not a flicker of puzzlement in her face at his name. Then she decides to call my bluff: "But surely there's one poem that stands out."

I say, "Not at all. It's like Cobb. Of all the times he's slammed the pill over short for a two-bagger, I could never say which one is my favorite."

The baseball slang should baffle Hettie some more. But instead, she can't quite repress a faint but discernible smile at the corner of her mouth. And she slides her eyes away from me, over to Colleen.

I realize the smile could be disdain. But it feels like amusement. It makes me wonder if she knows about baseball. About Ty. With my circumstances in this city since I stepped off the train, I still haven't gotten down to Comiskey Park. The Detroit Tigers have even been to town since I arrived. But I've never seen Cobb play except in my imagination, by reading newspapers. As a gal ducking marriage and testing the modern times in Chicago, Hettie could have actually gone on her own and seen him in person.

She returns her gaze to me.

She's serious again. The sadness has also returned. "Were you an officer?" she asks.

I figure she's starting to compare me with Paul.

"Yes."

"What was your command?"

"Myself."

This narrows her eyes.

I regret my response. Though it was the truth, what I said. I'm not trying to prolong our little tussle. "Sorry," I say. "That sounds odd, I know. I was a sniper. I commanded only my scoped Enfield rifle."

Hettie sits back. She sizes me up once more, factoring this in.

And a waitress appears beside our table.

Colleen takes command of the conversation between her two friends, like a downright police reporter interviewing witnesses, and I talk about newspapers, reading them since childhood and loving them and pursuing them now to give me a chance to work for them, and Hettie talks about Hull House, the settlement house complex on the West Side where she works on staff to support the massive, hardscrabble, widely scorned immigrant community of Chicago, especially the women and children, and about Jane Addams, the Hull House founder. At Addams's mention, Hettie leans toward me and says, "Our Ty Cobb."

I lean to her. "Can she hit a fadeaway?"

"The best that Matty could spin," Hettie says. She knows her baseball. Even Christy Mathewson's best pitch.

I stretch out my hand to her across the table. We shake, though without showing a smile, either one of us.

"Sounds like good work you do," I say. "When I get my news job I'll be sure to drop by the Hull House for a human-interest story."

"You do that," Hettie says.

Soon after, the girls have to get back to work.

I linger a moment at the table, watching their two fluffed bobs recede in the direction of the diner door.

But then Colleen touches Hettie's arm to stop her.

She circles back to me and says, "I knew you'd get along."

"Did we?" I ask this in all sincerity. I really haven't been able to tell.

"Yes," Colleen says, and her voice catches in an emotion I would be hard-pressed to identify. It makes me worry again that she invited her friend to induce a wooing.

The night of our lunch, I have job search news for Colleen, but she doesn't get back to the house until late. When the front door finally unlatches and begins to open I find myself sitting beside the davenport in the living room, waiting for her, and not until I hear Colleen's entry underway does it strike me that I've been waiting for her in Paul's favorite chair.

I jump up to put myself elsewhere.

I turn.

She is standing in the archway to the front room.

As when I read her my story, I realize the chair is not an issue for her. But it continues to feel so for me. Still, I do not move.

She comes to the davenport and sits.

"Please," she says, motioning me into the chair.

I comply.

The electric lights are on in the room. I can see her face clearly. It is flushed. Her eyes are puffy. She's recently been weeping.

"What is it?" I ask.

She folds her hands in her lap and leans back into the davenport. "Just a moment," she says.

"Of course," I say.

And we are quiet together for a while. Comfortably, it feels to me. No matter what the tears are about, we are comfortable together in their aftermath.

Then Colleen says, "I knew she would approve of you."

She looks at me and smiles and then looks contemplatively at the cold fireplace as if into a billowing winter fire.

It appears she will be silent for a time.

I try hard now to figure this out.

To no avail.

Is it a sad thing to her, Hettie's approval of me? A happy thing? Somehow both? Or is it ultimately a trivial thing and something else has happened?

I can only wait upon her.

Until I can't wait. I am a very young man, after all. Too soon I say, "Did you see her again this evening?"

Colleen blinks and refocuses as if she's forgotten that I'm here. But then she squares around to me and says, "Yes. Lunch was the first I'd seen her for a couple of weeks."

"Are you okay?"

"Yes."

I hesitate. But I ask, "You've been crying?"

"There are always tears," she says. "We've known each other too long."

Of course. I feel stupid and blundering. I figure I know what this was about. Hettie knew Paul. They spoke of him. I was just now sitting in his chair, after all. "Sorry," I say.

"You were concerned," she says, softly.

"Yes," I say. "That's right."

"Thank you," she says.

At least I now keep my young man's foolishness in check sufficiently to let our conversation end. She goes off to bed. As do I.

At breakfast the next morning, when we are seated across from each other and finished with our food and are slowly drinking our respective second cups of coffee, as has become our habit together, I say to her, in a quite casual tone, "In four hours I'm having lunch with the city editor of the *Chicago Independent*. His invite."

I have tried to wait for the best moment and have still mishandled the announcement, for she has just raised her cup and I interrupt it halfway to her mouth and she goes wide-eyed and twitches just enough to slosh the coffee.

Her left hand rises to secure the cup.

Her ring finger is empty. For the first time since I've known her.

"How wonderful," she says.

"Not fully," I say. "Not yet."

Meanwhile it's dawning on me that the lunch wasn't to introduce Hettie Harper as an alternate girlfriend. It was to have me pass muster with the other important person in Colleen's life.

As I'm thinking this I'm saying, "The *city editor.* That I should draw *his* interest I think is unusual."

"This is swell," Colleen says. "You'll do great. You must have already. Did you drop off your boatman story?"

I did. And we talk now about the *Independent*, how among the Chicago big dailies it is the hardest to identify, being a little of everything, editorially. But strongly inclined to be progressive. It is maybe the only one in town where my sympathetic colored boatman story would get me an audience with a real editor.

I keep up my end of that conversation with Colleen, but I am still caught by her gesture, the removal of her expired wedding ring following Hettie's evaluation of me.

Through all this I empty my cup, and in a pause in the conversation I find myself on my feet with the intent of heading for the coffeepot on the stove, briefly forgetting the incident of the touch.

I take a step and am about to pass her.

I remember.

I stop.

She looks up at me.

She says, "I am on the verge of jumping to get your refill for you. If you wish to put a restraining hand on my shoulder, I encourage you to do so."

I am a bit breathless at this whole thing. But I manage to lift my hand and steady it and gentle it, and I place it on her shoulder. Meaning: *Please stay seated, I can serve myself, though I am also—in fact, I am primarily—happy to have an excuse to touch you.*

"The last time wasn't about you," Colleen says.

"I understand," I say.

I take my hand away and get the pot and bring it back and fill both our cups.

And four hours later I approach the Independent Building on West Monroe, ten stories of white terra-cotta with steel bones underneath, sharp corner angles, and big plate-glass Chicago School windows in bays.

In the main lobby a young woman receptionist notes my name on a list and she uses a telephone to call upstairs. She asks me to wait for Mr. Kirchner. The lobby is polished granite, and I take this as a daily reminder at the *Chicago Independent* of the goal for every story leaving the typewriter of every reporter. Make it polished granite. I tuck this thought away to possibly use—I fancy impressively—at lunch.

I will never get around to doing so, and in the dark, as I am dying, I pause in relief that I never did. Whatever Mr. Kirchner saw in me from the outset, it wasn't the sort of fancy represented by this strained metaphor, and in my excitement it could easily have led me into alienating ad libs of more of the same. Not that restraint from good judgment unexpectedly prevailed in my young brain. I just forgot.

How drastically did that small lapse of memory alter my hundred years to come? No doubt for the better.

I think to ask God. But He has lately made himself clear. He wants me to polish the granite.

I wait in the lobby.

And then Arnold Kirchner finally appears, at nearly half past the hour. He is a substantial, newsroom-casual man, coatless, a bow tie askew, his shirtsleeves rolled to the elbows, his suspenders working a little too ardently, holding his trousers all the way up to what is probably the bottom of his rib cage, which itself is lost beneath a well-rounded, life-in-a-swivel-chair middle section. He is smooth-shaven and balding, with beacon eyes, the latter finding and shining on me instantly after emerging from one of the half dozen golden-doored elevators.

Arriving before me, he says, "Samuel Cunningham, I presume."

"Yessir."

"Sorry I'm late," he says.

"It's a newspaper," I say. This being a much better point to make, thank goodness, than the one I prepared.

"Around the corner we go," he says, and he strides off, with me to follow.

My career begins at a café on Canal Street with a roast beef on rye and Arnold Kirchner holding forth at a corner table small enough for him to loom large in my face and in my brain. Which—no doubt for the best—keeps me quiet.

"The story you dropped off," he says. "It shows you can write. You can find the beating heart in the breast of a citizen. He is a convincing colored man—convincing to me in both his color and his larger humanity—and so the story speaks well of your eye and ear and perception. However, if published as it is written, it would not speak that way to all of our readers. Not even, more to the point, to the *majority* of our readers at this moment in the twentieth century, especially with the recent uproar in town and what that says about our citizenry both white and otherwise. I point no fingers here. The *Chicago Independent* is just what its name says. Independent. But, Samuel Cunningham, you must understand that the editors at our paper are high up on a tightrope strung across the Great Gorge of Niagara Falls, feeling our way across every day. Our passage on that rope is tenuous, to say the least, as we bear so many contrasting weights, trying to balance them, trying to draw the readers to us in sufficient numbers so that we can stay alive and yet do it with an editorial philosophy that gives us a distinct identity. Our newspaper is a vast, comprehensive thing. For thinkers and emoters both. At once sensationalist and progressive. Big drama and real tears that are earned legitimately, but idea pieces that insist on being read.

Bannering our sordid human flaws but propelling humanity forward. Pal up with the pols but rake the muck. Have you read Walt Whitman, Samuel Cunningham?"

Kirchner has not taken his eyes off mine through all of this. And with this abrupt question, he pauses and waits for an answer while those eyes drill into mine.

"I have," I say. "I read the whole of Harvard's Five-Foot Shelf as a boy."

Those drilling eyes do not blink at this, not at the credential of it, not even at the lameness of my dragging it in.

Instead he says, "Then perhaps you know his great declaration. 'I am large. I contain multitudes.' He says it of himself. He says it of America. I say it of the *Chicago Independent*."

With this, he pauses, his eyes remaining fixed on mine, but the drilling is over. Then he says, "Samuel Cunningham, can you take editing without complaint even if it hurts, for the sake of my balance on that wire?"

"I can, sir."

"And what would your reply be to the offer of a job?"

"Sir, I would sound a 'barbaric yawp.'"

I see, at the further quoting of his Walt Whitman, my first Arnold Kirchner smile: a slow nod of approval consisting of a single cycle of gently dipped and raised face with the merest puckery hint of the smile at the very center of his mouth, never unleashed to the edges, never with upturned corners. But oh, its powerful impact every time I will see it in the next few years.

He says, "Though we clearly both appreciate the Good Grey Poet, please save the yawp for the street."

And so that afternoon I wait on the living room davenport for Colleen to arrive from work.

She knows at once what's happened. She rushes to me as I rise and our arms are around each other and my face floats cheek downward on her soft-bobbed curls.

"The *Chicago Independent*," she coos.

"Cub reporter," I say, emphasizing the *cub*.

The pillow of her hair shifts away and her voice is suddenly at the very portal of my ear. "Oh, so temporary," she whispers.

As is our first hug.

She fries us some chops and we open a bottle of wine from the back of a cabinet, and I think briefly that it was stored there by a young married couple that she was once part of. Then Colleen and I, having eaten our dinner and exhausted the topic of my new job, talk instead, appropriately, about News—capital *N*—and how my life will be covering it and how news resonates even in the toasting clink of our glasses: the constitutional amendment banning alcohol from the United States of America has recently been ratified and a battle is presently underway in Congress to work out the legislation, featuring a confrontation between the "Wets," who would let this bottle of wine we are drinking remain legal, and the "Bone-Drys," who would criminalize even that by next January.

We are a little loose-limbed and muddle-minded by the time we must part on this night. Contrary to the assumptions in the prohibition pulpits of America, the wine we've drunk has actually helped inhibit any further embrace. Colleen and I stand before each other in the kitchen and I am about to withdraw to my little back-room bed, and we look at each other until she takes a step closer and thrusts out her hand and we shake. We both are relieved at the resolution for this night.

But I lie awake in spite of the wine. And as my head clears, my feelings grow complicated. I move in combined anxiousness and ardor from thoughts of the job, to my celebration with Colleen, to our embrace, to marriage, to physical intimacy, to Paris. Paris holds me for a time, even as I lie in my bed in Chicago, with Colleen asleep somewhere above me.

In postwar Paris as both a professional killer and an eighteen-year-old virgin, one who has relinquished his rifle yet still wears a uniform and who waits in the City of Light to return to a life drastically altered but utterly unimaginable, I finally take action to alter the incongruous thing that I still am. I find my way to the Rue Duvivier and a brothel in a small hotel near the École Militaire, where uniforms are common and the girls understand soldiers.

Over the bright blue doorway is a terra-cotta mascaron, a gape-mouthed, heavily bearded, demon-vanquishing face, with a head of sausage curls flanked by ram horns.

Through the door is a salon lined with mirrors and red velvet davenports and, arranged in its center, drinking tables.

I have arrived in the late afternoon, finding what I hoped for, the working girls in lacy nightgowns and satin stockings but mostly still smoking and talking or playing checkers or sharing with each other an unlabeled bottle of wine. Only a couple of men. One is a Zouave in baggy trousers and an open-front jacket, sitting on a davenport with his arm around a woman and sipping at a glass of something pale green. The other is a Frenchman in his horizon-blue uniform dozing on another davenport, his head back and turned to the side, casting his breath onto the mirror.

A tall, gaunt *garçon de tolérance*, the brothel waiter, appears beside me. He speaks in French. I know just enough of the language by now to understand he's soliciting a drink order.

"No drink," I say. "Merci. Une femme, s'il vous plaît." Though I have anticipated these words asking for a woman and have practiced them, I no doubt have pronounced the French badly, for he raises his eyebrows as if they were his hands and I've just pulled a pistol on him. I am a criminal assaulting his language.

"American," he says. He already knew that much from my uniform when he spoke to me in French.

"Yes," I say.

"You wish one conquest."

I suspect his English is tailored for his military clientele. "Yes," I say.

He extends an open hand generally in the direction of the lounging girls.

I look to them.

I realize I have come here by much the same unthinking, aim-and-shoot process as governed my previous sniper self. The reckoning for that has now arrived. As I look at these female faces, any one of whom is ready to newly introduce me to my body, a tremor passes through me that is part divine judgment from a childhood of Sunday church in Lake Providence, part tumescent terror from the prospect of a woman's body nakedly available to my touch.

One of the smokers has turned her face my way.

A waifish, small young woman in need of a meal—a few months' worth of meals—but with vast dark eyes such that if I am to have a woman look upon me and touch me, I want her eyes to be like these.

She stubs out her cigarette in a coffee cup before her without taking those eyes off mine.

The garçon notices. "Mais oui. Mademoiselle speak English."

I have to consider whether this is good for me on this occasion. Perhaps actual communication is a complication I should avoid. Though the girl's eyes stay upon me in the few moments I've paused to have this thought, her face flits very slightly to one side in querying reexamination.

I decide.

"Yes," I say. "Oui."

He gestures to the girl. She rises and holds out her hand for me to go with her, her nightgown falling a little farther open, stifling the religious tremor in me but enhancing the tremor of anticipation, though the terror of it is quickly vanishing.

The lace of the nightgown is thin. I can make out the pale-eyed stare of her breasts there.

I step toward her.

She pulls back her hand and gestures for me to follow.

I do, along the davenports and into a dim hallway and then into a staircase. And as we begin to rise, something that has stuck in my head prompts me to say to this English speaker, "I did not come to conquer you."

She slows.

I continue: "Though I said yes to the man about choosing you, *conquest* was *his* word. Not mine. I did not agree with that word. It's not what I'm feeling."

She stops.

She turns to look down at me. She is in shadow, so I cannot read her face. I regret this, as she does not speak for a moment.

I go on: "I took it to be a comment on my uniform. Or perhaps just imprecise English. Either way, it was pointless to correct him."

And she says, "Thank you for telling me this."

Again, I regret not seeing her expression.

She turns away, continues to lead us upward, and we emerge into a corridor lit in red-veiled electric light and gatewayed by a corpulent woman in low-cleavaged ruffles sitting at a table with a cash box.

"Dix francs," the woman says to me.

"American," says the girl.

"Ah," says the woman. "Ten francs."

At this week's exchange rate that's one dollar in American money, that dollar worth twice as much as on the last day of the war.

I pay, and when I turn back to the girl, she is looking at me. The muted red light makes her not much easier to read, but her gaze is fixed and intent.

She extends her hand and takes mine.

Flesh on flesh.

She pulls me gently along and transfers her hand to the crook of my left arm. She presses her side against mine as we pass along the corridor, and she says, "I am Beatrice."

"I am Sam," I say.

The windowless room is small and sparse: an iron bed, a nightstand with a porcelain basin and a jug of water, a chair set beneath a peg on the wall. An electric lightbulb hangs from the ceiling, and though I know the sun presently shines on the streets of Paris, this room is all jaundice and shadow.

Beatrice glides ahead of me. I stop in the center of the floor. She arrives at the bed and turns. Her hands rise and she sloughs off her dressing gown and she is—except for her black satin stockings tied off just above the knees with red ribbons—breathtakingly naked. A darkly befurred arrow in the center of her body points to the woman part of her the like of which I have never yet seen and, from where we stand, I still cannot.

"Beatrice," I say.

Her face again turns slightly to one side, as if to reconsider a man who would address her by her name at this juncture. Not typical of her usual clientele, I infer. She quickly comes to some sort of conclusion and unfurls a small smile. "Sam," she says.

We let this do for a moment.

Then she says, softly, confidentially, "Beatrice is my real name."

She does not add, but I think I hear, *Which I do not usually divulge.*

"Sam is *my* real name," I say.

She laughs softly.

"You speak English," I say.

"Yes."

"How is that?"

"I am from Canada," she says. "My father was an English-speaking Canadian, my mother a French immigrant. I was born in Montreal."

For now, though my body at its center feels a scrabbling desire for Beatrice in her nakedness, I feel a stronger impulse to talk. I want to ask her follow-up questions, though none immediately yield words.

A few moments of silence pass between us.

Then Beatrice says, "They will knock at the door in thirty minutes."

Having slid into what will become a lifelong pathway in my mind—that path of questions and answers, of sentences constructed and refined and copyedited—I reflexively fill in the only available antecedent for the pronoun in her declaration. Her English-speaking father and her French immigrant mother will soon come knocking.

Though I hear it this way only briefly, it must be long enough to show on my face.

And Beatrice is a smart girl. She has heard her own ambiguity and knows what has just happened in my head. She is a girl with a sense of humor. She laughs. This naked girl who has just sold me thirty minutes of intimacy with her body throws back her head and laughs.

As do I.

When the laughter fades she says, "You know who I mean?"

"I do now."

We laugh a bit more.

Then fall silent.

And we remain motionless, looking each other in the eyes.

Until she says, "Sam, I am naked and you are not."

I look down at myself, though I know already that she is correct. And as things have gone, I am moved to say, "Beatrice, this is my first time."

"With anyone?"

"Yes."

She softly draws out a sympathetic-sounding "*Huh*" and nods at the chair beneath the peg. "Put your clothes there. That's the first step."

I comply, and then we are ready for her lesson and it is successful, with my active part in it proving to be brief. Quite brief. But I am present enough in the midst of it for the biblical phrase "one flesh" to come to mind, though in a secular and personal and localized way, and I am keenly conscious of how all the preceding looks and words and laughs that have passed between the two of us are very much present for me in the act.

That the act itself is brief turns out to be a benefit, as we have more than half our time to lie naked together and speak some more, which she is willing to do. I ask why she is not in Canada. "My father was a soldier in the British army, as good Empire Canadians were." She takes a big breath after this declaration and lets it out slowly. She says, "He died in the ninth month of the war. At Ypres. He was one of the first to be poisoned by mustard gas. My mother had no true family except in France, so we came to Paris. I was sixteen. Then circumstances brought me to this place and to this bed now to speak my father's name to you. It was George."

Speaking the name, she turns her face to me on the pillow, and I read her as she has read me several times. I say, "George." Softly.

"George," she says. And then: "Thank you for speaking it."

"Of course," I say.

"We have time enough," she says. "I am sure you have more in your body to give to me. Shall we try?"

"Yes," I say. "To supplement our words."

She smiles. She brings her face near mine and kisses me on the lips, a thing I realize she has not yet done.

So we join once more.

And having done all these things, having thought of them on the night I first fleetingly held Colleen in my arms, I lie in the bed at the back of her house and feel a need to apologize to someone. To Colleen. To my mother. To Beatrice. At least over her father. Apologize to God, though the only one I knew at the time was presiding over the First Baptist Church of Lake Providence, Louisiana, and I'd already parted ways with him.

I open my eyes briefly to the dark of my deathbed, thinking *this* is the God I need to start apologizing to. But His most recent commandment was for me to forget that He's listening and just fill the pages of this late city edition of the *Cunningham Examiner.* Though I now understand this isn't a family newspaper. Not with a banner headline of **Sniper Sam Loses Virginity in Paris Bordello**.

But the *Cunningham Examiner* will begin as the *Chicago Independent.* In working my job there, in becoming who I will become, what I witness and uncover and find words to tell will be the stories of my city and of my country and, consequently, inextricably, of me.

Strikes. In the news from my first days in journalism.

Workingmen struggling with low wages, dangerous conditions, and even jobs vanishing to machines and looking for a way to fight back. American strikes by American workers but thought by many to be stirred up by outsiders with no allegiance to this country, especially by the Reds from Russia. **New York Piers Idle by Strike of Longshoremen** and **Illinois Coal in Grip of Miner Strike** and in Boston **Armed-Gang Riots Fill Police Strike Void**.

Not that any of those were my stories, of course. On the day of a near-to-home miner strike, I'm still paying the dues of an aspiring cub reporter, assigned for that issue to cover a Great War veteran falling down three flights of steps and breaking his neck while visiting a girlfriend. A story stripped down for publication to eighty words, with neither foul play nor battlefield infirmities suspected. A small space filler at the bottom of a page-five, column-five jump from a front-page story about the next big anticipated labor strike: steelworkers at half the mills in the country, including the local one in Gary, Indiana.

Which, however, provides me an inspiration that will eventually propel my career forward: the steel story identifies a local union luminary as the chairman of the national committee for organizing the strike. John Fitzpatrick, president of the Chicago Federation of Labor.

At this point Kirch—I am now allowed to call him that—has taken a shine to me. Organized labor is always of keen news interest to the *Chicago Independent*, and Kirch puts me on John Fitzpatrick.

The Chicago Federation of Labor is the powerful local branch of the American Federation of Labor. I've already identified its headquarters location, a sixth-floor suite of a seven-story brick building on West Washington Street, a block from city hall and near the Independent Building as well.

So I set to work.

In our paper's photo morgue I find an image of John Fitzpatrick so I can recognize his mug when I see it.

I read the clip file on him. He was born in Ireland. His family immigrated to America when he was eleven. He became a horseshoer. Became a progressive. Became an official in the International Union of Journeymen Horseshoers. Which propelled his career forward.

The city saloons are fortunately still a few months from going dry, and I locate the nearest one to the C. F. of L. headquarters, a block north on Wells. Mick's. I am confident it's his: over its bar hang photos of the Chicago Cubs' Three-Fingered Mordecai Brown, the Chicago White Sox's Shoeless Joe Jackson, and the A. F. of L.'s Samuel Gompers.

I make it my after-work hangout, replete with a workingman's kersey cap on my head.

In a few days I'm on a nodding acquaintance with John Fitzpatrick. I even spot him with a copy of the *Independent*, as befits a Chicago progressive whose very job depends on news.

In this private, parallel pursuit of my job I wait. For what, exactly, I am not quite sure. Especially since my official news work has lately involved writing photograph captions for the upcoming Sunday rotogravure.

And then across the full width of the front page the **Big Steel Strike Begins** and on the lead column **Gary Starts Walkout at Center of Row** and **Fitzpatrick, Here, Gives Orders for Fight**. Related stories flurry on through the next several pages and all of them, including the ones on page one, carry a "Staff Correspondent" byline, which means reported by many, written by several, and assembled by a desk editor.

I read the coverage carefully. I have solid colleagues. I am content to learn. But the next day I read the multiple follow-up stories in our paper and recognize an opportunity. The strike has spread, and an official at Carnegie Steel in Pittsburgh has put out an "authorized statement" that includes a couple of assertions that are nowhere addressed in the story or anywhere else in our bulldog. That evening I'm at Mick's, and as soon as he enters, I follow along at Fitzpatrick's side.

I say his name and catch his eye and I whip off my kersey cap out of respect, hoping, for once, that I look closer to, rather than further from, my real age.

He pauses. A clean-shaven man with the face of a prize-fighter, not from bump-and-scar evidence of previous fights but from a massive squareness, a manifest ability to take blows.

I say, "I'm a young laborer whose tools are words in the newsroom of the *Chicago Independent*. My paper, as I wager you know, is deeply sympathetic with you and the C. F. of L. and I noticed yesterday that Big Steel claimed the men you fight for aren't actually Americans. In working my job, may I respectfully ask you for your thoughts on that?"

He gives me a smile, places a workingman-sized hand on my shoulder, gives me a tooth-jarring comradely shake, and then he gives me some words.

Half an hour later I am sitting at an office Oliver in the Independent Building with the late city boys busy around me and I am happy to see Kirch still in his office.

Soon thereafter I knock at the frame of his open door and I hand him a story I have already pared down to the classically tight cub reporter length so as not to overstep my place and yet to show him what a cub reporter story can be.

He puts on his pair of wire-rimmed, late-in-the-day reading glasses and he lifts my story before him.

It says:

> John Fitzpatrick, president of the Chicago Federation of Labor and chairman of the national committee for organizing the steel strike, strenuously objects to yesterday's statement by the Carnegie Steel Company calling the strikers "in every instance foreign" while "95 per cent of the remaining workmen are American."
>
> Fitzpatrick told a Chicago Independent reporter, "In point of fact, there are no Americans presently working in the steel mills."
>
> He explained, "The only real American is the Indian, and there are no Indians working in the steel mills. We

are all foreigners compared to them. And that includes everyone in management at every steel corporation."

Kirch finishes reading and lays the story before him on his desktop. Rather deliberately. Squaring up the copy before him. He pries the glasses off his ears and places them upon my story.

He looks at me.

I find I can barely draw a breath.

"As I anticipated," he says. And he pauses.

I have stopped breathing altogether.

And then he unfurls another of his carefully rationed and modulated and therefore quite powerful smiles. "You have the gift," he says.

Months will pass. For Colleen and me to work our jobs, to let time reveal who we are to each other, to act out between us the chaste seemliness of the age, which we have inevitably assimilated. And meanwhile, not only am I now quickly advancing in the writing of news, it is still my way—will always be my way—to sprawl in the evening with the competing dailies and quaff the news, swill the news.

In the beginning was the News. News is life. Life is news.

And the pages of the Chicago newspapers riffle through that first year, most typified by the *Chicago Daily Tribune*, which arrives at Colleen's front door, routinely leavening its biggest news events with coverage on its front page as well, of a parallel city and country, admittedly just as real to its half a million readers, just as intensely lived and felt and raptly embraced. **Can He Kiss? This Girl Says Pershing Can**, for instance, laid out cheek to cheek with the Boston police-strike riot, a story about the country's beloved General John Joseph "Black Jack" Pershing who has conquered the kaiser and who grabs a pretty stranger when she presents him with flowers at his New York City parade and kisses her full on the lips like no man ever has ever kissed her before, and the world riffles on as a **Vast Mob of White Men Burn Down Omaha Court House** and beat and unsuccessfully lynch the white mayor after he tries to prevent them from lynching a Negro inmate, whom the mob successfully lynches shortly thereafter, and the **President Is 'Very Sick'** and it's not about lynchings, he's physically sick only a week after his having to cut short his futile League of Nations speaking tour "on the verge of nervous collapse" while two columns over, **Wife Sues Broker Found with Girl** the girl being unfazed in the subhead *'I Don't Care,' Says Betsy, 'I Guess I'll Marry Him'* and the Democrats **Pick Cox and Roosevelt** repudiating the reputedly paralyzed President Wilson and the Republicans choose **Harding & Coolidge!** exclaimed in eight columns over a center-four-column cartoon with Warren G. Harding's massively bannered face hanging before an upgawking gathering of Americans, each pondering a question about this candidate who has been *Chosen in a 'Smoke-Filled Room'*: "I wonder if he'll beat a Democrat" and "I wonder if he'll be a demagogue" and "I wonder what labor can expect from him" and "I wonder what his Mexican policy will be" and "I wonder if he'll reduce my cost of living" and "I wonder if he'll reduce my profits" and "I wonder what he feels about the Reds."

And seven weeks after the conventions **Wilson Greets Women Now 'On Equal Footing'** the story of the final ratification of women's suffrage rendered thus indirectly on the *Tribune* front page without being a characteristic eight-column big-font bellow but on a single column with its headline in modest font and all of four paragraphs long. Indeed, it appears on the same front page as **Body and Baby Held for Unpaid Hospital Bill** which has twice as many paragraphs and the subhead *Widower Says He's Unable to Raise Cash*, and the eight-column screamer headline on the suffrage ratification front page is about mob unrest in Ireland provoked by the English Crown ignoring the hunger strike of the mayor of Cork. I have this particular newspaper before me on the kitchen table near the end of a long summer twilight, and Colleen must have finished her mending in the chair across from me as she rises and circles the table and stands behind me.

I continue to read, as she always encourages when she does this. As always, as well, I feel a sweetly nibbling warmth spread from the center of my chest and up into my face as she bends near me to read over my shoulder.

"So it's really all about Woodrow Wilson, that whole event," she says. "His magnanimity."

"So it seems," I say.

Colleen humphs, to underscore our shared irony.

"Not in *my* paper," I say. Today's *Independent* spanned its front page with **Women's Suffrage in Force** in eighty-four-point type.

"So I saw," Colleen says. Then she chuckles, a one-note, soft-edged chuckle as if she has just shared another irony with me.

She remains behind me, over my shoulder. I turn a little and look up at her.

Her smile is as small and soft as the laugh.

"What?" I ask.

"'*Your* paper,'" she says.

I instantly hear how it sounded.

In this past year I've grown from cub to ravenous young bear of a reporter, assigned to the police blotters of Chicago. Colleen is proud of that. But she has a point.

"You're right," I say. "It's still the other way round. I belong to the paper."

Her smile expands. "Ah, the implication of *still*," she says. "Suggesting the state is temporary."

I shrug. "I have prospects."

And she lays her hand on my shoulder.

I look down at it. Another irony for us. In this first year of ours, since the recoil incident was resolved, we have comfortably touched in casually quotidian ways and in formally congratulatory ways. But in no other way.

Her hand remains. I lift mine and lay it over hers. I look up at her.

I hesitate. But it's time to speak. I do so gently. "*Do* I have prospects?"

She knows what I ask.

I feel her hand stir beneath mine. I expect it to withdraw. Instead, it turns upward and our palms touch and we are holding hands upon my shoulder. Searching each other's eyes. My question, it seems, having been answered.

Indeed, this very evening we sit side by side on the living room davenport, that chair empty at last and bearing sightless witness to the kisses of Colleen and Sam, our thighs tightly and unwaveringly aligned, ardent but chaste, as our shoulders square around to each other and our lips speak wordlessly of what we have become.

Between kisses we say little. The world is but eight months into the third decade of the twentieth century, bobbed hair barely yet offsetting the newly shuttered saloons.

The next afternoon, a Saturday, with Kirch having sent me home early after a rigorous week of three page-one stories ranging from dead bank teller to police dragnet to dead bank robber, I am pushing an Acme lawn mower over Colleen's front yard. Aware, however, of that very phrase in my head: *Colleen's front yard.* Turning it over the way Walter Mandel might at his copydesk, finding it somehow imprecise.

It is at this moment that I reach the sidewalk and wheel around to mow back toward the house. I raise my eyes. Dim behind the screen door Colleen stands watching. I mow my way up the yard, the blades whisking like the wings of a low-flying bird re-created in metal by Henry Ford.

Colleen remains motionless as I approach, as I stop, as I draw out my handkerchief and wipe my brow, as I cock my head at her gaze, questioning if she has something on her mind. Given the recent kissing, I trust she does.

I leave the lawn and step up to the door.

The screen remains between us, but our eyes are unflinching.

We do not speak for a while.

Finally she says, "Thank you for the grass."

"I was feeling domestic," I say.

"So was I," she says. "Watching you."

"Perhaps," I say, "we should get married."

And she says, "There's a three thirty train to Crown Point."

Crown Point being the well-known marriage-mill town just across the border in Indiana, where there's no waiting period, no blood test, minimal paperwork, an optional sixty-second sermon by Judge Henry B. Nicholson, justice of the peace, and an average of ten weddings for each day of the year, annually matching nearly the entire population of Crown Point, Indiana.

"I have no ring," I say.

"There is a jeweler next to the courthouse. It's open late on Saturday night."

"You have given this some prior thought," I say.

"Since I realized I love you," Colleen says.

"I've realized the same thing," I say. Which requires a bit of copyediting: "About me. Loving you."

We share a brief, further clarifying silence.

Then Colleen says, "There is a porch screen presently between us."

I open the door.

We kiss.

We catch the 3:30 on the Chicago & Erie Railway and snuggle up at the end of the car. Given the improvised life we have lived so far on Wendell Street and our present quest, there are things we have not yet said that need to be said. We both seem to realize this at the same time and without preamble Colleen begins.

She says, "My father was a bad man. After he brought my mother and sister and me to America and we'd been here for a decade, he died in a bar fight, though that was by no means fully indicative of his badness, which, however, is all I will have to say about that, and when he rightly died, my mother and sister went back to Ireland. I did not go because I was about to marry Paul. That's why you will be, in effect, without in-laws. In case you were wondering."

And I say to Colleen, for it is time, "My father is a serious problem as well. I am the emigrant. From him, more than from Louisiana. But my mother's life is bound to his. Inextricably. Regrettably. Though perhaps someday you will meet her. I hope so." I pause. I consider whether I am, in fact, finished in this exchange, but shortly there will be formalities and I am reluctant to falsify them—most of all to her—and so, even as she lays her head upon my shoulder, I say, "One other thing."

She lifts her face to me.

And I declare, "I am—in some superficial sense, though hardly in some larger reality—nineteen years old."

She draws away. Not far. And gently so. Just, it seems, to look at me anew, which she does, her eyes fixing keenly on mine. "How?"

"I lied," I say. Then quickly: "Not to you or your friend. I was indeed a sniper in the war. That's the larger reality. I lied to the U.S. Army."

She narrows her eyes a bit—in thought, it seems. In those eyes, which now relax once more, I can see conclusions being drawn. Upon her mouth are signs of her wanting to smile but deliberately holding it back. She says, "So I'm to be the corrupter of youth."

I repress my own smile at my twenty-three-year-old soon-to-be wife. "Do you say this in aspiration?"

She returns her head to my shoulder.

By ten o'clock that night Mr. and Mrs. Cunningham arrive home.

She declines being carried across the threshold.

She takes me by the hand and leads me to our bedroom upstairs.

She declines any light in the room other than the minimal bit of moon and stars along the edge of the window shades and I decline inwardly to press the matter, though I regret not seeing her eyes one more time on this day. This time particularly. Which leads me to regret Beatrice of Montreal and Paris. Which leads me to regret that regret, out of consideration for Beatrice, her words more than her body.

And on this first night with my wife, Colleen, as we join our bodies together, I sense a vague tentativeness in her. From this and from her subsequent silence and from what I feel as the lifting of her hand to her face, perhaps to wipe away tears, I understand how complicated this must be for her.

But she puts her arms around me.

I am, though nineteen years old, wise enough not to ask about the complications. Instead I say, quite softly, "I love you, Mrs. Cunningham."

She replies, softer still, "I love you, Mr. Cunningham."

We fall silent and we cling gently to each other for our passage to sleep. And because what we have just said is true, I now realize that this joining of our bodies on our wedding night—though tentative, though complex—that this joining renders simply preparatory the small bed in the small room in Paris where I joined with a smart girl, whose father was named George, as she lived through her own complexities. A preparation as important but forgettable as a toddler's first steps.

And I am in the nursing home corridor once again, Maintenance Man Duke's face still turned in my direction but not seeing me, his lips still compressed with strong feeling, and he snaps his head back to confront Head Nurse Bocage.

He says, "You ask how we come to this? Even if you don't want an answer I'll give you one, Head Fucking Nurse. Because the answer is I finally *got* an answer and you gotta hear it. No shutting me up like it's always been. The president of the United States knows who I am. That's how. Me and enough of the rest of us to finally elect a fucking president who really knows us all. Even though he made a billion bucks out of the system, he still has the mind of one of us, like a guy who's actually got jack shit and he's pissed about it. Just like us. He's *our* goddamn president. So he can do and say what he fucking wants."

Duke finishes.

He lifts his chin at her.

Nurse Bocage stands rigidly tall in silence.

Peaches, tough gal though she is, has gone a little wide-eyed and has drawn back a bit from the desk. Even the nurse in the outer lobby has turned his face to view the altercation. His eyes are clear to me. Quite large and dark but not widened at the scene, not fearful. Calm. Seemingly unalarmed at Duke.

And I am back in my bed.

The darkness is absolute. I feel it as a weight upon my open eyes, light but palpable. God must be near.

"I did that on my own again? Drifting back to the front desk?"

"Yes," God says.

"What now? It felt like closure."

"What did?"

"Not the election of Duke's president."

"I know what you meant. I just want you to say it for yourself."

"Closure," I say. "The end of Lake Providence. The end of the war. The end of my apprenticeship to write the kind of words I'd been reading since childhood. The end of my solitude. Journey's end to the arms of my wife."

"Tell me, Sam. Why don't those all feel like the beginnings of things?"

I say, "Because you're not letting me see what's next."

"You know how this works."

"Sorry," I say. "It's not on you. It's me who doesn't want it to go on from there. So I just turned myself into a feature story for the Sunday supplement. A nice little feature that whispers to the reader, *You won't read any more about this. It'll be sweet and complete in you forever, no matter what happens next.* But not knowing what's next fits who I always was, doesn't it? The newsman.

The reporter of *hard* news. You put it all in the story by today's deadline and tomorrow you wait for further developments."

I pause. I'm not sure where I'm going with this.

God says, "That's pretty much how you all live your lives."

"And that was fine for me," I say. "That's the way a newsman likes it. But now here I am lying in this place with substantially more than a century of life come and gone. And the full hard news stories of everybody I've ever known have all been bulldogged to their stories' end. I float out to the front desk because maybe a benighted part of me figures somebody I used to know will show up there. But there's nobody. There's been nobody for years. I've apparently long ago accepted that. *Apparently* because of your tinkering with my memory. My wife would be a hundred and nineteen. My son would be ninety-three. I get that. But I don't know if there's anyone else who followed who's simply not showing up."

God says, "So shall we get back to the matter at hand?"

"Is that a rhetorical question?"

"You prefer another commandment?"

"No. I get it. Back to dying."

God says, "Just accept what your memory gives you now. Whatever it is. However selective. Beginnings leading to middles leading to ends—the longing for that structure is an inescapable part of who you all are. Your life may return to you that way. But it may not. Just stay in the moment, Sam."

This sounds to me like God's about to slip away for a while. No doubt He's having a typically busy night on planet Earth.

He answers the thought. "Don't worry. I'll still be listening. And I'll be back."

I'm seized by the impulse to pick a bone before he goes. "Speaking of a moment, since those two buildings in Manhattan came down in my hundredth year, my country's gone veeringly mad. And now this thing that you let me witness tonight on the television up there. It feels like there's worse to come. Couldn't you have taken me yesterday? Or even a couple of hours ago?"

"Who knew?" God says. "I didn't create the electoral college, Sam. But be calm. At this point, this isn't about him or them or anyone but you. Just don't be deceived about the *you*. Far more remains inside the circle of who you are than that bed you're lying in."

He pauses for that to sink in.

It does.

He says, "I'm going to let you do this now."

And I find myself entering the La Salle Street station, the Chicago Police Department's First Precinct headquarters. At the end of a scorching August, 1922. The heat has baked up the smells of cigar smoke and old oak and man-sweat and the place is bustling as I approach the ankle-high platform at the far wall beyond the booking desk. The presiding sergeant, Dermot Gallagher, is there at a desk of his own, sitting beneath an oversized photo of Hizzoner Big Bill Thompson, whose fleshy head is barely balancing a bowler. Gallagher sees me coming, knows me well by now, and he strips off his reading glasses as I approach.

He's a good cop. I know how it galls him to sit beneath Thompson, as corrupt and corruptible a mayor as Chicago is capable of producing, which is saying something.

Yesterday evening I saw a Teletype from the City News Bureau, the city's cooperative news agency staffed with a few old pro editors and a horde of hotshot wish-I-were reporters looking to do some apprentice time and move on. I recognize the young hotshot cockiness going on in my own head; I probably would have ended up at the CNB myself except for Kirch. The horde certainly knows how to Mongol a police blotter for leads. Half a dozen of the city's dailies lean on the CNB for quick, light rewrites of below-the-fold crime fillers. The *Independent* never indulges in the CNB shortcut, but we take the Teletypes to avoid getting bit on the backside if the pack of pups finds something.

I figure this happened last night. I saw one of their items come over the wire and this morning the *Tribune* has quickly picked it up. Clearly not because they saw it as important. I doubt they could have. They gave it a few inches at the bottom of page three because the story has some exotic touches, but they picked up the CNB's misspelling of the principal's name. A mug about whom I've been keeping my eyes and ears open for a few months. I've never yet seen his name in a newspaper. I know of him from my street source on the South Side, a panhandler and odd-jobber who haunts Wabash Avenue.

"I thought I'd see you this morning," Gallagher says.

I stop before him, not stepping onto his platform without permission. Gallagher lifts a forefinger and gives it a come-hither flutter.

I ascend.

"You know me well, Sarge," I say. It became somehow clear to me early on working with Gallagher that he likes me calling him familiarly by his rank, though I later learned I'm one of the rare few he allows to do it. He knows what I did in the war and he was old enough to have missed out and he likes the spin of *Sarge* coming from an officer of the American Expeditionary Force. I think he also likes this young first looey knowing to obey his rules of ascension to his desk.

"You playing catch-up?" Gallagher says. "It was in one of the morning rags already."

"The *Tribune*," I say.

"That one."

"I saw. The story got some things wrong and I think I've heard of this guy."

"I hadn't," Gallagher says. "Booked here because he chose the corner of Wabash and Randolph to drunkenly run his auto into a parked taxi and threaten the cabbie with a pistol. The story was right about him flashing a deputy sheriff's badge at our boys and claiming pull. Bogus badge, but he does have pull. Had a Dago shyster in a stiff collar here in no time to bail him out. Tightly mobbed up he is. He'll walk."

"One of Johnny Torrio's boys," I say. "But they got his name wrong in the *Trib*. Straight from the Teletype."

"What?" Gallagher opens the ledger book before him to find his blotter entry. He finds it. "Christ's wounds," Gallagher says, faintly but vehemently. It was obviously the same one as in the newspaper. "Not Alfred Caponi?"

"Not quite," I say. "His name, in Chicago at least, is Al Capone."

Gallagher snorts. "If he wanted to make up an alias, even the worst moron working for Torrio is going to do a better job at it than that."

The growl that punctuates this insight suggests that the duty sergeant who took the booking yesterday morning is going to catch Gallagher's wrath.

But we don't mention it.

He and I compare details on the incident and the arrest, and I'm left with nothing much other than a possible us-too filler story with a few corrections. So I exit the precinct figuring it's time finally to go over the top of the trench and introduce myself to Al Capone.

It's the last day of August and I wait for the late sundown to end before I head south to 2222 Wabash. The so-called Four Deuces, a four-story brick row building with columns of bay windows flanking its facade. The central entrance leads straight into the main business of the place, a brothel. Capone runs the joint, a detail even the *Tribune* got right. To one side is the entrance, improbably, to a furniture store. Capone has his name stenciled as proprietor in a lower corner of the front door, a thumbed nose of an alias in its transparency. He has a sense of humor, I figure. On the other side is the Four Deuces saloon. I'm betting Al will make an appearance on this day when he's flexed his muscle with the Chicago Police Department.

I insert my press pass in the hatband of my fedora. The mobsters have never bumped off a newsman, to anybody's knowledge.

On the contrary, their singularly most profitable business in Chicago is quenching the city's Prohibition-challenged thirst, and since many of the mugs in charge tend to romanticize their quest for self-definition, the newspapers are considered by some of them to be useful. A stick to draw a line.

So I step in. The heat of the day is still here, baking up some more than vaguely familiar smells: cigar smoke and old oak and sweat, though gangster sweat instead of copper.

I figure out I need to stop for the muscle just inside the door. He looks me over, sees my press pass. I offer my straight gaze to his, though he narrows his eyes. He begins to frisk me.

"I'm just packing a pencil," I say.

"Don't use it unless somebody tells you it's okay," he says, and he finishes the frisk. Then he says, "See the man behind the bar."

I figure that's not standard for everyone entering. Any newsman simply here for booze doesn't fly the flag of his profession on his head.

I nod and move to the back of the place, a nice mahogany bar with a couple of available spots. I lean into one and the barman comes over.

I say, "I'm here to see you. Your man's instructions."

He's already noticed my hat.

I assume he's also seen the morning's news item.

"You on the job?" he says.

"Not what you think," I say. "Sure, I'd like to see Mr. Capone. But not what you think. Not to write a story. If he's available, tell him I think he got a bum rap from the press today, starting with his name, which is known on this street with respect. Mine is Sam Cunningham. Of the *Chicago Independent.*"

The barman has pulled back through all this in slow-accumulating surprise. Now he flashes me a small smile that whiffs approval.

"Can't promise anything," he says.

"Then draw me a beer in the meantime so it ain't a wasted trip," I say.

He does and puts it before me and slips away, vanishing through a door in the back wall. Another guy in shirtsleeves and bow tie who's been working the tables shows up at once to pinch-hit for him.

I lean into the bar and sip the beer, which is surprisingly good, suggesting the word on the street is correct, that the Torrio gang has one of the big, previously legit breweries making the real stuff for them sub rosa.

I nurse the beer almost to the bottom and suddenly the first barman is before me again. "This way," he says.

So he leads me through the rear portal and into a dim staircase and up one floor and down a corridor to the rear. After the barman's double-knuckled signal rap on a door, I'm in a small but proper-looking business office.

At the opposite wall Capone sits facing me from behind a desk in a cloud of cigar smoke. He's got a ledger book open there like a proper business accountant. Or a police sergeant before his blotter.

He rises.

He circles the desk. A heavy man and a heavy mover in this tight space. Heavy but natty in a chalk-striped vested suit and silk tie, both in shades of gray. As he moves I catch a clear glimpse of two prominent scars: a long one emerging from his sideburn and angling far down toward his mouth, and another from ear to jawline.

The face is young, temporarily carrying its weight as puff instead of jowl. His suit and the still-tight knot of the tie and the careful trim of his pitch-dark eyebrows speak of a precocious young gangster with big-time executive ambitions, a sense already of a careful image in the making. An image perhaps ready to go public. My young newsman self with ambitions sees all this as exploitable. This guy and his needs can complement mine. And I'm willing to bet Capone's ambitions go far beyond the primary wares of a Wabash Avenue brothel. The big money is in the stuff on tap and in bottles downstairs. That's why he wants his name right when it goes public.

All this flashes through me in the little time it takes for Capone to circle the desk and settle himself before me.

And for one more moment we both prepare ourselves.

Me once more reminded of going over the top.

Him making a final quick calculation about me.

I am watching his mouth. His outsized lips are set in a determined calmness that verges on the sinister, as if he is about to do to me what he was brought to Chicago by Torrio to do to competing gangsters.

I am certain he sees in me a calmness as well. He may not recognize it as learned in the war, but I hope its aspect impresses him.

And now his face dilates into a smile and he takes a step to me and offers his right hand and I take it and his grip is intense and his other hand falls on top of ours. He keeps the shake going through our first exchange of words.

"Sam Cunningham, huh?"

"That's right, Mr. Capone," I say.

He nods and tightens his grip on my hand a little. It feels like a comradely squeeze. From my use of his correct name, I surmise. "Right," he says. "Those lousy rat fucks. Who hires mutts like that in your racket? Get a guy's name wrong."

"Not at our paper."

"They wouldn't work for me."

"Not for long," I say.

Capone barks a laugh at this, gives my hand a final squeeze and lets it go. "They're a danger to themselves," he says, attaching to his words a chuckle that appreciates my knowing what his managerial style entails.

"Sit," he says, waving his hand to a pair of overstuffed chairs facing each other at a side wall.

We sit. He fills my view. Capone's private space for cordial intimidation.

He says, "Eddie's got a good memory. My barmen all have good memories. He gave me your pitch just like you said it. I liked it. See, if you was of a different tribe and you came to me for a job, I'd say, *Give this man a chance.*"

"I appreciate that, Mr. Capone."

"But you're better off where you are," he says.

This is a complicated little declaration. Part of me construes it in my own personal way: I'm lucky to be at the right newspaper, where I can become what I seek to be: A real newsman.

A reporter who will record as truly as he can what the actors in the world are doing and saying. Objectively. Let the story tell itself. Keep a paper's opinions and agendas on the editorial page. Banish the lies and distortions of sensationalism. That's not the norm with circulation-hungry big city dailies. But in Chicago it's more or less the norm at the *Independent*. And I have a gut feeling this might appeal to Al Capone. Make him useful to me. But right now he doesn't know that's what I'm after. He can't even imagine it. Still, I hear his declaration consciously opening the question: What exactly are we going to do for each other?

I've given all this a swift thought. I start to figure out how to explain. But before I can, he says, "Are you a right guy, Sam Cunningham?"

"I am," I say. "Something happens that involves you or your boys, or you have something on your mind or you got something to let me in on, I write down what you say exactly as you say it. And that's what goes into the newspaper. I *am* a right guy, Mr. Capone. So I've got to tell you I'm going to give the same treatment to the cops or anyone else directly involved in a story. Being a right guy means no twisting and lying to sell newspapers. No high-horsing. No taking sides. Everybody gets to say and be who they are. The people you want to talk to in our pages will hear you straight. They'll know who's got what they want."

Capone has been perched through all this on the edge of his chair. He eases back now, expands, dips his thumbs into his vest pockets. "We can live with that," he says.

He continues to intrigue me. I am not sure if he's as nuanced as I'm hearing. The ambiguity of the "we can live." Meaning he and his organization are willing to accept that agreement? Meaning *me* continuing to have the privilege to remain among the living along with him, as long as I abide by that agreement? Or both? I have an immediate and strong intuition that *yes*. In his own way, he's every bit that nuanced.

"You want to shake again on that, Mr. Capone?"

He chuckles and leans forward and we grip hands as firmly as we each can without inviting a competition, and we shake.

He offers me a woman upstairs.

I respectfully decline out of love for my wife.

He expresses his admiring approval of that sentiment.

He offers me free drinks downstairs.

I compliment the quality of his beer and accept one more that I promise to lift toward these two chairs as a toast.

And so Al Capone and I begin.

And I am in the dark, approaching our house on Wendell Street. Is it this same evening? I think it is. I told Colleen I'd be late, though I only said I was developing a news source, leaving the Mob out of it so as not to worry her.

She should be in bed. I go up our porch steps with a silent tread and I muffle open our door and I find the front room tinged by light from the kitchen.

I expect to find her at the table there. Perhaps with a cup of warm milk. Tomorrow is a workday and her work begins early. Nevertheless I ease the door shut before I begin to cross the room.

And then I find her curled asleep on the davenport in her bare feet and her nainsook nightgown.

I wonder whether to cover her or to wake her. I think of something in between, soothing her into a half awakening and taking her gently into my arms and carrying her upstairs. She does hard work at the Mutual Life Insurance Company of Chicago. Increasingly responsible work. She's typed her way up from the office pool to secretary for a rising young executive.

I think, *Of course she has.* I know the quickness of her mind.

But still. Long, hard work.

I think, *She deserves to be carried up the stairs.*

I kneel beside her.

She opens her eyes.

After a brief moment of disorientation, she says, "Darling."

"Shall I carry you?" I say.

"No." This is firm. She is fully awake now.

She sits up. I rise and sit down beside her.

I ask, "What brought you to the davenport?"

She squares around a bit to look directly at me. Her face is in shadow.

"A little sleeplessness," she says. "A few too many thoughts."

I wait.

She waits.

I wish I could see her face more clearly to read it. Her answer does not quite explain why the davenport was her destination.

I take a guess. "Anything you want to talk about?"

"Yes," she says. She shrugs. "But I didn't realize how late you'd be. This was an accident, me falling asleep here."

"Wouldn't you rather go to bed now? You're the one who's up with the birds in the morning."

"You're right." She pauses, and I expect her to rise and head upstairs in anticipation of the birds. But she has circled back to my guess. "I do want to talk about it," she says.

This seems not to be a small thing. I want to see her face. "Just a moment," I say. I turn and pull the cord of the floor lamp beside the davenport, hoping to stop the faint wobble of concern that has begun in me.

But she has assumed her furrowed face, and my fingers itch to smooth the place between her brows. "Tell me," I say.

"I have never lied to you," she says. "But there's one thing that hasn't come up between us and my omission of it gives me a pang."

She pauses.

"What sort of pang?" I ask.

"A more or less mild one," she says. "Can a pang be mild?"

"I think so."

"A mild one then. Though the subject is important."

She pauses again.

The furrow persists.

I say, "You do know, don't you, that you're giving *me* a mild pang? Drawing this out?"

"Sorry," she says. "How to say it?"

She has asked this of herself and it takes a moment to silently find an answer. Then: "We neither of us adhere scrupulously to the religions of our upbringing. Or even unscrupulously for that matter. Especially Catholic me, who's had even further to fall."

With her next pause I try to help out. "So you downgraded the sinfulness of lies of omission, yes? I'm all in favor of that."

"Ah, there's that," she says. "But I cite my abandoned Catholicism not about the omission itself but about the thing I omitted. Well, the omission too. But that's not how it started. I married Paul when our entry into the war seemed imminent. Margaret Sanger was already in my personal panoply of saints, and it was clear to both Paul and me that it would be wise to limit our family, as she champions, but more pressingly to postpone it. He did not want to be away on the Western Front as his child was starting to grow up. And so I learned the ways of birth control."

I suddenly understand. "Which you've been employing with us."

"Mea culpa," she says, and she thumps her fist upon her chest. And thumps it once more. "Mea maxima culpa."

I overheard this bit of Catholic Latin a couple of times, in France. Each time from a dying man to a trench priest. I knew what that moment was about. And how private it was meant to be. Each time, I turned away.

"What does the priest do with that?" I ask.

"He offers forgiveness."

I remember a gesture. I lift my hand and make a cross in the air for Colleen.

"That's it," she says.

"You're forgiven," I say.

"I want you to understand," she says. "It's not your fault that nothing has yet come of our intimacy."

I hesitate at this notion.

She misunderstands. She gropes a hand toward me. "Really. I'm so sorry. Of course you couldn't have known. I use a device inside, a pessary it's called, a little internal cap I place squarely over my contribution to the process. I was in control. I hope you didn't think it was you."

"I hadn't thought about it at all," I say. "We've both been busy starting up our lives. If I thought anything, it was to be grateful for not having to manage a family." I pause. But I think to add a reassurance. "Temporarily."

I see a flicker of something in her face at this last word. An anxious something. At once I say, "I understand."

"You do?"

"It's time now," I say.

She looks away, unsquares herself from before me, leans back into the davenport.

"My ambition made me oblivious to your needs," I say. "Mea culpa. You didn't want to put the burden on me of supporting you and a baby. Not while I was working my way up from cub reporter."

The furrow returns to her brow. I'm not sure why.

She looks at me.

I say, "It doesn't bother me, the omission. Really. You were being considerate."

All this seems not to be brightening her. I expected a little surge of relief from her. It's all okay. I can begin to support three of us now. *She's tired,* I think.

She says, "It's more complicated than that. I'm truly enjoying the job. And it's becoming more important as my boss climbs the ladder. The cap was for me as well. That's part of *mea* mea culpa."

I delay a moment to work at a complex task, keeping my voice neutral in preference, warm still in my engagement with her. A shadow begins to pass over her face, no doubt over mine as well, but I'm ready to say, "Perhaps we should wait a little longer." It comes out okay.

Her shadow vanishes. "No," she says. "Really. I am ready—more than ready—for our baby. Along with whatever else, I've always wanted to be a mother. It's time to make this inevitable choice. Time for both of us. I have no regrets, my darling."

And the shadow lifts from me.

I stand up before her.

I say, "Then the time is right. Doff your cap."

Colleen draws a deep breath and says, "Yes. Consider it doffed and tossed."

I offer my hand.

She takes it and she rises, and we walk together up the stairs.

And my son is born. It was a difficult birth, the doctor tells me, and Colleen is sedated though she will be all right, but my son is brought to me swaddled, and I hold him in my hands, his face floating there like the bloom of a flower, and I am struck that he is mine. Not as a material possession, this new-fledged human, but that he has my face. The eyes are a lighter blue—though I know this is a phenomenon of his newness and I foresee that they will darken to the blue of a forest shadow on snow—but they are slightly narrow set in a familiar way and are in familiarly proportioned triangulation from their outer edges to the tip of his nose, and they are underscored by an equally familiar fullness of lips. And I edit myself: He is not *mine.* He is *me.* A forever externalized me. Free, yes, inevitably, in his independent existence. But carrying a recognizable me upon him, within him. The circle drawn around me has been cast outward. How far and to where it extends I do not know, however. And by a hand that is not mine. I stand through a ripple of unease about all that. Which passes. I edit myself again: not *passes.* Which settles permanently in, but deeply, unobtrusively. Perhaps not *un*obtrusive. Perhaps disguisedly obtrusive: I am vulnerable now in a new way. Knowing that he is vulnerable.

Colleen is vulnerable too, awake after her arduous birthing, her face floating on the pillow like my son's, her eyes turning to me, recognizing me as I step to her, and I take her hand. We hold to each other even as the nurse arranges pillows to help prop her up and then goes out.

"Have you seen him?" she asks.

"I have," I say.

The nurse returns and Colleen lets go of my hand as our boy settles into her arms and she looks down upon him and says, "Ryan."

Colleen and I have spoken about names, though we agreed to look the child in the face before deciding. One of them on the short list was Ryan. One was Samuel Junior.

She lifts her face to me. "Sorry," she says. "But isn't he our little king?" Citing the Gaelic meaning of the name.

I feel it's just as well, that he not have my name in addition to my face. For his sake.

"He's already you," she says. "Look at him."

"In his love of you, most of all," I say. I nod toward Ryan.

She turns back to him and he is focused fully on her, wide-eyed, unflinching.

"He's entranced," I say.

She pulls him closer, kisses him in the center of his forehead.

And she lifts him just like that enough months later that he has begun to go up on hands and knees and rock as if to crawl, our son, but it is early evening and he is on the cusp of sleep and we three are together on our davenport before the fireplace, and she lifts him to her and kisses him in the center of his forehead and then she lays him on her chest, his cheek against hers, and her eyes are full of tears. This day her doctor has told us of the fibroid tumor growing in her womb. A womb she must now relinquish. We will be man and wife fully again, no more pains in her back and legs, no more seemingly ceaseless blood in her time of month. We will have the pleasure of our joining restored, but there will be no more children. It will be the three of us, and no one else. Not that I have looked that far ahead anyway. Nor, I think, has she.

"It's all right," she says, and her voice does not waver, does not even harden to repress a waver. Her voice is steady and calm and I believe her. And I find that if she is indeed sincere in this ready acceptance, so am I.

"If it's truly all right for you," I say.

"It is," she says.

"Then here we are, the three of us," I say.

"My boy!" I cry. In the dark. From the dark. On my deathbed.

I am full of dread. And I don't know why I have cried out as I did, though I feel I should know.

I revisit these moments in my life. At the behest of God Himself, for Chrissake, and then I can't see how they go next, how they turn out, though it's all already happened long ago. But that's the way He wants it. Obviously. Part of this process, right?

"Right?" I cry. I hear the jagged edge in my voice. I repeat it in a reasoning tone. A supplicant's tone. "Am I right?"

From the dark: nothing.

"Hey!" I shout. "Hey."

Not exactly the classic summoning for Him.

I should not be surprised when it doesn't work.

God doesn't show.

Instead, Al Capone scares the bejesus out of me. A couple of his thugs appear before me on the sidewalk of West Monroe as I come out of the Independent Building, Al's natty thugs in their high soft collars with fashionable points framing immaculate four-in-hands.

"Sam Cunningham," one of them says.

"Yes," I say.

"Mr. Capone says you is to come with us."

A Ford sits muttering at the curb with a third thug behind the wheel.

"Where are we going?" I ask. A natural question, of course, but I regret asking it.

"He just says to give you a ride," one of the thugs says, and that's an answer I prefer not to have elicited. This is a well-known and much-feared thing, being *given a ride* by a Chicago gang. Is this Al's sense of humor at work? Applying it to me? I realize that I'm not sure.

So one of these two thugs sits beside the driver and one sits beside me in the back seat and we mutter on west on Monroe.

I've been covering Al's rise for a couple of years, and though his mentor and titular boss, Johnny Torrio, is still around as the chairman of the board, Al's the chief operating officer now. He's in full control of the South Side and the de facto overlord of the West Side. Since the Volstead Act created this all-American big-business operation, there's been a three-way Torrio truce with the Sicilians in Little Italy and, combustibly, with Dean O'Banion, boss of the Irish-run North Side Gang. In his ruthlessness and his sense of irony, O'Banion always seemed to me a bit of an Irish Al, not reluctant to personally put a bullet in the brain of an enemy with his ruthlessness and to run a florist shop with his irony, though, indeed, he has spent far more personal time with his flowers than Al has with his used furniture. But finally—inevitably, given his temperament and his hatred for the Italians—O'Banion started overreaching in the West Side. Two days ago four men came into his shop, and Dean O'Banion, with a pair of flower shears in his hand, took two bullets in the chest, two in the throat, one in the left cheek as he lay on the floor among his flower clippings, and a sixth and final bullet, fittingly, in his own favorite target, the brain.

I wrote the page-one story to a fare-thee-well, with exclusive access to the florist shop's Negro odd-jobman, who witnessed it all. I had the hit men's blue Jewett sedan. I had brown overcoats and brown fedoras. I had O'Banion initially mistaking them for customers, there for flowers for the funeral of a Sicilian gangster who lately died of natural causes, that mistake eliciting a handshake just before the shooting. Which elicited a great subhead: *A Handshake Rub-Out*. And I had much more of the same sort of detail in my story.

I did not, however, have a comment from Al, as I knew his strong preference to stay out of the breaking news of shed blood. Nor did I mention him by name in the story's background matter on gang politics. My scrupulousness about such things is my hope, as I am being taken for a ride, not to end up dead in a pit of quicklime out in the prairie west of the city but perhaps alive before Al himself who is ready for a talk.

We turn south on Ogden Avenue and west again on Twenty-Second Street and I feel better. I know we are bound for Cicero, a factory town just west of the Chicago city limits, where—by major bribes and serious muscle and a carefully selected, recently elected, comprehensive group of governing officials from mayor to town clerk to town attorney to, no doubt, dog catcher—Al and his boys have taken over and are creating an oasis of saloons and gambling halls in the wasteland of Volstead.

We stop in front of the Hawthorne Hotel, three stories of brick horseshoed around a roofed courtyard with a frontage of small-town businesses—a laundry and a smoke shop, a barber and a restaurant. This is Al's Cicero headquarters. The head thug from the front seat of the Ford leads me down a long central passageway and we emerge into the lobby.

The front desk and all the chairs and divans and settees, the cigar counter and the telephone switchboard and the bellhop desk—everything—faces the corridor I've come down, as if I've just stepped up from the audience and onto a stage set. A dozen boys like the ones who brought me here are lounging about on the furniture and their faces all instantly turn or rise to focus on me. Some of their shooting hands even reflexively slip across their chests and into their suit coats.

All of this is wise. Dean O'Banion's comparable boys are no doubt being marshaled to reply to Al's move. My personal thug keeps on leading me, around the front desk and into a back office, where I find Al sitting in one of his preferred side-wall face-to-face setups, this one with a couple of leather wingback chairs. But his suit coat is off and his vest is half unbuttoned and his tie is loosened.

"Sammy," he says.

"Al," I say, the use of which he encouraged early on.

"Want a beer?" he says.

"After we talk," I say.

And Al flips his chin at my thug, who apparently is still standing behind me.

I hear the door close.

"Were the dice good to you?" I say, nodding at his dishabille.

He glances down at himself and laughs. "Not till sundown," he says. He expands at the shoulders and even undoes his remaining vest buttons. "I ain't never felt the need to be formal with you, Sammy."

"Only when you say so." I always grab a chance to remind him why he trusts me with exclusive quotes. Even his occasional intentional formality is still great copy, often merely a curbing of his reflexive profanity.

"You've always been a right guy," he says.

"You've always been a straight shooter," I say.

He laughs again.

"*Speaking* of Dean O'Banion," I say. And he laughs once more.

"*Somebody* can shoot straight," he says.

"Who's next in charge over there?"

"Bugs or Hymie," he says. Meaning, respectively, Moran or Weiss. Al persistently refers to his rivals only by their reductive nicknames.

"You have a preference?"

"Neither will last," he says. And this comes out so offhandedly that I clearly hear his intentions in the matter.

Not that I would write that.

"Do I have to tell you?" he asks.

"I already thought it, Al. Not for print."

"See? You're a right guy."

"But something's on your mind for the record." I say this as I take out my notebook and pencil.

"People in this town are thirsty," Al says. "You can't make a man's thirst go away with a phony law. That's when a good businessman comes along and provides a public service. I ain't afraid to say this in the open. They call those businessmen bootleggers. But it's only bootleg when it's on the trucks. When a million hardworking men sit down in a friendly place to relax at the end of a hard day, bootleg is reward for a job well done. Or when their million little ladies want to make nice with their sewing circle, bootleg turns into hospitality."

He pauses. Lets my pencil catch up with the quote. It does. I look up.

He's not looking at me. He's staring down at his two hands, palms up, floating before him. He's slowly flexing them into and out of fists. He says, "Your family comes to this country as immigrants, poor as tenement rats, and you become a millionaire. They should give Al Capone a medal. He is *la grandezza dell'America* is what he is."

I've been around the Italians long enough and this is simple enough a phrase that I know what he said. Al Capone is *the greatness of America*. But he's talking mostly to himself at the moment, as he does not translate for me, which he usually does if he shoots me a bit of the language that suckled him in Brooklyn.

I wait for Al to come out of the reverie. I need to draw on his tolerance of me for the story at hand.

He lifts his face.

I say, "But not all the would-be businessmen with bootleg on their trucks are right guys reflecting our country's greatness. Wouldn't you say?"

"I know what you're driving at, Sam," Al says. "It's a shame not everyone plays square. But in this business when things get out of hand—and of course, I am personally opposed to that—but when they do, the mugs involved only go after each other. They're all very careful about keeping the civilians out of it. The good people of Chicago and vicinity don't got nothing to worry about on that score. As for those of us inside the thirst business, we know how competition can go sometimes. The ones who end up departing the business were plenty ready to arrange the departure of the ones who survive. We all of us know how that goes. We've always known. So it ain't lawless at all. We just got special laws with each other."

He waits.

I write.

I can sense him thinking.

As soon as I finish, he says, "There's fucking honor in that much of it, even for the guys who ain't right with others of their own kind. Honor because we don't rat on each other either. Never. None of us do. That's because we all came from nowhere with nothing. The *real* bad guys with money in our great country, the fake guys, they never worked for their stake to start with. They had rich daddies. Or granddaddies. For them it was all meaningless money to start with. So they don't have the guts to play for keeps with each other. They got no code to live by. Not for each other. Not for their customers either. Those mugs are the ones who ain't part of the greatness. They're fake Americans is what they are."

Al rolls his shoulders a little at this declaration and I know this gesture is intended to indicate an end to his comments. I write the words down with exaggerated care, letting him bask awhile in his own rhetoric, knowing in these situations that he would at least indulge, if not actually answer, one last boundary-pushing question.

Which I now try: "What do you expect either Bugs or Hymie to do next about O'Banion's demise?"

"I expect them to wise up," Al says.

Which they don't.

And the newspapers are the witnesses.

Torrio Is Shot; Police Hunt for O'Banion Men this not three months later, in front of Torrio's own house, shot in crossfire as he emerges from his car, taking buckshot and .45-caliber bullets to jaw and chest and gut, which he survives and which lead him to retire to Italy, his wife having witnessed it all a few yards away—though unhurt by the honor of thugs—and Johnny puts Al in complete charge at last and thus **Cicero Hotel Shot Up, Target Capone Unhurt** Al's fortress shot up indeed, taking a thousand machine-gun rounds in a minute and a half from a slow-moving convoy of eight Hymie Weiss sedans, and thus **Hymie Weiss Slain** *Machine-Gunned on North State Street* and this done, no doubt from Al's sense of humor at work, just a few yards from O'Banion's old florist shop, with Al greeting the police shortly later at home in shirtsleeves and slippers, not knowing a thing about it, and Bugs Moran wises up for a time but, business being business among the true American self-made businessmen **7 Gang Members Massacred** *Moran Staff Wiped Out* machine-gunned against a wall in a parking garage on North Clark, the staff having been politely lined up by Al's hired Sicilian hit men arrayed in fake police uniforms, Bugs himself having been lucky enough to miss the event by arriving late and noticing the apparent police car and passing on by, lucky for his life but unnerved enough at last to retire and leave the whole of Chicago to Al Capone.

I do not get to actually write that story, since many months before—soon after Al got his revenge on Weiss—Kirch moved me along to cover the gangland that is Chicago politics. That was late summer 1927. The massacre occurs on Saint Valentine's Day 1929. I see Al only in my mind, sitting alone in one of the paired overstuffed chairs in his office, his tie loosened, drawing on a stogie, his head shrouded in its smoke.

Ryan now. My son.

Sitting beside me on an elevated train. The Northwestern Line. Though I can't see him yet. Not clearly. Instead I feel the abrupt collision of Al Capone and my son, a realization that holds me back. The abruptness, I assume, a product of my dying brain.

My son and I are sitting on a plush green transverse seat of the latest model of elevated rolling stock. I'm explaining the new train car to him. I know that much about this moment, though on my deathbed I can't yet hear my voice. My brain is lagging. Perhaps from my news reporter's proclivity for chronology.

But no. I realize it's a proclivity that might still be at work. The massacre in the parking garage was on a Thursday. This is two days later, Saturday, and I have the day off. My contribution to yesterday's front page was at the top of column one but beneath the full-page banner headline about the massacre, whose story dropped into column eight. Mine is **Thompson Declared Unfit for Office** *Voter's League Calls for Removal.* Not totally unrelated to the banner headline, as Mayor Big Bill Thompson—back in office for a third term after a four-year hiatus of diversified pocket-lining on the Waterways Commission—has long worked closely with Torrio and Al and their boys.

And abruptly I am afraid. Recognizing how my thoughts have just wandered from my son to a long since meaningless news story I published nine decades ago. Even to the detail of its very headline.

I am afraid. That this present haziness about the L train rushing northward and my son sitting beside me, that this very haziness suggests why chronology persists in my dying brain. I neglected him. And time has rolled on with no way to make it up.

I spent too much of his first years on earth apart from him, in my work, in my preoccupations, in my focused attention, even as he passed from an infant floating in my hands to a smart, articulate, rapidly growing boy sitting beside me on a Saturday morning nearly six years later.

I loved him all along. Through that whole passage. I truly did. And I know I told him so. Overtly. Now and then at least. As I had never heard from my own father, nor felt. And I spent what time I could with my son. I sense all this from the cold and freshly besnowed Saturday morning that my memory has chosen for me, even if I'm presently prevented from remembering any specifics backward or forward from it.

But I didn't do enough for my son. I realize that. Even on this elevated ride. I wasn't present enough with him. Surely that's what God wants me to understand.

A testament to my neglect sits sidewise in the aisle, propped vertically against me, my arm around it to keep it steady. Weeks ago Ryan woke to Christmas morning and to the object I am presently clutching upright. A Flying Arrow sled, with a horizontal backless seat of hardwood slats varnished red and blue and its name writ large in the center and with runners made of tempered spring steel fully controlled by a steering-arm slat across the front. This swell sled has sat propped against the wall of Ryan's room for this past month and a half, during which Chicago has been filled every day with snow and I've had several of those days off and it did not previously occur to me to instigate this outing. The sled was given on Christmas morning with a promise that he and I would learn to use this wonderful thing together, seeing as his Louisianan dad never had one. And Ryan has been a good boy—a very good and courteously indulgent boy—not to push me about that promise. He waited for his dad to feel on his own that the time was right. Though my son's courteous indulgence shames me now.

Which dispels the haze.

And I turn my face to Ryan.

He is watching the flash of second-floor windows at the back of the brick three-flats, our elevated track nearer a flat's window than its front door. Most are curtained, some are not, and when a figure is visible, Ryan lurches ever so slightly toward it and flips his face ever so slightly to follow its passing. One window frames a boy pressed there watching the train and Ryan sees him and starts to lift his hand, but the gesture he wishes to make is stymied by the quick vanishing of the boy.

Ryan turns away. He realizes I'm watching, and he looks up at me.

"Were you going to wave at him?" I ask.

"Yes."

"He was gone too fast," I say.

"No," Ryan says. "*I* was gone too fast."

I laugh. He's right, of course. My smart little man. I have never talked baby talk to him. Colleen has picked that up too. Tender talk but not baby talk.

I say, "That happens sometimes with people."

Ryan nods gravely, looks away outside, but I sense him thinking.

The mood is catching. I am surprised to find the Black boy from Lake Providence come to mind. Cyrus Dobbs. *Dobbs*, and his voice: *Not rightly our name, seems to me.* I turn my head to look at him and he is striding away on the crest of the levee.

My head clears.

My son still sits with his thoughts.

"What are you thinking?" I ask.

"I'm glad we've got all day," Ryan says.

"Me too," I say.

"That boy doesn't care," he says. "He just watches everybody rush by. He doesn't expect to make a friend." And Ryan rolls his shoulders a little. Shrugs off this topic.

"I can't wait to get sledding," I say.

He nods at this and looks away again. He squares around and presses close to the window to watch some more.

I find myself briefly, faintly surprised. In spite of seeing my little man in my little boy, I expected the prospect of sledding to make him bubble. I now hear his invocation of the long day ahead as a subtle rebuke for the long delay.

But I let it rest.

He wants to watch the passing city and I turn to the sled leaning against me. I never had one as a boy, snow being unknown in Lake Providence, Louisiana. But I've done my reportorial research on all of this. He and I will learn together.

So we ride to the end of the Northwestern Line, passing from Chicago through Evanston, until our train finally descends from its elevation into the Linden Avenue Terminal in Wilmette. I've learned of a place with good sledding in otherwise flat Chicago and its flat environs. Ryan and I walk north and then east and across Sheridan Road and into a woods where slopes lined in ash and maple run down toward the lake.

There are other boys and sleds busy at their sport. But there are several slopes, and I find one for us that's lightly populated. It's a gentler slope, without a dogleg and with a leveled foot in plain sight. Perfect for a couple of beginners.

Ryan is quiet still, focused and studious but perhaps darker than that, perhaps even fearful. I need to adjust my plan. I thought we'd go straight to belly flops. We'd laugh at our failures. He would bubble. This isn't happening.

So we discuss the sled for a time. Its relevant parts. Discuss and examine it closely. We prepare for this the way a smart and articulate five-year-old has decided things should go. And he participates fully in the discussion, though thoughtfully, observing how the runners have grooves like skates and admiring the arrow shot through the *Flying Arrow* name emblazoned on the center slat, how clever a design that is.

I talk sliding strategies with him, discounting the belly flop, with the sled held vertically before you and a running, diving start. A more moderate approach would be perfectly fine, with a few pushing steps while bent forward into a grasp of the sled on the ground and a belly-first easing onto the seat. He nods an understanding of this.

Then we have talked as much as we can talk. It's time to actually sled. But. Though he has participated in our discussion with the precocity I admire in him and which I know he enjoys in himself, his somber mood persists. The little man mood. But I have expected my little boy to appear, bubbling at last about this adventure.

And I suddenly worry about all the time I've spent away from him. He's had a full-time mother but far less of a father. Less, no doubt, than most other boys, even those who have hardworking fathers. The jobs of those men can be left easily behind in the office or in the factory. My job is to observe life—everything about life that is striking or dangerous or influential—and to give it daily voice to four hundred thousand Chicagoans. I have trouble turning that off when I arrive in the life of my child. In my head, at least, there is no end to my workday.

So now I see a problem in Ryan's life. I blame myself. I helped create it. A problem with his being a five-year-old little *man* is you can miss the risk-taking of *child*hood. You miss the chance to teach your body and mind to be brave. To fool them forever into thinking there's no price to be paid in order to be fully a man.

"Are you all right?" I ask him.

"Yes," he says, unquaveringly. But he says no more.

"I've never done this before either," I say.

"Because of Louisiana."

"Yes. So this is a new thing. The world is full of new things." I hesitate. But I add, gently, "Be brave now. You're a brave boy. I know who you are."

He looks at me. He looks at the sled, which I have placed between us. He looks down the slope.

"Shall I go first?" I say.

"Yes," he says.

"I'll test our plans."

"Be brave," he says. And he shoots me a sly smile. I am glad to see the soberness dispelled.

"I will," I say.

"You're a brave papa," he says.

"I am," I say.

And he steps back and I bend to the sled from behind and grasp it and push it along into the slope in an awkward little crouching rush and I flop forward onto the seat, my torso fitting okay with my legs bent straight up at the knee, and I'm gliding along headfirst, going faster than I'd expected and gaining speed, and I grasp the handles of the steering slat for stability but it's too much of a temptation to try to feel I'm in control and I try to steer, which of course I overdo badly and I veer and tilt and now my man size on this boy's sled prevails and I find myself on my side in the snow and then on my back.

I jump up, forcing a laugh even as I'm rising, to reassure Ryan. I realize I'm a little disappointed that I feel the need to do this.

I look up the slope.

I don't see him.

I pick up the sled, climb the slope, not worried but puzzled.

And there he is. Lying on his back, his arms and legs extended. I am oddly relieved. He's making fun of his old man. Good. That's a spirit he can grow up on. He's even moving his arms and legs in an arc in the snow, as if I were thrashing after my fall. In slow motion yet. I laugh an unforced laugh.

But I'm wrong.

Now that I've seen his little parody, now that I've laughed in appreciation, he should be looking at me, sharing my pleasure at this joke. But he continues the slow thrash and ignores my presence.

I do not know what to say to my son.

I stand in silence.

Then he stops his arms and legs.

Now he looks at me. "Papa," he says. "Wait and see."

And with meticulous movement of legs and torso and placement of feet and hands, Ryan slowly rises and rotates to the side and lifts one leg and takes as long a stride as he can and then quickly another as if not to disturb something. Now he briskly comes to me and turns to stand at my side.

He directs my attention to where he was lying.

I see for the first time what is there.

An imprinted outline in the snow.

The imprint of his stocking-capped head and the length of his body. But instead of extended arms, the image is of extended wings. Instead of legs, the image is what can only be described as a gown.

All this I perceive but I am struggling to put these elements together.

"It's an angel," Ryan says.

And so it is.

I wish to find words. Instructive words somehow. Corrective words. Failing those for the time being, perhaps even carefully circumscribed approving words. Fatherly loving words. But in spite of words being my profession—even my life now—I have none for my son at this moment.

He's bubbling beside me.

"Isn't she beautiful?" he says.

I do put my hand gently on his shoulder. A gesture he might well take as approval.

But I am unsettled.

And Ryan rushes forward, lies down beside his angel in the snow, and he begins to make another.

The particularity of the scene begins to fade now. But I am aware that I will go on to teach myself to sled on this day, as Ryan creates a choir of angels in the snow. Out of what I consider pitying consideration for his papa's enthusiasms, Ryan joins me once, to ride on my back after I've mastered the sledding. But in that single run down the slope I sense his deep unease, and I press him no further. He returns to the snow to play on his own terms until we head back to the elevated.

Ryan presses against the window on the trip home. He has led us to sit on the left-hand side of the car, viewing the same three-flats that he watched coming out. It occurs to me that he's looking to see if the boy at the window will be there.

But as I sit beside him, I vanish from the train. I am in France. I am barely seventeen years old. I am still a boy. And I am a killer. I see my weapon in my hands, my Pennsylvanian Enfield, and I lean into a broken wall, chest high, and across a rubbled field before me is a road and beyond is a tree line of oak and beech. The Bois-le-Prêtre, the Priest's Wood. The September offensive has not yet begun. I am forward on reconnaissance. But also to watch for a target of opportunity. A passing German staff car is the prize. Or a German sniper coming forward to us.

And he emerges from the trees. I put my eye to the scope and my forefinger to the trigger. I see him clearly. But what is fully there lags a fraction of a second behind what only fits my expectation. At first a German soldier—armed, alone—emerging cautiously from the trees, square before me, and, as I see him through that veil of expectations, he is professionally alert enough to spot my flimsy cover and evade me or crouch and aim and pose a mortal threat. And so he becomes an immediate target. I see his forehead clearly in my scope and my crosshairs are upon it and the process begins, the tip of my forefinger lying soft upon the trigger, my knuckle aiming, my breath calmly suspended, but in the next fraction of a second, just before the squeeze, I see him fully and I know he is not a fellow sniper. His rifle is slung on his shoulder, his emerging step is not cautious but fearful, his assessing first look is unsystematic, inept. And his face is the face of a boy. Perhaps seventeen. Perhaps a prematurely thoughtful boy. Perhaps a boy who's had a neglectful father. A boy who is ill prepared for what the world is. And all of this next-fraction insight rushes into me even as my forefinger, trained effectively for this world as it is, does its work and the spot on the boy's forehead between his eyes explodes.

I am beside my son and panting hard.

I can hear myself clearly. My desperate, labored breath. I look to Ryan. He is unmoved, watching the distant three-flats rush past, his limbs comfortably weary from making angels in the snow.

And I am afraid.

I am in the dark again.

I cannot see forward from that moment in France.

And I realize I do not know when this fear actually was felt. Ryan did not hear me panting. And as I heard myself, I did not hear the rush and clack of the train. Did the memory and its insight visit me upon the train or only just now?

"Didn't I understand my son?" I cry to the darkness. To God.

I didn't. Not then. Not fully. Whatever my fear for my son was at the time, it didn't move me to adequately teach him about the world.

"Was that my sin?" I cry.

God does not answer.

Instead I'm on another train. Not the elevated. That's still to come. This is the Illinois Central's *Louisiane*, heading south. Ryan is pressed against the window. But he is on his mother's lap, getting a bit too big for that, having turned four some months ago. He's growing rapidly but he's not quite a little man yet.

He is enchanted by the view.

Colleen is leaning into the window with him and the two of them are seeing everything and naming everything and discussing what everything is for.

I am sitting across from them. I've looked up from a sheaf of newspaper clippings. News items that have caught Kirch's eye. He is now the managing editor at the *Chicago Independent*. I've been dispatched to a news development tailor-made for my attention: in my Louisiana, the dramatic rise of a flamboyant politician with a progressive agenda. And the aftermath of massive river flooding in the state this past spring. And there are matters of my own. By now a desk drawer at home nearly full of letters in my mother's familiar hand; and that growing little boy in the opposite seat as well.

All of that has diversely accumulated to put the three of us together on this train, heading for Louisiana. In those letters was my mother's hand, but also Colleen's handiwork.

Soon after Ryan was born, Colleen poured my coffee at the kitchen table, and as I was in mid-sip, she pulled her chair near to me. When my cup was down, she laid her hand gently upon mine. She said, "May I ask you a very personal question?"

"That's part of the Crown Point deal," I said.

"Seriously."

"Of course."

"Will you promise to answer with all honesty? Knowing that whatever the answer is, I fully understand? I suspect for *both* of us that the unsaid things about our fathers are much stronger than the said things. Which is a terrible complication in several ways."

She was serious indeed. "Yes," I said. "I promise."

She asked, "I know why you had to utterly separate yourself. But do you miss your mother?"

I hesitated. Not because the simple answer was a difficult thing to say. I said it at once to see if it would be enough. "Yes."

"Does it bother you that there seems no way to communicate with her?"

"It does," I said. The answer was sincere, as far as it went. Of course I missed her. But this second question nudged me closer to the thing I wished not to confront about myself.

For a moment I flicker a return all the way to my deathbed. I sense I am near another moment I am meant to reckon with, even as I also sit before Colleen while she seems to wait for more of an answer. Missing my mother, loving her, should not have been outweighed by my struggles with my father. I understand how my mother—as a wife, as a woman, especially in her middle age—was convinced she had no viable identity other than the middle-aged wife, the woman, of her husband. That fate was decided when she married him in the state of Louisiana in 1898. But perhaps I should have remained in Lake Providence. After all, my father had stopped beating me. If I had remained, perhaps I could have figured out a way to keep his ongoingly abusive hands off her.

But then who would I have become? A small-town assistant banker and a bodyguard of my mother. As her bodyguard, however, since I also would have lived an adult life physically apart from my parents—even if only down the road—I would have inevitably failed. And indeed, having failed to adequately protect her, and because my country and a world at war would still have given me that alternate identity—though conditional, that identity was still operative in me—at some point, I likely would have killed him. Killed him in fact. Personally. Not just by proxy as a sniper from a cottage window in France.

My mother understood when I had to go away from the two of them. She blessed my escape. She wished for my escape. I tell myself, *Surely she felt that a part of her escaped with me. It was the only way she could.*

But I sit once more before Colleen at the kitchen table, her hand still on mine, and in this moment I curse myself, silently. It is to her that I must make my reckoning. She has asked a question that is not rhetorical. Even though it was the only way to break with my father, do I suffer for leaving my mother behind? In all the time Colleen and I have been together, I have said and done nothing that would have answered this for her.

"I may not actively show it," I say. "But yes, it bothers me deeply."

Colleen gently squeezes my hand and says, "Now she has a grandson. She should at least know."

"But what can I do? As long as she must be with my father, reaching out would be dangerous. Certainly the risks would make life much harder on her. If he finds out we're communicating she'd become my surrogate for even more beatings."

Instantly I wonder if all this is a lie. Conveniently improvised self-justification for simply accepting this state of things. But tears brim in my eyes now, just short of expression. Colleen squeezes my hand once more. She already believes the thing in me that

I myself still wish to believe. That what I have just said is true. That the nascent tears are not for me, in my hard-heartedness. They are for my mother.

"I have a plan," Colleen says. "Your father the banker is very rarely at home when mail is delivered. Am I right?"

"Right."

"Does your father insist on opening all the mail that comes in, even if addressed to her?"

I give this a moment's thought. "I never saw any evidence of that. I'm sure he believes in his established control of her. She gets very little mail. She has a friend or two downstate who write her and she does mail order. I think he sees all that as beneath him."

Colleen pauses briefly for a thought. "Then we only take a small risk. I will write to her first. I'll introduce myself. I'll work out a carefully timed plan to correspond. I'll always address the envelopes. From just another friend downstate. I'll write to her and you will too."

Now it's my hand that squeezes hers. "Yes," I say.

We neither of us say anything more.

And so we begin, one risk at a time.

Until we are on the *Louisiane*. Rushing with my son to his grandmother in what once was my home. The risks have grown complex. My son's grandfather, of course, will be there as well.

Now he stands half a dozen paces away on the platform of the pitch-roofed Lake Providence station, his hands out of sight, clasped behind his back. Mama has met the three of us at the bottom of the train car steps. She and Colleen embrace and then Mama gently descends to her knees before Ryan, who is bouncing around with hellos, and they hug. As they do, Colleen bends and puts a hand on Mama's shoulder.

I feel the circle around them drawn not in dirt but glowingly in the air, and I ease away a step, happy to leave them to their connection.

I turn my face to my father.

His face turns from them to me.

He and I do not move.

Nor do we go on to speak more than a few necessary words about luggage and such until we are all in the house of my childhood and Mama, Colleen, and Ryan are boisterous in the kitchen and I stand in the place on the front-room floor where each day as a boy I would spread the *Times-Picayune.*

I lift my eyes, and through a front window I see him in one of the twin oak rocking chairs. I am inclined to back quietly away from where I stand, prolonging the mutual avoidance this man and I have instinctively established.

But it cannot last. I am here for four days. And on a couple of those I will be downstate doing my work.

I step onto the front porch.

He must see me in his periphery but he does not turn his head.

The near rocker is empty. I step to it and sit.

I look to the place where he has been fixedly staring. Our magnolia tree at the foot of our fieldstone walk. A hundred feet high, predating the house itself by perhaps a century.

He is dimly visible in my own periphery.

I regret having sat down here.

Now that I have brought my family to Lake Providence, I find things beginning to shape in my head that need to be made clear to this man.

But for the moment, instead I say, "The flood would have killed it. The magnolia."

And my father says, "It likely would have stood. But the roots would have started to die."

I have no more talk ready.

When that becomes clear to him, he adds, "Do you actually care?"

"About the tree? Of course," I say.

Through this exchange there has been no movement in the edge of my sight. He has not looked at me since I sat down. He still refuses to do so.

He says, "Do you wonder why God chose to spare Lake Providence from the flood?"

I look at him. "Because you're here?"

Finally he turns to me. He says nothing for a moment. A long moment. And then: "He's flighty, isn't he?"

"God?"

"The boy."

This catches me off guard. And it unsettles me, his even referring to my son.

"Careful," he says. "He may fly off from you someday."

I realize that every word my father has said so far has actually been, in some oblique way or other, about him and me.

I let him know I know. "You got my postcard," I say.

"Oh yes," he says. "You broke your mother's heart."

Good, I think. *He did not suspect her complicity.*

"I'll be sure to apologize," I say. "But it could be done no other way."

"Is that so? To sneak off in the night? Look at you. The grizzled war veteran. Mister Sniper with notches on his gun butt. But this overgrown teenager didn't have the guts to stand up to his father or even say goodbye to his mother."

"I could have told Mama goodbye but she would have told you, and it's you I didn't want to see." I'm happy to double down on my mother's innocence, even if it momentarily encourages him.

My father barks a loud, single-note laugh.

He thinks I'm afraid of him.

Of course he does.

The plosive power of that phony laugh means he's even trying to convince himself that his failing to go off to a war and my going off to one have come to nothing as leverage between us.

It's time to make things clear to him. I say, "Thanks for the newspapers. They gave me important things you never expected they would. Thanks for a couple of lessons about who we are, though you were more villain savant than wise man. And thanks for making it easy for me to enlist in the army. Even as you were already jealous as hell that I could do this and you never could. But don't fool yourself about what I became or failed to become over there. I'm a killer. I've killed a hundred men, one-on-one. More. Way more, actually. There are no notches because it quickly became so natural, so easy, became something I could do so expertly that it was amateurish to count. No matter what else I do in my life, whoever I become, I will always be that too. You hear me? I am a fucking killer. And don't ever forget it."

I pause briefly to let this sink in. His face is as superficially smug and stern as it has always been, but he is turning even whiter than the whitest of the local boys inside his drawn circle. An intimidated, blood-drained white.

I say, "And you sure as hell better not forget it while my wife and son and I are in your house."

I pause again. Stiff-spined, I lean toward him with serious deliberation. He takes a quick breath, draws back from me ever so slightly. I say, "Understand clearly, old man. I am about to go off to work for a couple of days. If I come back and find out that even once you have lifted a hand to my boy, that you have tried to discipline him in any way—and I will find out, I assure you—I will kill you."

My father does not blink. Does not twitch. Does not breathe.

I say, "It is what I have learned to do. What I have learned to be. I learned it well. I do it expertly and I do it easily. Whatever the consequences, I will kill you."

He still does not move, though I hear a faint, jagged whistle of air coming from him as he carefully exhales.

"If you believe me," I say, "nod your head once."

He does.

I rise.

I leave him.

The next day, outside of Tallulah in Madison Parish, press pass conspicuously displayed in my hatband, I stand at the front of a gabby, chaw-chewing, all-male, all-white crowd. We are on the edge of a field that should be full of the stump stalks of harvested cotton but instead is simply a flood-leveled barrenness. For every guy in a suit and tie among the hundreds, there are a dozen in denim overalls and flannel shirts. Even some bareback under their bibs in the mild Louisiana November air. One of the latter is standing next to me and I look to him as we wait. His profile has been sun-blasted into an indeterminate, hardscrabble age, anywhere from thirty to sixty.

I lean a little toward him so he can hear above the chatter around us. "May I ask you a question?"

He turns his face to me, his far cheek presenting a bulge of tobacco. He gives my press pass a glance, and he says, "Yessir, you rightly can."

"Is Huey your man already?"

"Yessir, he is."

"How's that?"

"Well, sir, he really knows what fellas like us are about. What we need. He's gonna talk up for us."

Before I can frame a follow-up question, a gathering wave of applause and voices calling out the candidate's name heads our way from the rear of the crowd.

And now Huey Long himself arrives with a couple of mugs flanking him in worsted three-pieces and slouch hats—bodyguards cut from the same cloth as Al Capone's—and Huey climbs up on the open back of a cotton wagon before us.

He's dressed like a dandy, but studiously an American one: his suit is the color of the amber waves of grain; his shirt, the purple mountain majesties; and his tie, the fruited plains, if the fruits were all strawberries. I would never pick him out of a lineup as the fella who knows what the fellas in this crowd are all about. But that crowd is now cheering to beat the band. And Huey responds by whipping off his amber coat and tossing it to a bodyguard below. He loosens his tie.

He smiles out to the huzzahs of the crowd. His face is fleshy and round under a dense shock of chestnut hair. Before he opens his mouth he seems almost smarmy, with his only striking feature a deep-cleft chin. This face is the face of somebody's bachelor uncle Hiram who sells Fuller brushes door-to-door where he can be quite a ladies' man if the ladies feel homely and desperate.

Then he begins to speak. "So tell me, gentlemen, who's going to give you a helping hand now? Now that the floodwaters have finally gone? Now that you tenants of the big plantations, who do the real work, and you one-mule farmers trying to do for yourselves, and you merchants and you trappers, are all suffering even more than usual? Who's going to give you a helping hand? The water at least is from the hand of God and you go on from that as you can. But the privileged polecats you got controlling you on this earth are the same skunks you've had to put up with forever. Those boys in the big houses are not going to help you out in this time of tribulation. They are taking care of their own to maintain the privilege they are accustomed to. Those boys are nothing more than blood kin to the boll weevils who have been eating away at you for years now, eating your cotton, eating the very food from your table. The moneymen and power brokers and corporations and plantation owners and most every politician are all hard-shelled boll weevils, sticking their long, skinny weevil snouts into your livelihood and sucking it right on up."

All of this comes from Huey in a rising floodwater of volubility and excitability, his arms rising high and waving to Heaven in the throes of churchy ardor or fisting up and then pounding down on an invisible desktop in country-courthouse prosecution.

I was prepared for this side of Huey Long from all the press clippings Kirch gave me to study. Huey the impassioned rabble-rouser, voicing the grievances of his working-class listeners with homespun metaphor and sharp-tongued invective. And he goes on like this for a while more, a proper hayseed demagogue, but you don't have to be very smart to be a demagogue and your demagogic ambition doesn't have to travel any farther than the state line.

But that's not Huey. I figure he might turn out, in an elected career, to be a self-serving demagogue all right. Likely will. But he is far from stupid. And I suspect his ambition is from sea to shining sea. As the speech goes on, his tone becomes practical, and in the transition between invective and policy I see his gaze turn briefly sly and penetrating. He shifts from calling out the boll weevils and polecats and trough feeders to invoking the real-life things his listeners are deprived of—with and by the complicity of Louisiana politicians—and he promises to provide them all. He would turn Louisiana's ubiquitous dirt roads and gravel roads into paved roads. He would build bridges, including the state's first across the Mississippi River. He would hire new teachers and start adult literacy classes and give free textbooks to schoolchildren. He would build hospitals that would open their doors to the poor and provide free health care.

All of these good progressive policies are the reason the *Chicago Independent* is eagerly awaiting my dispatches.

And he concludes by saying, "Now I want each and every one of you to look at your neighbors. The one to the right of you and the one to the left of you. Go on now."

And they do. The whole crowd rustles with the turning of heads and torsos in obedience to Huey's command.

When that's all done and the rustling fades into the rapt silence he has long since earned from his cotton-wagon pulpit, Huey says, "You have just now looked into the face of a king. Two kings. As have they. You all are kings. Every man is a king, just no one wears a crown. You deserve to be treated like it. Every last one of you. That is long overdue. And I stand before you with the solemn promise to make that happen." At this he lifts both arms high, fists clenched, and he waves them like flags as he cries, "And the low-down, vile politicians and the vermin in full-dress suits and the grafters and money boodlers and the corporate bloodsucking field ticks are not going to stop us!"

The crowd cheers as one.

And after his speech, I come close to the wagon as he climbs down to one of his bodyguards holding up his amber coat for him while the other blocks the crowd from surging in. I am at the front edge of that crowd and the intercepting mug sees my press pass. "Stay close," he says to me.

So now I settle in with Huey Long on a bench in the Tallulah train station as he awaits the Vicksburg, Shreveport & Pacific to an evening rally in Monroe.

Huey loosens his tie and says, "You a *Picayune* boy up from New Orleans?"

"I'm an *Independent* boy down from Chicago," I say.

Huey cocks his head in surprise at that.

"We are a progressive paper," I say.

"I am well aware," he says.

That he knows our paper should surprise me, but it doesn't. He's smart all right. And that makes it easier for me right away to say, "My paper's point of view is why I'm here. We believe your ideas will be welcomed outside of your home state. Outside of the South. After you fix Louisiana, do you see the country benefiting from what you know to be true and right?"

Huey shoots me the same sly look that I watched emerge in his speech. A little bit smile, a little bit come-hither, a little bit *I am in complete masterful control here and never doubt it.*

And a freewheeling interview follows, both of us racing ahead of the imminent train that will take him away, Huey glad to talk to another part of the nation, his long-range plan clearly in mind. He talks about his policies. He talks about his enemies. He talks about his constituents, the fellas who feel deeply understood at last by Huey Long.

And I approach a question that has been shaping up in my mind since the big catchphrase climax of his Tallulah speech.

He has just now said, "All I care about is what the boys at the forks in the creek and ends of the cow path think of me."

I write that into the notebook I've been using, and he watches me as he's done with every colorful phrase he coins—making sure I get it right no doubt—and I slow way down on this one, meticulously writing it out word for word, while I prepare to ask my concluding question.

I close my notebook. Any answer he gives me will appear to go unrecorded.

I say, "I was quite taken with your oratory and your policies, and I was particularly struck by the way you led the men in your audience to look each other in the face and see each other in a bright new light. Every man a king."

Huey is faintly nodding at me, thoughtful and approving of how I see him.

"But I know you understand all those men as they exist day to day in their humanity. They are farmers and mule drivers and field-workers, but they are also, some many of them, drunks and brawlers and wife-beaters and cheats. All of them are flawed. As have been all the kings recorded in history."

Huey has stopped nodding. Though his face can no longer be read as approving, neither is he jumping to any defensive conclusions.

I say, "And for that very reason, don't these kings need some great, vested personage who sees them for what they truly are but can also preside over them, lead them, manage them, protect them, even from themselves at times? Don't they need a king of kings?"

Huey's eyes are brightening.

And I say, "Isn't that what this election is about? Are you to be the king of kings?"

For the third time today I see that sly Huey Long look. I suspect that each time it's been a satisfied gesture, more to himself than to any of us. Because his invective and his policy are all one in service to his ambition; because that ambition knows no boundary; because he finds "the king of kings" to be just about right. He expected any bumpkin kings in the audience who happened to notice his look simply to feel his confidence. He twice expected the progressive journalist simply to accept his look as a respectful nudge in the ribs but otherwise as an insuperable *no comment.*

The interview is over.

The train arrives.

He hopes the great city of Chicago will continue to follow all the great things he has in mind for the great state of Louisiana.

Huey Long heads on down the line to his future.

But even before the smell of coal smoke and valve oil from the departed train has faded away, I know the opening sentence of my opinion-page accompaniment to my front-page feature story. *Huey Long, progressive-minded candidate for governor in Louisiana, said as much about himself and his future in three silent looks as he did in all his spellbinding oratory.*

I return to Lake Providence.

I do not have to kill my father.

While I was gone, Colleen did not even have to try to prevent private time between grandfather and grandson. My father kept his distance and Ryan seemed not to wonder at that, happily content with the full-time attention of his mother and grandmother.

On our last morning, things conveniently get very busy at the bank. My father is properly, if stiffly, regretful to all of us that he must go to the office early and that his final goodbyes are brief. He is standing already halfway across the front-room floor. The rest of us gather as if into an inspection rank before him. Colleen has her hand on Ryan's shoulder, but even so, he seems content to make no move toward his grandfather at the man's departure.

Nor do I.

My father and I both know this may be our last goodbye. But we maintain our distance.

He turns and goes.

My son and his mother and grandmother retreat chattering to the kitchen.

I do cross the room and look out the door at my father striding down our sidewalk without a glance back. I ask myself, *Would I have actually killed him? Or perhaps simply beaten him badly?* I take the question seriously and ponder it a moment, and with reasonable certainty I answer myself: *Yes. For the degree of the offense he was capable of, I would have killed him.*

And I sit up in my deathbed. "Is that it?" I cry to God. "I would have. I wanted to. I regretted not having the chance. No. Not that. Because that would have required harm to my son. But yes, I would have killed my father. You know it. I know it now. Is that what you wanted me to come to understand?"

No answer comes from the dark.

"Well, I understand it," I say.

Silence.

Abruptly I think I know why. "And I am sorry," I say.

Nothing.

I realize I'm not sorry. The regret I acknowledge having felt while watching my father vanish at the far end of our sidewalk was not limited by that time and place. A residue of the fuller regret remains scattered into the corners of my brain even as I lie here in the dark. Scattered there perhaps by the breath of my sniper self, the breath of the killer in me, but it is there even now. The ongoing regret of not having had a sufficient excuse to deliver an obliterating blow to my father.

And of course God knows all this.

I am fucked.

And I think now, *Rightly so. Rightly fucked. After all, my father surely was who he was because of his father.* I suddenly have no doubt that Granddaddy Ezra beat my father into the man he was, and so the deeper reason for why I could kill my father was how he himself was shaped beyond his control to become a father who would then beat his own son into a man who would be capable of killing his father.

I try to think: *Poor Papa.* I try to think: *I forgive you, Papa.*

But the best I can do is to cry out into the dark, with what feels like legitimate sincerity: "I am sorry that I'm not sorry that I wish even still to kill my father."

I wait.

God lets me. Then He says, "I believe you."

I'm glad. As far as that goes.

I'm glad His eye is openly upon me once more.

I wait for more.

He does not offer more, but I sense Him still present.

I'm being stupid. "Okay, okay," I say. "It's on me. You told me to start with my father. But you've come back to me now that I've arrived at this issue. Fathers and sons. Is this about fathers and sons? Of course it is, right? I learned that long ago. So many of us have. Heaven is about fathers and sons."

And God says, "Now, Sam, listen to your copydesk. I already cautioned you about pronouns."

"Parents and children," I say.

"Closer," God says.

"I had a child," I say.

"Yes."

A prickling unease blooms from my chest into my throat. I say, "Why won't you let me look ahead now to what's already happened? Long ago happened."

"I have my ways."

"Then stop acting like you're the copy editor," I say. "You're the chief. The old man. Pardon my pronoun. Send me on a goddamn assignment."

That results in a thump of silence between us.

The wrong epithet entirely.

"Oops," I say.

"You *are* starting to prickle, aren't you?" God says.

"Yes. If I knew how to effectively pursue the blame I deserve, I'd do it. But isn't that what I'm here to learn? Can't you give me an assignment?"

"You had a child," He says. "Open yourself to that and then see where it takes you."

Okay. I stir.

But He reads it in me, of course. At once He adds, "I said *open*. Don't try to lead the story. You know how to report. Just fill your notebook. Don't assume the outcome."

My son's hand falls gently onto my shoulder.

I am sitting on our back steps. But I remain as well lying in my deathbed.

I feel his hand. Then he sits beside me on the steps. "Poor Papa," he says.

In the dark still, I wait for context.

"You're sad," my son says.

I am frightened, is the truth of it. But I do not say this.

Hindenburg Dead, Hitler in Charge and **Hitler Supreme in Germany** and **German Military Swears Allegiance to Hitler**. And the lead editorial in one of the Chicago papers is headlined **Fool Rules**. It begins: "For now a ranting, blathering ex-army corporal is in charge of Germany, but he is unlikely to survive the confirming plebiscite vote he has demanded. Nor would he survive his manifest incompetence, recently demonstrated over and over in foreign policy and domestic planning."

The fool, I am afraid, is the editorial writer.

The dark around me is dissipating. The back steps are of our brand-new, bay-windowed, pitch-roofed brick bungalow out the Fullerton streetcar line in the neighborhood called Hermosa. We are only recently unpacked.

It is Sunday afternoon.

I've hardly come out here since we moved in, but I wanted to separate myself in my thoughtfulness. The last few days' newspapers are all stacked away in my dormered attic office.

Ryan has found me here at once.

I put my arm around my son.

I am frightened for the world. I am frightened for him.

He would not seek out the newspapers anyway. He has never shown an interest in them. Or in the welter of what they chronicle. But still I hid them.

I turn my face to him and he is looking at me in what strikes me as pity. He is eleven years old. He has my squared chin, more clearly similar now as he grows, but his eyes are his mother's gray, though resonant not so much of Louisiana storm clouds as of Louisiana mourning doves.

He has a good heart. This I know. But those who died first in the Great War, who died most readily, were the pure of heart. And in those who lived, the purity died.

My father and I hunted doves together.

My arm is still around him.

I hug him gently against me.

"Am I wrong?" he asks.

I don't understand.

He picks up on that. "I think you're sad."

"I'm just thoughtful," I say. "About work."

"Want to see my house?" he asks. "It's all done now."

I've hardly glanced in the direction of the garden shed. It is very much like a little house, with a door and a window and its own pitched roof, something Ryan saw instantly, and he had to joyfully ask only once before Colleen agreed to banish her gardening tools to our new basement and I hired a workman who converted the shed into our son's hideaway.

"Yes," I say. "Please show me your house."

He jumps up and takes my hand to hasten my own rising and then he leads me across the yard. As I follow him I examine my complicity in allowing my son to remain ignorant of the world as seen and reported in newspapers, an enterprise to which I have devoted my life. At his present age I was each day, by way of a newspaper, devouring the world in all its tumultuously unsettling complexity.

Why have I let this happen to him? For the sake of my convenience, ironically in service to my all-absorbing identity as a newsman. And by my neglect, as I deferred entirely to Ryan's impulses, like angels in the snow. Though my deference was empowered by my trust in Colleen and her identity as a mother, which she has ardently embraced. A legitimate trust. But I left most everything to her, and she is a woman, while her child must become a man.

When a man? How long will it take the ranting but somehow persuasive Adolf Hitler to fully revive the German people, given their single-generation passage from unification to murderous self-aggrandizement to abject national humiliation to obeisance to a newly minted führer? Long enough for Ryan to come of age?

He welcomes me into his little house.

In the center of the floor is a small hardwood camp table flanked by two camp chairs. He stands behind one of the chairs and invites me to sit. I do. He sits across from me. Between us is a reed basket of red roses and maidenhair fern.

"Aren't they pretty?" he says as I stare at them. "They're made of cloth. Mama will grow them someday along our fence. But these will never wither."

"Indeed," I say, feeling the need to say something, as his voice is eager.

"They're happy in the shadow," he says, and he laughs lightly. "Which is good. Mama said we can see about putting in an electric light. In the meantime I can read my books by the light from the window."

I avert my eyes to the window as my son gushes on: "I love my house, though I hope I'm not being ungrateful, Papa, if I say I would be very happy if it was in a tree. Like in *The Swiss Family Robinson*. That's my favorite book."

The window is hung with lace curtains.

Once Kaiser Wilhelm took over the chancellorship to reign supreme, as Hitler has just done, it took him fourteen years to start the Great War. A war that is no longer exclusively called by that name, which suggests a singularity, but just as commonly called the more generic *World War.* To start another will be simpler for Hitler. If it takes him half the time, Ryan will be eighteen.

Ryan has paused.

I turn to him. I say, "Did your mother do the decorating?"

He cocks his head, not quite understanding.

I say, "Did she choose the pretty flowers? The curtains?"

"*No*, Papa," he says. "She took me to Marshall Field, but this is *my* house."

I return to the window.

A blue jay spanks past.

Ryan says, "You still seem sad, Papa."

I look back to him.

I think, *It's not too late. Surely it's not.*

"Thank you," I say. "You're very kind, my son. I treasure that in you. Do you understand?"

He doesn't seem to, quite. His brow furrows. Of course he doesn't. That comment fits this moment only for me. And even for me, there is an undercurrent of irony. That his kindness as it presently lives in him is admirable but also deeply worrisome.

"I understand," he says. "I'm glad."

How to begin?

He says, "It's your work that makes you sad?"

"Not always. Not sad exactly. Sometimes I learn something that makes me thoughtful."

I pause. I will not say it by its proper name. *Fearful.*

He waits.

"You love to read," I say. "But never newspapers."

"I like the funnies," he says.

"Not the news," I say, but gently.

He considers this a moment. "I like my books. Long ones . . . I'm sorry, Papa. I'm proud of my papa, writing in the newspapers. But somehow, what I like . . . Am I a foolish child?"

"No," I say. And I reach my hand across the table toward him, pushing the basket of flowers aside. He slides his hand into mine. "Not at all," I say. "But you're such a big boy now. And I'm very sorry that my work has so occupied me that I've not spent more time with you. Not guided you. Taught you some things I know. Do you forgive me?"

"Papa," he says, squeezing my hand. "Don't be a silly goose."

I return the squeeze and gently withdraw my hand.

Every phrase he chooses now unsettles me.

I say, "Do you remember how I used to call you 'my little man'?"

He laughs. "I do. Was I like that?"

"Yes," I say. "In flashes. But what you have become since then is fine. Just fine. A fine boy. As you should be."

"I am *eleven* now," he says, the emphasis sounding prideful. "By two months."

"Just so. Manhood comes into view. Don't you think?"

He looks to the side for a moment, thinking. "I'm sorry, Papa. No. I haven't thought about it. I should. I should think."

"It's time for me to help you do that."

"Yes," he says.

"After all," I say. "You have your own house."

He laughs.

I say, "Shall I tell you some things right now?"

"Yes," he says.

I pause and confront my neglect in a new way. I realize how little I've spoken with my son about the events I've lived through, the events I've witnessed and written about, in this city, in this country, in the world. I have deferred to Colleen any talk of those sorts of things. Out of my respect for the mothering circle she has rightly drawn around herself and her son. And out of what I feel has been a respect for my son's childhood that I first acquired by sledding alone in the snow. Expressed by benign neglect. A fatherly respect I would have been grateful to settle for from my own father, to have just been left alone. Perhaps this is why, whenever I've found the time for my son through his childhood so far, I've been content to offer him this, the simple attendance to his whimsies: reading a chapter together in the endless everyday saga of the Five Little Peppers growing up; helping him furnish a shoebox cage for a pet katydid who inexplicably did not fly from his touch; the brush-grooming of our indoor cat—*Ryan's* cat, for the animal readily but exclusively accepts my son's attention to a task any right-minded cat would prefer to handle in its own way.

I recognize the irony in all that. I refused to become *my* father to father my son. But the way I chose to do that involved neglecting Ryan, prevented me from passing on the necessary adult lessons that my father at least—in spite of his flaws or sometimes even inadvertently *through* them—ended up teaching me.

So I say to my son, "When I was your age, my father was already teaching me the things I needed to know to become a man."

"Grandpa," Ryan says.

"Your grandfather," I say. "Yes." I heard a knowingness in his voice, an engagement, that makes me ask, "Do you remember him?"

"Yes."

"What did you think of him?"

Ryan pauses briefly to consider this. But without a trace in his expressive face of anything disturbing. And he says, "He is a very busy man with his work and is full of thoughts."

I cannot help but ask the question: "So did you find *him* to be sad?"

Ryan straightens a little, taking the connecting leap with me. "Yes," he says, brightly. "Just like you, Papa."

"Did you ask him about his sadness?"

"No. Should I have?"

"I'm glad you didn't," I say.

I see in Ryan's eyes another quick consideration and he asks, "Did I do wrong to ask you?"

"You are such a smart little man," I say. "With a kind heart, to ask that. But no. You didn't do anything wrong. You have awakened me. And I'm embarrassed that my own father should have done right by me in a way I have failed to do with you. I'm sorry for that."

Ryan is about to protest and I lift my hand to stop him. "It's all right," I say. "Just listen now. So your grandfather took me in hand, and for one thing, he taught me to shoot at an early age. Much younger than eleven. He taught me to handle a weapon. A rifle. He took me hunting with him—often—and he gave me this skill with a rifle and the nerve to hunt with it. To use a powerful weapon with precision and finality . . . Do you understand?"

I ask this because his face, usually animated by his concentrated listening, has gone blank, even though I sense that he is still focused on me. I ask this because I now hear my loss of nerve in speaking to him. *Finality.* I used the euphemism in talking about killing animals. Because he has become a boy whose characteristic instinct is to domesticate a katydid. Which speaks to how I have failed to prepare him for the world as it is.

And the failure involves having missed the chance to teach that lesson when he was at his most impressionable. Before he learned to love an insect. Euphemisms won't work now.

I say, "I learned how to shoot a rifle by hunting doves and rabbits and squirrels and deer."

Ryan has gone as still and focused as that briefest of moments when a deer first picks up the scent of a hunter. But the deer runs. Ryan has nowhere to run.

So be it. He needs to hear this.

I do try to mitigate it. I say, "Once my father and I hunted a bear. With some other men. But the bear was hunting too. He was killing our neighbors' sheep and goats."

"Papa," Ryan says, very softly. He has more to say, but I am afraid he will soon come to tears and put an end to what he must hear. Enough about animals.

I say, "I'm sorry. This isn't about killing animals. You don't have to kill animals. But in this world a boy has to become a man. This is about a man's skill I had to learn to be a man. To save my own life. To save the lives of my friends. To protect our country. Before you were born, when I was not much older than you are now, the world went to war. Do you know about that?" I ask this question after realizing, with a little shock, that I don't know the answer. I have spoken very little about the war to anyone, much less my son. In school he has surely heard about the war by now. His mother may have spoken of it to him. Other children surely play at war. But I know none of this for certain.

Ryan is still piercingly focused on me, offering no answer. At least there are no tears.

I say, "It's what people call the World War. In Europe. Started by the Germans against most everyone else, including our country. Have you heard of this?"

"Yes," he says. Very softly.

"I fought in that war," I say. "The world would be a terrible and much more dangerous place if people like me had not fought in that war. I chose to fight in it, but only a few months ahead of being *forced* to fight in it. As a young man. Chosen by the government and *forced* to fight. To carry a rifle and to kill other men who were trying to kill me."

I hear myself.

If only I had long ago made his man's skills natural to him.

I am too blunt now. He is not ready to hear this. But when will he ever be?

Tears are filling his eyes now, preparing to express themselves.

My time to speak is running out. At least on this day.

Part of me wants to justify all this by saying what I know in my bones is coming to this world because of the heartless ranting of a self-glorifying moron of a man who's been put in charge of a major country. But I cannot do that.

"I don't mean to scare you," I say. "It's my fault for the way I'm telling you these things now. It's harsh. But I had to say this. You have to hear it. You are destined to be a man. And there are threatening things happening in the world right now. In the same way as before."

I catch myself.

"But that's not something you have to think about. I'm trying to teach you what men have always been and what they must be. I just want you to have the best chance to fully become what you are."

His tears begin quietly to fall.

"I love you, my son. You are strong. You are so kind as well, and that's good, but that doesn't mean you can't also be strong. That you can't also be a man. I'm confident in you."

My son says, gently, "May I be excused?"

As if he's asking to leave the dinner table.

"Don't feel ashamed of your tears," I say. "Even a man can cry. Tears are not actions. Tears can just be a recognition of how the world is."

I pause. He waits, utterly unmoving, weeping soundlessly, not wiping it away. I realize I haven't answered his request.

"Yes," I say. "You're excused."

He rises.

He goes.

I feel myself capable of tears. For Ryan's suffering. For how I have mishandled this all along. For how badly I handled this today. But I do not allow the tears. This had to be said. I tell myself, *His tears show me he has heard the truth.* I wonder, *Has he heard enough to awaken his nascent self? His true self?*

He's smart. Very smart. He's capable of nuanced reflection. Even self-criticism. I have just seen that in him, in our conversation. Should I have told him about Adolf Hitler while I had the chance?

No. I've said too much already. And the worst I fear may not come to pass.

But now I see my son at the kitchen table. In his pajamas. The newspaper lies spread open before him on the table.

I have just come home from the *Independent*. Earlier than usual, which is to say just before his bedtime. He's reading news. Pages two and three.

He looks up. It's less than three weeks after our talk in his playhouse. We've spoken only in brief passing since then, returning to our customary hello-see-you-later warmth. For the usual reason, however. My work.

Perhaps he's preferred it that way. Still. He's been reading the news.

And he says, with great solemnity, "I understand, Papa. Everybody needs to figure out the world. Because the world is sure going to try to figure *us* out."

He looks away, across the kitchen. Colleen is here as well, at the stove heating Ryan's bedtime milk. She receives Ryan's glance and nods at him.

I know what he's been reading on this day. The plebiscite vote in Germany is heralded on the front page. **Germany Backs Hitler 10 to 1** *Absolute Power Is Won* and this with a voter turnout of 95 percent. And next to the continuation on the jump page, a name familiar to me **Al Capone Is on Way to New 'Devil's Island'** as he's transferred to Alcatraz Island in California from Atlanta, where he's been in jail for three years now, finally sent up for the only thing the feds could pin on him, tax evasion.

And just missing inclusion in the paper that's open before Ryan but appearing in tonight's late city edition: **New Managing Editor Named at Independent**, that being Sam Cunningham, with Arnold Kirchner moving up to editor in chief.

I say to my son, "If you want to talk about anything you read, let me know."

"I will," he says.

Though my elevation at the newspaper is the reason I'm home a bit early tonight, I immediately recognize that it's the same reason I will be able to fulfill that offer only very occasionally from now on. I think, *I will fail him again.*

And I'm standing near the front desk.

Duke and Nurse Bocage have squared off and are staring each other down, with Duke's chin still lifted.

The nurse in the outer lobby, the high-tan man with the bun of hair, has just turned to the altercation and begins to move toward it with a softly gliding gait. I can imagine what Duke makes of him. I expect Duke momentarily to jostle him roughly along in the spirit of the election. But as the nurse passes between the combatants, those two do not unloose their bonding glare, do not even acknowledge his passage. This is Duke's routine reaction to the man, no doubt, finding him unworthy even of a jostling. And Nurse Bocage is too deeply engaged at the moment with the politics of this janitor to be distracted.

The nurse continues into the corridor where I stand. Not *stand*, of course. The nurse moves toward the space where my consciousness lingers.

But now the headlines I have expected for nearly seven years rush into me, five months ahead of the schedule I once roughed out in my head. From the Sunday papers of September 3, 1939: **Britain and France Go to War Against Germany** and **Nazi Troops Smash Through Polish Corridor** and **Americans Seeking Way Home Besiege Embassy in Paris** and even **How Can Hitler Sleep? Mrs. Roosevelt Wonders**.

I have put in a long forty-eight hours at the *Independent* but make sure I am home, on this darkly momentous night, before Ryan goes to bed. As I enter our house and move from living room into dining room, I find Colleen and Ryan standing in the door to the kitchen, having no doubt heard me come in.

He is sixteen years old. He is as tall as me. He is within a few months of my age when I went off to war. Colleen says to him, "Go to your father," and as he begins to step toward me, she catches my eye. She gently nods him into my care.

I stop and motion my son to follow me back into the living room. I sit in my reading chair, Ryan close on the near end of the davenport. He angles around to face me.

He says, "Papa," in a voice whose tone, from its incremental maturation, I hear on this Sunday night without surprise; but revisiting the moment from my deathbed, it comes as a shock. It is the tenor voice of a man. He says, "Like you've always warned."

"Yes," I say. "Though America will not go to war. In a few hours our late city has a story about Congress drafting a proclamation of neutrality. The president will sign it. An act that formally keeps us out of the conflict. I don't see that changing anytime soon. Compared with the Germans', our military is feeble. It's been a tough economic decade for our country. That makes it very difficult to adequately rearm ourselves. But in the meantime, American companies can manufacture arms to sell to the Brits and the French and anyone else over there who takes on Hitler."

This is all true. This is what our Washington bureau has told us about our government's thinking. But I am still fearful about the future. More so than ever. In this moment, however, sitting before my son—whose near manhood remains devoid of any transferable skills or habits of mind or inclinations of heart that he needs to go to war—I am prepared to soothe his mind, and the mind of his mother, who is sitting in the dark at the dining room table listening to us.

"If not *soon*, then when?" Ryan asks.

I don't answer him at once because I take a moment to appreciate the selective leap of my son's mind, the unabashed skipping in his question of all the rest of what I said so he could focus on my vagueness about the most crucial consideration.

But my delay, though brief, leads him to explain. "Till our neutrality changes," he says.

"I know what you're asking. I just didn't have an instant answer to that. I don't really have an answer at all."

"What do you *think*, Papa?"

"It's not something I can think out. But my *feeling* is this thing will be long and messy. And if so, there are certainly ways for us to get drawn in."

Ryan nods, almost imperceptibly, as if it was the answer he expected.

"You worry," he says. "About me."

Again I hesitate. This time because he's right.

I try to put a mask on it. "Any father worries if his son may go to war."

He says, "It's more than that, isn't it, Papa? You're afraid . . ." And now he's the one to hesitate, but before I can intervene with what should already have been my reflexive denial, he says: "You're afraid I'm not a man."

I say, firmly, "You're still barely sixteen. Of course you're not a man. But you're going to be. It's just that if you end up being a man who goes to war . . . I don't mean to harp on that. I just want you to have the tools . . ."

"Papa," he says. "I've been thinking about all this. Wars are fought with more than rifles. You'd be proud of me in the navy, wouldn't you?"

The answer is so obvious that I realize with a small, grave thump in my chest that rifle skills have been a subordinate worry, something theoretically fixable for me to focus on instead of my deeper concern about a draftable young man's sensibility, his temperament. Those things about him might be just fine in another world, but in this world, at this moment of history, it's dangerous for him. The navy might be the answer. Of course. I need to put my army bias aside. Both branches of service are comrades in arms. And navy service is possible without exactly the same personal requirements.

"That would be fine," I say. "Of course . . . If it comes to that."

"Just in case," Ryan says, "I have a plan . . . I know you'd buy me my own rifle, if I asked. So I'm asking for this instead. Take me to Lafayette Radio. It's a big shop on Jackson Boulevard just outside the Loop. Buy me a kit to build my own shortwave radio. If I have to go to war, I want that to be my weapon. Radio. Ships have to communicate to fight. When I'm about to come of age for any draft, I can enlist. The navy gives you an aptitude test if you enlist. They talk to you. I can prove myself to them. I'll have built my own radio and mastered it. I'll learn Morse code. I can persuade them to make me a radioman. If America goes to war, radio is a big gun on a ship."

His rush of words ceases. His hand reaches out toward me, falls on the armrest of the couch. His eyes bear in intently on mine.

I know what he needs. It is easy to give. I mean it sincerely. I realize my son has the basic courage to go to war. He's proving it right now.

"What a good plan," I say. "I'm proud of you."

I flicker back into the dark.

I am a little puzzled. I wonder if this memory is faulty. If, in fact, I failed to say those words of pride in him that Ryan needed to hear. Or perhaps I even failed to feel them. But no. I'm sure I have just relived those moments as they happened.

Here in the dark I've been expecting to review only my failures. Surely this wasn't one. Can I hope for this accounting to include my successes as well? Or was there something in this memory that I've missed?

These are questions I mean to ask only myself, in my head, but God says, "Stop it."

"Sorry," I say.

And I am sitting next to my son at the table in his little house, a structure no longer for play but for him to listen to Europe and its war and to prepare for his possible role in the conflict. It's June 14, 1940. The war has been going on for nine months. Ryan turned seventeen years old yesterday.

Before us is the radio he's built: a low chassis of knobs and tuning panel and with an open top that holds a brimming garden of coils and tubes and condensers. He's fitted the radio with a separate speaker for this very sort of occasion, when the two of us can listen together in the dark, when the shortwave signals are at their best. Colleen has let Ryan stay up late tonight as the war has blitzed its way to a terrible milestone.

Ryan has tuned in a mellifluous and unflappable British male voice: "This is London calling in the worldwide service of the British Broadcasting Corporation. Here is the news, and this is Alvar Lidell reading it. Tonight the city of Paris echoes with the hobnailed boots of German troops. The capital city of France has fallen, and the German High Command has announced that the second stage of their western campaign has been successfully completed. The French resistance in the northern fronts has been broken, and the Germans claim that the remaining French forces will be destroyed within two weeks. Reliable sources in Berlin confirm that this is a realistic expectation. The British government has pledged to continue giving the French government the utmost aid in her power, but made it clear that if France is lost as an active ally, the British will fight on alone against Chancellor Hitler's war machine."

With imperturbable detachment Alvar Lidell continues to the details of the French debacle and to the Germans' openly announced plans to do likewise to Britain, with a prediction that its army will be on British soil before the end of July.

When the news shifts to the latest in the Far East, Japan's bombing of Chungking in its ongoing conquest of China, Ryan switches off his radio.

I turn to him and his head is slightly bowed. He is looking in silence at his hands, which have settled one on top of the other on the tabletop.

I do not interrupt him.

Then he says, quite softly, "You told me once that you had to kill men in the World War. When you went off to do that, you were younger than I am now."

It's been a half dozen years since Ryan and I had that conversation, when we first sat together at this table. He shortly thereafter began to read newspapers, and we have spoken now and then about the events of the world. But over those years I have not said another word about my own war. Nor has he asked.

He hesitates to frame a question from that preamble. But then he asks, "You killed with a rifle?"

A rhetorical question.

"Yes," I say.

And now he lifts his face, turns in his chair to face me.

But he hesitates again.

I turn to face him.

"Are you sure?" he asks.

"Sure?"

"Shooting from the trenches. There were trenches for the riflemen, right? All of you shooting from there at once, did you know when you killed someone?"

It would be simple to explain the facts of what I did and how I did it. My impulse is to do that. But with the following beat or two of my heart, it seems anything but simple. Still, I cannot bring myself to lie.

At least I can *say* it simply. "Yes. I knew."

Ryan's eyes move ever so slightly, from my eyes to my mouth, which has just affirmed this terrible thing, and back to my eyes.

I wait, afraid he will request the details that he seems just now to have minutely searched for in my face.

But he asks a question I do not expect: "Did the killing change you?"

No answer comes to mind.

He says, "Who you are? Forever?"

I do not have an answer.

I do have an answer.

I do not have an answer I know how to speak. Or even know how to understand.

He watches my face as I struggle with this.

I admire the subtlety of my seventeen-year-old son. I am afraid of his subtlety.

"Not forever," I say. This is true and it is not true. True literally. I have killed no other man since, nor would I ever. Untrue in some deeper way.

My father unexpectedly comes to mind.

He had no issue like this, having had no war to fight. He never said anything that would seem to bear upon it. But now I realize his intrusion has to do with his picking up that stick and drawing the circle of self on the ground. He has come to mind with the truth of that lesson. And with the drastic oversimplification of it.

I am of the men who had to kill alongside me.

I am not of them.

I am not of the men I killed.

I am of them.

Ryan is still focused on me intently, but his gaze searches my eyes, one at a time, restlessly, the left, the right, the left again, as if to catch the one that tells the full truth, that betrays the evasive shrug of my answers. He is asking, *How could the killing not have changed you forever?*

But he does not ask this. Though I know the question is in him. His subtle mind makes a leap from it: "The Germans all chose Adolf Hitler. Almost every last one of them."

"Almost every one of them," I say. He remembers one of the first stories he read when he finally turned to newspapers.

He says, "Mama and I saw a newsreel at the movies last fall. Just before the war started. A crowd for him. So big. It looked like a million people saluting. What do they see in him, Papa?"

"They see themselves writ large. Something they can all be together."

And he says, "So then they can see each other more clearly too."

My son. I affirm his insight by clutching his shoulder, shaking him gently with a nod of assent and approval.

"That makes them feel it's a good thing, doesn't it?" he says.

"It always does. That's the danger."

"How do you know when it's a bad thing?"

"I don't have an easy answer. Just know that sometimes a bad thing can be shared by multitudes. While for a good thing, there might be only a few of you."

This thought jolts him. He straightens. He considers. His eyes fill with tears. He says, "Thank you, Papa."

I'm not quite sure why.

Not that I let myself question it. The circle has been drawn around just the two of us. And it is better than a multitude.

But the moment vanishes.

Into headlines . . .

France Surrenders *Nazi Terms Signed in Full*

. . . the bannered intrusion of the wider world that I've spent my life watching and reporting and editing and experiencing in newspapers . . .

Battle of Britain Begins *Air Fleets Clash over Sea and Shore*

. . . the wider life I've lived from a distance while missing so much of the life right before my eyes . . .

Japan Joins Axis Powers *Alliance Seen Aimed at U.S.*

. . . and my having missed the life that was near to me is why, I suppose, instantly upon his embrace, my son vanishes from my recollection. Because that was how I failed him.

And the flurry of headlines now comes from issues of the *Cunningham Examiner*:

Sam Returns to Oblivious Ways

Ryan, Colleen Have Serious Talk *Grow Glibly Light When Sam Enters Room*

Ryan Certified in Morse Code *'I'm Ready' He Tells Mutely Proud Father*

Sam Wakes in Night with Regret *Realizes Acute Fear Can Silence Him*

Even over his pride in his son.

Ryan Turns Seventeen & Six Months

This from the December 14, 1940, issue of the *Examiner.* I know what his plan is for that morning, know where he will go and what he will do. Join the U.S. Navy. He has built and mastered a shortwave radio. He has mastered Morse code. He is six months past his seventeenth birthday. The navy will listen to him.

They do.

And they take him.

It is now 1941.

Ryan Cunningham Turns Eighteen *Arrives Bainbridge Island to Become Radioman*

On this very same day, from the Chicago newspapers: **New Details of U.S. Freighter Sinking** *Survivors Tell of Nazi Torpedo Attack* and **Germany Defiant, Threatens New Sinkings** *Warns U.S. to Cease Selling Arms to U.K.*

And in the following few months U-boats indeed continue to sink American freighters. The *Longtaker* and the *Pink Star.* The *Meridian* and the *Crusader.* And more. And whenever the sinking of an American ship clarions in my brain, I invoke the same litany: *I should be proud of where he is, what he's doing. I am proud. No. To Hell with your pride. You shouldn't have rushed him into this. To Hell with* me. *But yes, I'm proud.* With a countering ironic response: *If you'd spent more time with him he would have ended up doing the same thing anyway but with a rifle instead of Morse code. The only American ships at risk are merchant ships transporting arms. He is safer on a U.S. Navy warship.*

And in November he comes home on leave, the first I will have seen him after all his training. He is now a navy radioman, at which he excelled, naturally, he being who he is and having prepared so well. Excelled such that he has already advanced from seaman to petty officer third class. Excelled such that the navy is sending him straight to our Pacific base in Hawaii for assignment to the U.S.S. *Indianapolis*, a Portland-class heavy cruiser that was once President Roosevelt's ship of state.

I am at work on the day he arrives, but finally it is evening and I can leave the late city to my staff.

I enter our house where I know my son and my wife are waiting.

How does this moment go? Even as I am crossing the living room floor the dying part of me separates at that question, and the most recent *Examiner* headline yawps at me: **God Assigns Sam to Son's Story** *'Don't Try to Lead It, Just Report' Instructs Deity.*

All right.

Ryan emerges from the dining room.

He is wearing his navy dress blue uniform with its low-knotted black silk neckerchief dangling long down the front of the jumper and with its wide-legged trousers and its flat-topped, brimless cap, which he puts on indoors now especially for me, adjusting it minutely to sit at an ever-so-slight tilt to one side, the precise angle of which I sense he has carefully calculated to be tolerated between inspections. And he touches the two pointed ends of his neckerchief, arranging them to some effect that is invisible to my eye.

He is proud of his uniform.

My son straightens at the spine, closes his stance, and he snaps his right forearm and wrist and hand into a perfect alignment that rises at a perfect forty-five-degree angle to touch the tip of his forefinger to the bottom edge of his cap, and his gaze rivets to mine.

He remains utterly motionless.

It takes me several moments of admiring his ramrod perfection to realize that as an enlisted man he is waiting for me—as if I were still an officer—to return his salute.

Which I do.

As perfectly as I can, though this was never a strength of mine, as it clearly is for him.

I release my salute and let my arm fall. He snaps his down.

"Permission to hug you, sir," he says.

I hesitate.

Ryan is now slightly but perceivably taller than me. He is a member of his country's armed services, and within forty-eight hours he will be borne from his home and off to sea in a world widely at war. He is a man.

These are relevant facts, but my hesitation is a reflex of the viscera to which these facts are relevant but utterly subordinate.

Does Johnny Moon stir in me? Probably. About the hugging.

But now this also rushes into me and this too is visceral: though it seems like long ago, only last year my son and I hugged and it felt proper and true and fine.

I do not know how to reconcile these two feelings at war in me as Ryan stands waiting, particularly under these factual circumstances.

So I say, "Permission granted."

He steps to me, ripping his cap from his head while I bend toward him from the waist, and we hug at the shoulders.

And now it's the next evening, the last of Ryan's home leave, and we sit down together in the living room, the three of us, I in my reading chair and Colleen next to Ryan on the davenport. He wears civilian clothes, including a light blue chambray shirt with a wide collar that he's favored for a couple of years, faded from washings and grown small enough that he's had to unbutton the sleeves and roll them.

He sees me noticing it and flicks the tips of the collar. "Doesn't it seem like the navy? But I've loved it since before I made my plan."

"Will it go into dry dock after tonight?" I ask.

"Worse," he says. "Decommissioned."

"High time," says Colleen, putting her arm around him and hugging. "We can find another you'll love."

Ryan angles his head to touch briefly on her hugging shoulder, then straightens again and their eyes lock and he says, "No need. I love the cut of the uniform even more."

Colleen lets go of him and laughs, though she looks away from him at once and I hear a taint of willfulness in the lightness of it. Ryan hears it too. As the laugh fades, he looks closely at her.

She is afraid for her son.

He reaches to her near hand, which has come to rest on her leg.

She looks back to him.

He squeezes her hand.

They do not say a word.

Ryan looks at me.

I am struck by all this, the deep and nuanced communion they share.

I am glad for it. I envy it.

I say to him, "I'm so sorry I've come home late again. I've missed so much of your visit."

His hand rises from his mother's and opens toward me. He says, "For the same reason I have to leave, you have to be absent. We all need to know what's happening in the world. Especially now. Desperately so. What you do makes that possible, Papa. I'm proud of you."

The lift in my chest at this, the prompting in my eyes, makes me pause and harden this feeling so as not to let it show. I cannot let myself be less of a man at this moment than my son.

I say, "Watching is all I do. You'll be out there actually protecting us. That's far more important."

"Papa," he says, his tone gently dismissing my deference.

The three of us fall silent.

I study my son's eyes. His gaze shifts inward. His mouth compresses. He follows his train of thought for a few moments and then says, "It's not just watching. It's vigilance. They would hide their victims from us. Your newspaper tells us that. Hitler's concentration camps, for instance. Hundreds of thousands are going. And nothing to say there won't soon be a million. All the Jews and Slavs and Gypsies and those the Nazis say are moral degenerates. What do we expect he'll do with all those people he hates?"

I know the story from the *Independent* he's speaking of. About the rumored horrors at camps in France and Austria, Poland and Czechoslovakia.

Ryan falls silent. Contains himself.

This time it's Colleen's hand that finds his.

Now he and I are standing before each other in the final moments before he leaves our home to go to sea and, I fear, fully to war.

He looks sharp in his dress blues. He prefers to say goodbye inside our front door. I understand. He is on his own from here, heading downtown to catch a bus with other Chicago sailors to be mustered at the Great Lakes Naval Station just north of the city.

He sets his stuffed but pristine seabag on the floor beside him. It is time to part.

For a few moments I find myself struggling as I have over the past two days. My son gazes at me and does not move. I try to read his face, whether the child in him will ascend and ask for something that I know I should give. I should give him a hug, freely and warmly and without concern. But I struggle.

And I separate from this moment briefly, partially, and I think, toward God: *Okay. I get it. I'm sorry. I continue to let him down. He deserves to be a child a last time before going to war. I do not fully understand my hesitation. I do understand that I'm wrong.* But all of that is the insight of the dying old man. Not the man who stands before his son at this crucial moment.

And my son, my dear son, makes it easier for me to be a fool. He is standing straight as his training has taught him, though now I perceive in him a subtle further straightening, a state he achieves and then holds, as if signaling an expectation, as if telling me it's okay to do this in the way that I prefer.

So yes. I too stand tall. I vow to do it properly. I lift my right arm, shoulder to elbow parallel to the ground, and I bend at the elbow and in doing so instantly arrange forearm and wrist and hand and fingers into perfect locked alignment and I touch the tip of my forefinger halfway up my forehead over the center of my right eye.

My son does the same to me.

I snap off the salute.

My son snaps off his reply.

And he picks up his seabag and turns and goes out of our house to begin the journey to his assignment on a ship at Pearl Harbor.

And I am in the dark.

And abruptly:

JAPAN STARTS WAR WITH U.S.
IN SNEAK ATTACK ON HAWAII

And I am in the dark again. For one moment. For another.

I cry out aloud to God: "So am I supposed to deal with the sin of impatience now? What do I have to go through to find out what's next? He was there."

My tone is not respectful.

I have shouted.

I am thrashing inside, though I have accepted the inevitable fact that in the present moment my son is already dead. I've surely outlived him and dealt with that no matter when he died. But I remain riled.

I'm not getting a response from the Creator of the universe.

I work on my presentation. "Okay. Sorry for the tone. And sorry for the impatience. And very sorry for the thought I just had, which was to sneer at your reputation for being loving."

God says, "Calm down, Sam. Nothing you've said or felt requires an apology. I do have my ways and they are sometimes mysterious. You've heard that reputation too, haven't you?"

"Yes, yes, yes," I say, somewhat impatiently in feeling, though my tone is simply weary now.

God says, "All right. I'll take a little of the mystery out of this for you. I needed you to sit briefly with those headlines. It's not to torment you. I have my reasons. The feeling you just had about your son was unconditional. Tuck that awareness away."

He pauses.

"I will," I say. "I will." I sound sincere. And mollified. I suspect I am on both counts.

God says, "He was at Pearl Harbor when the attack came, but he was quartered onshore, waiting for the ship he would join, which was out on maneuvers. He was unharmed. He would join his ship two weeks later."

"Thank you," I say.

"Now get back to your assignment," He says. "It's time to open yourself to your wife."

Our front door has closed.

Ryan has just left, his seabag slung over his shoulder.

His footsteps recede across the porch, down the steps, remain briefly audible along the brick walkway, and then vanish into silence.

I take a breath. I let it out.

I turn.

Colleen is standing in the dining room doorway.

With our next breaths we cross the floor and embrace, pressing each other as close as we can. For a long while saying nothing.

Then we are turned to each other on the davenport. We still don't speak. I remain silent out of deference to her. Something is going on behind her eyes.

I want her to lead us now.

She no doubt can see things behind my eyes as well. But I won't open myself to those things for fear they will make me speak before I know what she needs.

Colleen breaks our silence. "He'll be okay."

"You had to work up to that," I say.

"But I believe it."

"I made this happen," I say with a dying fall, expressing my self-doubt, my regret, which, I now realize, have both begun to roil in me.

Colleen puts her hand on mine. "It's the world at fault," she says. "Between you and Ryan, you figured it out. He's done the smart thing. If we can stay out of the war, he'll have learned useful skills and had a maturing experience. If we go to war, that means it's become so massive the whole world's involved, and a boy his age would be forced into it anyway. But with far less control over his fate. On that ship right now, doing what he's doing, he's as safe as he can be in these times."

I turn my hand and squeeze hers, gently, thankfully. "The smart thing," I echo. If not firmly, at least evenly. Stanching the doubt.

"Yes," she says. "The smart thing."

We pause.

We are still holding hands.

Which of us, without letting go, initiates our rise from the davenport? It's difficult to say. Because I suspect we have each of us risen on our own at precisely the same moment. Certainly we have the same intention.

We walk hand in hand into the dining room and through its sidewall door into the hallway that runs from our bedroom to Ryan's.

We turn toward ours.

In between the two bedrooms is the bathroom. Avoiding, at least, a shared wall. But our bedrooms are still too close. They have always been close, the Wendell Street cottage having been even more compressed. During virtually every hour of our son's life, when he was away at school, his father was reporting and editing the news. And when Ryan was home, his instinctive strong attachments and interests almost always kept him there.

All of this is what animates our steps now along the hallway, intensifies our joined hands in these commencing moments of our rare shared solitude. But animated as well in defiance of death, the devastating possibility of which has come to dwell with us for the foreseeable future.

And now we are in bed. No longer secretive. No longer restrained. No longer hushed. No longer in the dark.

But even as we join and move and are not afraid to elaborate and proclaim the act, I become aware in my deathbed that those freedoms, though taken advantage of to some extent at the time, register in this revisitation only in a general way.

I inhabit my forty-year-old self fully now, through our eyes, hers and mine, she beneath me and I above, our eyes holding, holding, no matter how we move. Hers hold steady on mine, steady but minutely expressive moment to moment, movement by movement, her eyes narrow ever so slightly and now widen and now flutter just briefly and then widen again and willfully hold steady again, concentrate as if behind them she is determined to see me clearly, to know me, and also to retain this moment and the next and next, to remember, to hold fast to precious things. But now my body makes a boisterous surge and her eyes close tight and her brow furrows. I've hurt her. I stop moving but remain within, and I whisper, "*Sorry,*" and her eyes open at once and rush to me and she returns the whisper as if returning a caress: "*No, my darling, it's all right, just go gently now,*" and I do.

And I return to the dark. Regretfully. Wishing to go gently with my wife for a while longer, after all these decades of circumspection. But now that Ryan has gone off to sea and I seem to be fully with Colleen instead, I find myself retreating to a more difficult night, just hours after I first set Ryan's eventual departure in motion. Seven years before, the evening of the day I confronted him in his playhouse. When we'd lately moved into our new home in Hermosa. A Sunday evening. Ryan has gone to bed now, and Colleen and I step out the back door and sit beside each other in wicker chairs on the sunporch.

Though we have had this luxury for only a short while and are able to enjoy it only intermittently, we already know to sigh and settle in quietly for a time and listen to the night. On our sunporch in the dark. What we've already begun to call our "moon porch." Which is bright tonight.

But very shortly she says, "You had a talk with Ryan this afternoon."

Of course. This has been on her mind ever since. He went into the house in tears. He probably went straight to her.

Still, she has said this gently, my Colleen. The tone of a loving mediator.

I ask, "How was he when he went to bed?"

"Better. But he was shaken up."

"Did he give you the details?"

"Yes." And she adds quickly, "But please understand. He and I are close in everything."

"I'm glad for that," I say.

My arm is lying on the arm of my chair and she puts her hand upon mine.

"I wish I could do more for him," I say.

She squeezes my hand.

"My job," I say.

Another squeeze. "I understand," she says. And she takes her hand away.

"All of which is why I needed to talk to him today."

"He's eleven years old," she says.

"Have you seen the newspapers?"

She does not reply.

I say, "Adolf Hitler has grabbed unlimited power in a country that not so long ago plunged the whole world into war. A war I fought in. He's already building an army. Have you been close with Ryan in regards to all of that?"

She turns her face sharply away from me.

I hear my tone.

But in the gesture I hear her answer. No, she has not.

She says, "He knows about it."

"Accidentally. He doesn't follow the news. Newspapers are simply the funnies."

Colleen looks at me. I wish I could see her eyes more clearly in the moonlight.

I say, "He needs to start learning about a world that will severely challenge who he is."

"I agree with that," she says. "I really do. I'm not a giddy toddler mommy who doesn't want her child to grow up. Ryan is learning who he is. But there's plenty to learn about that before it involves a war in Europe."

I say, "When that war finally gets going and then gets big enough to involve our country, he will get drawn in. And *that's* who he will be."

I pause.

Colleen's eyes are still unreadably upon me.

I say, "He will be a *man*. He will *need* to be a man. Fully so. We have to prepare him to be a man or we are preparing him for a body bag."

I pause again. Briefly, but long enough to let her reply if she wishes.

She does not.

I say, "When he's in, he will unavoidably—necessarily—learn how to kill. *I* had to learn how to kill. And I survived the war only because I was good at it. Does that mean it's who I am? Am I a killer?"

I stop at this turn in my words.

I did not expect to go there in this conversation.

Colleen's hand is on mine again.

And I say, "There was a man in the war. I fought beside him. A fellow sniper. An American. His name was Johnny Moon. All that I told you about my skills, my way of killing, it was his too. And he was good at it. Very good. He did it coolly and bravely. He was a man. In every way a man. But just as the war made us both killers, it also did another thing to him. And to some others in the trenches. Other men. When an attack came and the assault was over, there were dead men among us but there were also men dying. Men who had been wounded by a shard of shrapnel or a rifle round. The wound was mortal but the dying was not immediate. We had medics who went through the trenches helping the wounded. But some of us, Johnny included, would go to one who was clearly dying and take him in their arms and speak low to him, and the soldier—who was out of his mind now from the pain and knowing it was the end—would mistake the touch as his mother's or his wife's or his girlfriend's, and Johnny would play the woman's role and would hold the dying man close and caress him and even kiss him. Do you understand? So is that who

Johnny Moon was? A moral degenerate? No. Though his actions and attitude were of such a one, he actually wasn't. Which is my point. The war moved Johnny to do certain things that did not define who he was. When the war was over, those things would be left utterly behind. Do you understand me, my darling Colleen? I wasn't a killer. But I had to kill. I had to be a man in order to kill. And I had to kill to survive. If I hadn't killed, Ryan would not even exist. Your son would not even exist."

I stop.

I am glad for the dark and that my wife cannot clearly see my eyes.

And I suddenly hear all I have just said.

For a moment I am astonished. How did I end up here?

Then I realize.

"My point," I say. "My central point is that Ryan may one day be required by his country to go abroad and do things that are not about who he really is but about a terrible yet crucial job that has to be done. I was not a killer. My close friend—he was a friend to me as well as a comrade—my friend was not a moral degenerate. We were men. We had to truly be men to survive all that and still be who we really were."

I stop speaking.

Colleen is looking at me but I have no idea what she is feeling. I cannot read her except to know that she is absolutely still.

And that's good. It makes me grow still as well.

I look away.

Ryan's childhood house is dark and throws a moon shadow across the yard.

I feel Colleen's hand on mine.

It remains there for a moment, very briefly, then withdraws.

And now he is a man, my son. He has slung his seabag over his shoulder and he closes the door and goes off.

I say to myself, *I have done what I had to do. He will do what he has to do. He will return and he will be who he truly is, and his ability to be someone else for a time—because he must—will become part of who he truly is.*

This is how I understand it. This is how I can hear his footsteps fade and vanish and yet I can be at peace. Such that my wife and I can move through an otherwise now empty house and make love and be at peace.

Then the Imperial Japanese Navy attacks Pearl Harbor and he survives. And when he sails, he sails off to war.

And he writes us in his first piece of Victory Mail:

Dear Mama and Papa,

I am somewhere on some ship or other doing something or other and writing only blandly to you so the righteous navy censors can assure the protection of the aforementioned ship and all of its crew and protect the crucial mission that the ship and its crew are performing without the censors having to delay themselves in the execution of their own crucial mission by my forcing them to employ their redaction pen on this, my loving letter to the both of you.

Your son,
Ryan

He is at sea. All the parents of all the navy men are allowed to personally know the name of their ship, but no amount of even a newsman parent's reporting, no news source carefully cultivated and judiciously harvested, will ever reveal where his ship is or what it is doing, which will be the case for all American sons on all American ships on all the seas for as long as our nation is at war.

I am happy, as the war goes on, that as a newsman I hear nothing of the U.S.S. *Indianapolis*. The only ships whose names we are occasionally, eventually, allowed to print are those that sink.

But in the *Cunningham Examiner* Ryan's bland letters are always important news.

Ryan Enjoys Ship's Hot Saltwater Showers
Too Hot for His Fellow Bathers But He Is Blissful

Ryan Ponders Tattoo, Alarms His Mother
Promises Flowers Not Anchors, Then Reveals Jest

Ryan Rises to Petty Officer 1st Class

And now. Now in this mental half-light that I've become accustomed to here in the physical darkness of my dying bed—the half-light where headlines flow, carrying briskly onward my life already lived, watching that life from a distance, reliving it from a distance, life distilled, managed—now in this half-light, instead of the headlines that I expect will safely, compactly, carry me through the Second Great War, I have a

Cunningham Newswire bulletin, a raw lead, in the form of a Western Union telegram.

> The Navy Department deeply regrets to inform you that your son Radioman Chief Petty Officer First Class Ryan Samuel Cunningham is missing in action and presumed dead in the performance of his duties. The ship he served on was sunk by enemy torpedo on July 30, 1945, and his body is not recoverable. I know that this results in added distress for which I offer my deep personal regrets as well. You should understand that the navy considers this result to be a burial at sea with all the attendant honors to that state. Please accept my heartfelt sympathy in your bereavement.
>
> Vice Admiral Louis Denfeld
> Chief of Naval Personnel

And now. And now. But surely there is no *now.* I am, after all, dying, and he has already gone, my son, my precious son, and before I started dying I already knew that to be so and I had long known it, but now Colleen and I are clutching each other close in the center of our living room floor, the telegram still clenched in my fist, and we are trembling into each other and we weep and weep and cannot speak and she does not blame me and I do not blame her, and now I have lived seventy-one years beyond the dying of my son, he has died so long ago he could have leaped from death to the womb of some just-impregnated mother and been born once more and then lived what easily passes for a full life in this world and still had time to die the day before my dying, and dying I am, dying now, and I care about dying, which perhaps hints at the *why* behind the headline in the current late city edition of the *Cunningham Examiner*—**God Reveals Withheld Memory**—withheld because if on my deathbed I'd retained the deep weariness of my long-lingeringly bereft life, it would have rendered this whole process meaningless, but now it hasn't been, my son has lived anew, and I have known him again, and so the headline clarions **He Lived, He Once Did Live** but he has also died anew, my son, and now I am myself in the midst of dying, and I can presume he went through this same process as well, and there is news to come, there is always news, now and ever shall be there is news.

The second day after the telegram about Ryan, in part to manage my grief, in part to remind myself who I am, in part simply to make it possible for me to rise from our bed and put one foot in front of the other, I take my reporter's hat out of a bottom drawer and begin to make phone calls to my best sotto voce sources in the military. The telegram was devastating in its unelaborated core message, but it was made even worse by its vagueness. Then a sympathetic and well-placed admiral speaks to me. Unattributably. But even that has a further condition. I cannot break the embargo for news of a sinking ship, a strict requirement that has been in place for the entire war.

But less than a week later, with profoundly complex feelings, I oversee the assembly of what is arguably the most momentous front page in the history of the *Chicago Independent*.

Bannered across it, dropping its story into columns seven and eight:

THE WORLD WAR IS OVER

And bannered in two decks beneath it across six columns, and presenting its story in columns one and two:

**Japan Emperor Accepts Puppet Role,
Addresses Nation, Blames Atom Bomb**

And featured in a three-column box below the fold:

**Heavy Cruiser Indianapolis Sunk,
Carried A-Bomb Parts to Guam**

Now the navy has made the news of Ryan's ship official, choosing to do so on the very day the war ends. But in the announcement there are unanswered questions, for which I know or can infer answers I cannot print. Answers that have a bone-deep connection to me.

Kirch emerges from his office to stand shoulder to shoulder with me and approve the galley proof of this day's thunderous front page.

We both take a deep breath before it.

Kirch says, "Too bad FDR didn't live to see it."

"Or do it," I say. "Likely would have gone the same way, though."

"No doubt," Kirch says.

Though in my head: *Not likely the same way. Not the same in every detail. Not in the granular timing of contemplation and discussion and command. If FDR had lived, these four months later there would have inevitably been some difference in all that. Even a small difference means that the freak rendezvous of the* Indianapolis *and a lone-wolf U-boat in the vast Pacific would never have happened. FDR died and therefore my son died.*

"It's ready to go," Kirch says to the press foreman about the front page.

The foreman whisks up the galley proof and I say to Kirch, "I want to do something out of the ordinary tomorrow."

We go to his office.

I explain at length how what I want to do is something of an editorial, something of a deeply personal meditation, something of a news story drawing on known facts, on facts that are soon to be known but are presently unattributable, on quasi-facts that will be plausibly inferred. All of these.

Kirch listens and his go-forth words to me are: "To honor what you have lost, my friend—primarily for that—but also for the *Independent* I described to you at our first lunch together, this sounds perfect. Regards the paper: thinkers and emoters both; pushing the boundaries. Let it contain multitudes, Sam."

I arrive home on this night and the lights are lit, but the house is still. It has been eight days since the telegram. Each night when I've come home from the paper, she has been waiting for me on the davenport. She has slept only sporadically and fitfully.

I remove my shoes and this is a hopeful gesture even as part of me thrashes in fear. I move across the room and into the hallway and toward our bedroom as quickly as I can while being as quiet as I can, and my passage is taking far too long, this is far too long to wait.

The door to the bedroom is open.

A small light is on inside.

Finally I enter.

She is lying on the bed in the plaid housecoat I see every day.

Her face is turned this way. Her eyes are closed. Her body is in fetal compression, her arms crossed at the wrists and clinched close and her legs together and drawn up.

I move to her, though softly, softly, in case my fear is stupid. Unable to draw a breath I bend to listen for hers.

And there it is. Soft and slow. She simply sleeps. Thankfully, she sleeps.

I turn off the table lamp, and I back quietly away.

I go upstairs to my office.

I turn on the desk lamp and look at my Corona portable on the desk.

The piece I must write ruffles my fingers and asks for a connection to all I have ever written.

I set the Corona aside.

I go to the closet, and from the floor, at the back, I heft the Oliver Model 9 and carry it to the desk.

I set it gently down.

I sit.

And I write:

News/Editorial/Memorial

Recent News Accounts Buried a Lede;
Our Managing Editor Sees It Differently

By Samuel Cunningham
Managing Editor

As the U.S.S. Indianapolis sank from a German torpedo on July 30, the ship's ranking radioman, Chief Petty Officer First Class Ryan Cunningham, heroically persisted in broadcasting an SOS, resulting in his death by drowning while performing his duty.

Recent news reports, including in this newspaper, gave a thorough and necessary and widely grievous account of the human toll from the loss of the heavy cruiser: 883 crew members died. 315 were rescued a hundred hours later, those being the only crew members left floating in the ocean by then, with as many as 500 more who had abandoned ship having already drowned or been killed by sharks.

Grievous indeed. But in my heart and the heart of my wife, as we are all that is left of our family, the true lead paragraph of the U.S.S. Indianapolis story sits at the top of this account.

Chief Petty Officer First Class Ryan Cunningham was my son.

My son. My son.

In this first wave of published stories, the navy gave only a cursory explanation for the devastatingly long time the ship's survivors were forced to float and die in the ocean. The official statement said that all major commands in the Western Pacific had replied in the negative when asked whether their radio logs showed the reception of any SOS signal from the Indianapolis.

However, I have in the past twenty-four hours reverted to my previous identity as a reporter, and I am told by an authoritative source that the Navy Department plans soon to release a revised report.

The report will say that although no ship, aircraft or shore station seems to have heard a distress message, there is "ample evidence" that such messages were in fact keyed in from the Indianapolis and may have actually been successfully transmitted on at least one (500 kc) and possibly two frequencies.

That was my son. He was the ranking noncommissioned officer on that bridge. It was his responsibility. Though a question remains if anyone actually heard those messages, what is undisputable is that no one acknowledged them. And simple navy sources readily confirmed that a radioman's sworn duty is to continue sending a ship's SOS until he receives an acknowledgment.

The Indianapolis sank in twelve minutes. "Ample evidence" suggests to any thinking person and fills his father's recent darkest dreams that radioman Ryan Cunningham was, with unwavering heroism, keying in an SOS in spite of the Pacific Ocean filling the bridge and finally taking his life.

Further evidence that this was exactly what happened is suggested by the climactic end of the relationship that the eight-year-old Ryan Cunningham forged one summer with a very large katydid he found sitting on the back porch. The insect chose not to fly when my son offered his hand. Indeed, the katydid crawled up on Ryan's forefinger and the two of them chirped like birds to each other. He named her Katie. Thus began the katydid's new life being fed and pampered and conversed with in a shoebox.

One afternoon a few weeks later, however, the katydid grew lethargic and silent. It was clear her life was nearly over. But Ryan refused to leave her. He took her up and held her gently in his hand and he chirped to her till she passed nearly two hours later.

She never returned his chirp that afternoon. But he did not abandon her.

There was a time in my life, as a parent, that I could force a smile whenever my wife waxed proud over this trait in our son. But it always seemed to me sentimental in an extreme way. It seemed unmanly. Inappropriately so, even for a child who was to become a man.

I say there was a time when I felt that way as if the time has long passed. In fact, I have fully come to understand my son as a child only within the last twenty-four hours.

> As a child he felt a sense of duty to another being in a critical time and he did not waver, he did not abandon the creature. He did what he had taken on to do even though he received no acknowledging response. He persevered to the end.
>
> I hear your keystrokes, my son. I hear the signal you are sending me even now from a vast ocean far away. As I write these words with love and shame and profound regret, I acknowledge that you were all along and will forever be a real man.

I sleep on the davenport and I wake before dawn to prepare for work. As I am finishing my coffee at the kitchen table and going over the text of my editorial for a last time, Colleen startles me with a hand on my shoulder.

I rise and I kiss her and she feels, she says, if not actually rested at least less overwhelmingly exhausted, and she sits with me.

Without a word I lay what I've written before her.

She lifts it and draws it close and reads it slowly.

She finishes it.

She places it before her, squaring the corners.

She turns her face to me and her eyes are full of tears and I know instantly that those are complex tears indeed.

We look at each other in silence for a long, long moment.

My eyes also fill with complex tears.

I do not wish to examine them. Not mine. Not hers.

I simply wait to see what our life together might now be.

Then she extends her hand across the table and places it on my forearm, which I thus discover is lying there.

After a brief moment she takes her hand away and says, quite softly, "My poor Sam."

She rises.

She says, "The sun isn't even up. I think perhaps I can sleep a little more."

"Good," I say. "Yes."

And then: she is not in the house. How long after? A year. Perhaps a little more. On this night we put the paper to bed early. After that first sleepless week of our grief, Colleen would always be asleep when I arrived home, and then she was able to wait up till later in the evening to say good night, and then at last we were able to spend casual time together, even in the room where we received the news. I would sit on my reading chair. She would tuck her bare feet up under her on the davenport, her housecoat and tousled hair vanished now from our evenings. We would say little but read together, I catching up on the other newspapers, she working her way through Edith Wharton.

On this night the lights are on in the living room and her novel is lying alone on a cushion on the davenport. More Wharton, the author's name in gold letters at the bottom of the book's red cover board. At the top, the title is also in gold: *The House of Mirth*. Which stops me momentarily, hoping Colleen has left this book here deliberately, to see it before I see her, marking the return of her refined sense of irony. I feel a nudge of love for her.

I call for her.

There is no answer.

I look in the bedroom and she is not there.

And the irony of the book title curdles into something dark.

I call out again.

I think of the back porch.

I stride there.

The chairs are empty.

But now I see a light in the window of Ryan's little house.

I take a few breaths to calm myself. No reason to taint her with my wrongheaded fear.

I move across the yard. I knock lightly at the door and speak her name.

Only silence.

But before the fear can rise in me again, she says, "Come in."

She is sitting in profile on a chair at the camp table. She turns her face to me. She has a lit cigarette in the upturned V of her index and middle fingers. On the table in front of her is an ashtray with several stubs. Beside it is a pack of Lucky Strike, with its round red target logo, and a book of paper matches.

"You're home early," she says, and tilts her head at the objects before her. "You caught me."

"I did," I say, but with the clear lilt of my voice that also says, *So what?*

I have never seen her smoke. I did not know she smokes.

She slowly manifests a small smile. A sincere one, I feel, an impression supported by her now lifting the cigarette to her lips and taking a drag on it. She turns her face from me and plumes the smoke toward Ryan's floor lamp just beyond the table.

"May I sit?" I ask.

"Please," she says.

I do. Not across from her but to her right.

"Do you mind?" she asks, lifting the cigarette.

"Not at all. You didn't need to hide it."

She ponders that a moment and says, "I didn't think of it as hiding, exactly."

I smile at her. "Then what's the occasional whiff of licorice about you late at night the last few months?"

Colleen humphs.

I say, "I just realized . . ."

"Okay. Okay," she says. "Sen-sen. But that was for you. You don't smoke, is all."

"I once did. When I went off to war. We got them in our field rations and from the Red Cross."

At this she takes another drag, a nodding, thoughtful one, while turning her face forward. She blows a tight stream of smoke before me.

"You willing to share?" I ask.

"I'd like that," she says, and she nods at the Luckys. "Help yourself."

I take up the pack and tap a cigarette out and place the pack on the table. I move my hand toward the matches.

She touches my hand. "Wait."

I pull back.

"Bring me your face," she says, squaring around to me, and she puts her cigarette between her lips.

I know what she's suggesting. My breath surprises me, catching ever so slightly.

I put the Lucky to my mouth.

We each steady our cigarette with thumb and forefinger, flaring the rest of our hand, and we draw our faces close, bringing the burning tip of her cigarette toward the expectant tip of mine.

Our tips touch.

I draw at her flame, and draw, and puff, and I am lit.

But we stay like this for one moment more than we need to, touching the tips of our cigarettes, and one moment more, and then we pull back.

I take a deep drag and I face forward to exhale. But when my lungs are empty, I turn my face even farther away from my wife. I cannot look at her in this moment.

It isn't about her. It's the cigarette.

A mellow tide has begun to flow through me. Shockingly mellow. Beginning in my head. From the brain within, no doubt, but also, it seems, from the very bones and flesh of skull and face, the tide flows into my chest and my arms and into my hands, my rifle-savvy hands, flows into my hips and groin and legs. A calming tide. But in this present domestic moment, my past need for cigarette smoke also flows in with it, inevitably, the terrible need for it in war, in the trenches, the need for its comfort, the need for it to fill my senses, especially my sense of smell, and so, by that imprint, the smells that made the smoke crucial in France saturate the smoke that enters my body even here with my wife, in my son's childhood house, these other smells are immediately alive again within me: the stench, always the stench, the stench of the rotting flesh of men, the blown-up bits of men overlooked after the gathering of their dead bodies, the stench that has joined inseparably with the earth all around us in trench face and landscape, and the stench as well of the shit and piss of the living, and of our unbathed bodies, and the grindingly bitter smell of nitrates from every shell that explodes anywhere near us. Even when they maim or kill no one, their savage stink finds us. Finds me now.

I take the Lucky from my mouth and begin to tap it out in Colleen's ashtray, saying, "Sorry. It's been too long." I continue tapping after it has already stopped burning.

"I understand," she says. "But I find it calms me, comforts me."

I quit tapping. I look at her.

"I smoked as a young woman," she says. "I stopped but took it up again for a time, after Paul died."

"And now the smoking's about our son," I say.

"Yes."

We fall silent together, Ryan having been invoked. This always silences us for a time.

Then she says, "But I've come to understand it's less about him now. His death has settled in more deeply. I can't reach it through the lungs."

She pauses.

"What is it, then?" I ask.

"The smoke also encourages me."

"That's good," I say.

"Yes," she says. "I need to find work."

This leap surprises me. But I instantly understand. "You need to get out of the house," I say.

She settles her eyes on mine and we look at each other for a time. It speaks of her pain that I have trouble reading her. I realize this has been so since Ryan's death, her opacity. Not surprising, surely. Her gaze has no doubt gone inward.

She puts the cigarette between her lips, though absentmindedly, her eyes not letting go of me.

The cigarette is dwindling.

The smoke curls up near to her face.

She blinks.

She takes it from her mouth, keeps hold of it. She looks down at the tabletop and reaches to the ashtray with her other hand. She picks up the nearly whole cigarette I tapped out there and puts it in her mouth. It's hardly bent. It seems I've been gentle in extinguishing it. She brings the tip of her cigarette to the cold tip of mine and draws upon the last of her flame.

She turns her head and blows smoke and then comes back to me.

"That's the lesser part of it, really," she says.

For a moment I'm not sure what she means. Then I realize: Getting out of the house is the lesser part. She wants the work for itself. Soon after I met her she became a twenties-modern workingwoman, but then Ryan became her work. Which she seemed devoutly to want. The classic workingwoman of that time, her profession being her children.

But there were to be no more children.

And then there were none.

"Yes," I say. "Find work."

I am in my bed.

In the dark.

All my paths lead now to the dark.

I feel suddenly weary.

"Is that the point of all this?" I ask aloud. Of God.

I wait.

Nothing.

I clarify. "That I'm in the dark? Again? And always?"

I wait.

Still nothing. If He's there, He's not letting on.

I think, *Okay. I'll just be content to talk to myself.*

God lets on. His voice is in my ear, as if very close: "Come on, Sam. This isn't the time to start pitying yourself."

He's right. I say to Him, "Okay. We're getting near a decision on my eternal fate. Yes?"

"There's no clock," God says. "But I'm *not* interested in your reviewing the whole hundred and fifteen years . . . By the way, I didn't will that long a run. In case you were wondering."

"Now that you mention it," I say.

"So yes," He says. "The decision draws near."

"Then how does it matter if Colleen took up smoking and wanted a job? I was pretty relaxed about both, and my attitude was sincere. So I had to confront how stupidly long it took me to understand Ryan. How I failed my son. I get it. I needed to deal with that. But why are Colleen and her work next?"

"Don't ask me," God says. "I meddle with all you creatures there below a lot less than most of you assume. Especially not in the details. You're setting the agenda."

"Me?"

"You. You know where your story's incomplete. You've already followed your father and your mother and your son to an understanding. You're a relic on your deathbed, Sam. Old enough to have been forged by simpler mores and simpler doctoring. For all your years you've had two parents, one child, one spouse. You've got one of those left to resolve. But you're setting the agenda. That's part of the point of all this, Sam. Just be aware. They were *her* cigarettes. It was *her* job."

He stops speaking and I instantly know He's taken Himself away again.

All right. It's on me.

I am sincerely glad for Colleen's intention, to find some other purpose through work, some other self. Not just because it lets me feel less guilty about my ongoing preoccupation with my own work. It does do that, I admit. But I'm also glad for *her*, for her new sense of who she is now that her beloved child has been taken away. Glad and concerned. I wonder if she can even find work, given her age.

I am obviously with her once more, as I have returned to using the present tense in reliving the tale.

But here I also am, in the dark. Still. Which is the ultimate present tense of my ongoing death. Long after she has died.

Why have I become so self-conscious in this?

Why do I struggle to summon her up in the body, in the moment?

She smokes. She longs for work. With the gaze of her son vanished forever, she longs to see herself anew.

I long to see her too.

Colleen. Colleen.

What's the news?

I turn to the *Cunningham Examiner* archive in my head. Stories swelling into me from the postwar years.

Colleen Consults Messrs. Oliver & Gregg,
Renews Expertise at Typing & Dictation

Colleen Finds Perfect Job at Age 49,
After 24 Years, Returns to Old Boss

And I read the naked ledes to some other *Cunningham Examiner* stories that made it impossible for the paper's copydesk to capture their essence in the confines of a headline.

[dateline: July 30, 1946]

Sam arrived home late on the first anniversary of Ryan's heroic death, having to oversee breaking front page news of four U.S. Marines killed in convoy ambush near Peiping and of four Negroes lynched in Georgia. He found Colleen drinking alone in Ryan's backyard playhouse.

[dateline: July 30, 1948]

Sam and Colleen lay awake beside each other last night. Through the window, on this third anniversary of Ryan's heroic death, they heard the ratchety calls of katydids and, in adjacent grief, they turned wordlessly toward the dark of opposite walls.

[dateline: August 2, 1950]

Sam sat reading last night on his living room easy chair while Colleen read on the davenport. Without raising his eyes from the page, it struck him how quietly comfortable they were in each other's presence at this moment, something he'd not felt in a long while. He turned to her and found her sleeping.

The next year, dateline February 10, 1951, a scoop at the *Cunningham Examiner*:

Colleen Rises with Her Boss,
Now Secretary to Chief Exec

And a mere two weeks later, across town at the *Chicago Independent*, another scoop about a promotion:

Independent Names New Editor-in-Chief;
Cunningham Succeeds Retiring Kirchner

And in the next fall, on the first of November 1952:

Entire Pacific Ocean Island Vanishes
In First H-Bomb Blast, 20 Miles Wide

On the morning of that story, as the *Independent* reports what men have created, Colleen sits down with me at the breakfast table.

She will, as has become her custom, drink her first cup of coffee before frying our eggs. Since our promotions, we spend time together here most days.

I have left the paper carefully folded for her at her place. As she often does, she unfurls it to gather a topic or two for our breakfast conversation. Her eyes go straight to the left-hand lead story.

She simply reads the headline, about the thermonuclear obliteration of the Pacific Ocean island, and she refolds the paper with slow-motion meticulousness.

She stares out the kitchen window.

I sip at my coffee. I watch my wife closely, waiting for her to speak.

When she finally does, she addresses her hesitation. "I'm trying to decide on a pronoun," she says.

She pauses, apparently still deciding.

Since the conversation will likely open with the H-bomb, an extended struggle for an opening pronoun seems odd and even vaguely ominous, which leads me to a lame response: "There aren't so very many to choose from."

"They. I choose *they*." And with this, she turns her face sharply to me. "They made him part of this," she says.

"This one is different," I say.

"No, it's not. It's the spawn of the other one."

I have the fleeting thought: *How quietly* UN*comfortable we are in each other's presence at this moment.* With no explicit context, we know exactly what we are beginning to argue about. And we know that we know.

"Ryan wasn't part of it," I say.

"Of course he was," Colleen says. "My blessed Ryan played a role. And the thing will end the world."

"He didn't choose the role," I say. "There were no more than two people on board the *Indianapolis*—if even that many—there may have been no one—who knew what they were delivering to Guam."

"I'm not putting *blame* on him," Colleen says.

Something strikes me now, delayed by the rush of our back-and-forth.

She continues: "He was victimized."

And my own continuation, flowing from my sudden thought, has me say, "Your decision on *that* pronoun didn't take any time at all."

"That's my point," she says.

"The pronoun?"

"What?"

"'*My* blessed Ryan,'" I say.

Colleen shakes her head as if to clear it.

I clarify. "You said '*my* blessed Ryan.' Yours. He was *our* blessed Ryan."

"All right," she says. "Shall I correct the other pronoun as well?"

"It took you long enough to decide on it."

"You'll see why."

"Okay."

She squares her shoulders to me. "Not *they*," she says. "I considered and demurred, but now you've pressed the matter, and so yes. The more accurate pronoun is *you*. *You* made him part of this. *You* put him on that ship. You and your 'be a man' crusade."

Colleen and I each have a familiarly contentious voice that we assume when we argue. But Colleen's has now turned hard. I don't want to follow her there.

We have never argued about this.

And so I soften my own voice to say, "It's been seven years since we learned the mission of his ship. Why is this just starting to bother you?"

"Dealing with his death obscured it," she says.

"The 'it' being what, exactly?"

She hesitates for a moment. Then she simply repeats the vague complaint. "He was made part of the advent of these bombs."

I have the impulse to question this.

Then abruptly I flash to my physical embrace with Colleen moments after learning Ryan was dead. An embrace shared deeply by both of us and without a word of blame. In that moment, a fear in me was instantly vanquished. But now I realize how deeply and enduringly runs the thing I feared.

I think, *This must be put very gently.* And so in that tone I say, "Now that you found the right pronoun, my darling, isn't there really more to your concern than the taint of nuclear weapons on the crew of the *Indianapolis*?"

She is not looking at me. Not speaking.

And I think, *Okay. Now I should let it drop.*

I don't. But with even more gentleness, I say, "I think you hesitated at the pronoun because you really want to say more. It's just difficult for you. More about me. More than my somehow helping to involve Ryan with the birth of nuclear weapons."

She does not reply. She keeps her face averted.

I wait. Not so much for her but for myself.

Then, in a near whisper, I say, "Aren't you really trying to say that it was I who drowned our son in the Pacific Ocean?"

Colleen turns back to me, and in a whisper she says, "I suppose I am."

Having both chosen whispers to come to this at last, we say no more.

We dare say no more.

Not a word more about anything.

Not until the night. Not until we lie beside each other in bed, our blankets layered against the November cold, our bodies not touching.

We stare into the darkness above us.

After a long silence, then not in a whisper but softly, Colleen says, "Because I feel something doesn't mean I believe it."

I try, for a time, to take the comfort from this that she intends.

But I fail.

I say, "I wish it were otherwise."

A faint rustling. She has turned her face in my direction.

I say, "If only, instead, you believed it but did not feel it."

The rustle again, her face turning away.

We are still.

I try at least to sense her presence. I listen for her breath.

I cannot hear it.

I cannot hear my own.

And I am once again in the corridor outside my room and partway along toward the front desk. I have resumed my previous moment out here, with the soft-edged nurse still heading my way.

I am to one side in the passageway and his face turns ever so slightly in my direction, briefly giving me the impression that he actually sees me.

But of course he does not. He at once resumes his forward gaze, and he passes near to me, almost entering the very space where I float. Almost but not quite.

And I feel my nostrils flare. I am aware of my sense of smell, expecting a scent from the nurse, perhaps of cologne. This consciousness has come quickly upon me as he passes by, and there is something, yes, but not cologne, sweet but sweet like wood, sweet like the cedar closet where my mother hung her clothes.

Then with his first step beyond me the scent of the nurse vanishes, utterly, and as he moves on away, another smell rushes into me. A smell like a vacant lot, all the smut grass cut down and starting to go musty, a smell of Lake Providence as the summer ends, and I know full well it's not the nurse I'm smelling. It's me. It's the smell of an old man.

And I float toward the nurse and I follow him and then I pass him to enter the darkness of my room.

And a clock begins to tick.

I am sitting at the desk in my office, the afternoon light coursing in from over my shoulder. I have exercised my editor in chief's prerogative of closing my office door each Friday afternoon, after the home edition is put to bed, in order to write my Sunday editorial.

The clock is on the wall before me. Kirch's old windup Seth Thomas.

I roll a sheet of paper into my Royal Quiet Deluxe and I let my first draft begin in a free-ranging voice from a free-ranging mind, as is my process, planning to nuance the piece the second time through with a cadence and argument more appropriate to my editorialist-in-chief persona. But for now it's me simply letting go to the page.

> This past week we reported on a Pacific Ocean island vanishing in an instant. By the hand of man. Just as, by the hand of man, large parts of two Japanese cities vanished.
>
> The eyewitness who saw the recent H-bomb test said that it was as if he were watching the end of the world.
>
> Indeed.
>
> And who in the world is empowered to initiate the events that would lead to that? Ultimately some individual man. For a current example of such a man, a Kansas City haberdasher who came to that power by way of the usually irrelevant office of vice president, brokered, in his case, by hacks in the back rooms of a Democratic convention.
>
> Or the other current example, a former Russian Orthodox seminarian who went on to the religious,

racial, ethnic, and political murder of as yet uncounted millions of his own people.

Moreover, one can imagine the present state of the world if the sophisticated scientists of Germany had been the first to develop an atomic bomb and thus put it into the hands of Adolf Hitler.

But in all the ages to come, in all the countries that will acquire or develop these weapons, who knows what tyrants or fools or incompetents, what heartless egotists of minuscule and reckless intelligence, might come to power and gain control of these weapons?

Haberdasher Harry is the only one so far to have actually dropped such a bomb. And he had his reasons. It was to be that or a land invasion of Japan.

He calculated all the deaths, both American and Japanese, that would result in the two alternatives. And that persuaded him, as he sat alone at his desk in the Oval Office, the door closed, the afternoon light coursing in from over his shoulder.

And I stop writing as my eyes fill with tears.
They puzzle me, these tears.
But I am weeping.
So I write.

Did Harry Truman shed tears in making this decision? I doubt it. Contemplating those two calculated sums was a process of abstracted decision-making logic. Or he could not have done it.

But he did. The decision was made abstractable, made possible, by the fact that he did not know—had never laid eyes on—a single specific actual person who would be incinerated by his order.

This editorial is about the military and about war and about death and about the head man, the commander in chief, the leader; about his profound responsibility, his inherent culpability, his inevitable human untrustworthiness; about the consequences of the actions of this leader of a nation, who is like the leader of a family, like a father, a father who was once of the military and is somehow forever of the military and who has been to war and has lived with death and has made decisions—through the very fingertip of his own right hand—that have over and over inflicted death upon individually visible men. And still he must lead. His actions have consequences. He is responsible for a life. The life of his son. His son. Not abstractable.

I stop writing.

And I know why I've been weeping.

I recover temporarily and I rework the editorial again and again until it becomes the voice of this other man that I am, and then I go home.

I turn into the walkway leading up to our house.

My eyes, for the moment, are dry.

As I climb our front porch steps I try to tell myself that the tears I shed at the office are sufficient for this day. But I know that's a lie. I am guilty. A hundred deaths are upon my head. And one more death as well, the culminating death, for me the quintessential death.

I step into my house.

I close the door.

And my eyes fill.

Colleen appears before me.

I stop. I begin to weep again.

For a moment she watches, and then she moves to me.

She stands close.

She watches my eyes.

"Ryan?" she asks.

"Yes," I say.

She lifts her right hand to a place that she now comprehends. To my cheek. She places her thumb upon the track of my tears and gently wipes them away.

Then she lifts her left hand and intercedes with those tears as well.

She withdraws her hand. "We both loved him," she says. "We did the best we could."

Now she puts her arms around me.

"And yes," she says. "It's what I feel. Both of us."

I put my arms around her.

We hold each other.

And I know when she will die.

Not as we held each other in the original embrace. Not even in the reliving of that embrace. I know it now, the *now* of my bed in the darkness. But in the knowing of it I don't fly off to her deathbed, though I also know that she will die with me sitting beside her. I know the *fact* of her death. For now, merely the fact of when and of my presence at her bedside. Not the sight of it or the sound, not the scent of it in the air or the touch of it on my hand or on my lips. But I'm surprised that I know even this much. Things God has so far deliberately withheld from me.

"So are we finished?" I call out to Him.

Silence.

It is an obvious place for us to end. Father, mother, son, and wife. My wife was my last assignment, so perhaps my final spontaneous dying vision will have been our reconciling embrace after seven years of dissolution. A vision of renewal. Of reconnection. The line redrawn around the two of us.

It's where I would end a feature story. A Sunday supplement feel-good. But this story seems to have stalled at the copydesk.

So have I. I'm not yet dead.

Twenty years of our life together remain after that embrace. Maybe I'm allowed to know this so I can see the void ahead. Maybe it's the void itself that has come to me now. An experience I've had continually in this nursing home. I've lived here for a quarter of a century in a matrix of daytime TV and ontological dread, down the halls and behind the partition drapes. After having lived alone in Hermosa and worked on West Monroe for nearly that long, until media conglomerates, twenty-four-hour cable news, and my creeping octogenarianism trashcanned both the *Chicago Independent* and its longtime editor in chief.

Even the years of Hermosa and West Monroe are a void in my dying brain as I strain for moments to examine, to cling to. A void like outer space. The scientists tell us it teems, the universe. A hundred billion galaxies in just what we can see. Each holding a hundred billion stars. No doubt true. But when I lift my eyes to the night sky, only a few thousand of those objects are visible. And even those exist for me only as indistinguishable specks of pale light in a vast darkness.

A book, a nap, a cup of coffee. A conversation, a touch, a front-page scoop. The smell of newsprint, the feel of typewriter keys, a friendly stray dog. A brief, striking silence outside a window on a summer night. A woman's smile, a newspaper hat, a distant siren. A scarf.

None of it yielding anything. No light. No heat.

But now.

I am aware of sitting on our back porch. Aware that Colleen is beside me, though she is only a dim presence: there is no moon; the lights are turned off in the back of the house; it is summer and even the stars have vanished, presumably in overcast.

She has been speaking. Still is.

"Would it bother you?" she asks.

She's been talking about her work. But I can't fit this question into what I've been picking up. The insurance business is up overall, but only by rich people buying policies, not the middle class. I realize, however, that I registered this a minute or two or more ago and my mind has drifted since.

She has paused, as if I'm expected to reply.

Can it be that she wonders if it bothers me that the middle class isn't buying insurance?

I look to her.

Reading her face is impossible in the dark, though I can make out that she's not actually looking at me.

The silence goes on. She's waiting. Expecting, I am afraid, a knowing reply.

I have to take a risk. "How do *you* feel about it?"

"How?"

"Do you feel."

She humphs. "Of course."

"Yes?"

"You're right," she says. "It's about me, after all."

I'm glad to hear that, whatever it is. I look out to the dim form of Ryan's playhouse, now a storage space.

She says, "Nineteen years."

She pauses. And then: "Right?"

"Right," I say. I'm doing the math in my head but nothing quite computes.

"What's it all been anyway?" she asks.

She pauses.

I wait.

"It's all about him," she says. "His endless bland words. I just take them down and fluff at them a bit."

She pauses again.

So the bothersome thing is the mundanity of her secretarial work.

"Even at that," she says. "After this many years, there's still only a small, finite number of things an insurance man will ever say."

Somewhere in me—through my reporter's ear for quotes, no doubt—I'm listening to her. But I'm not actually comprehending. I hear the words but my mind is also flowing away, like a cup of coffee tipped over on my desktop.

"Even most of the fluffing has long since been done and just needs repeating," she says.

The nudge that tipped the cup being her first comment: Would it bother *me*? I've been editor in chief for as long as she's been a secretary. And I have lately pondered my own version of that dilemma.

"I know what you mean," I say.

"And good Lord," she says. "How many times have I typed his rah-rah platitudes to some agent in the field?"

"Damn, but I've missed the actual gathering of news," I say, though low.

"They're always the same," she says. "Like: '*Sometimes you will work rather indifferently but success will come easily.*' "

"I occasionally look at story copy but others do the editing."

"And: '*Sometimes you will work yourself diligently but without results.*' "

"Even that's still one level removed from actually digging out the stories."

" '*It's like planting grain,*' " Colleen says.

Which makes me pause. She seems to have spoken to my point. I vaguely try to understand, as my mind works onward with its own agenda. "'Planting'?" I say. Perhaps planting instead of digging.

She says, "'*You sow and plow and labor, but you don't immediately see the end of your work.*'"

"Yes," I say, though her meaning is still vague.

"'*But just keep on,*'" she says.

"I don't plant," I say, "I don't harvest . . ."

"'*Diligently,*'" she says. "'*And you will inevitably reap a harvest.*'"

"I just manage the farm," I say.

"It's always the same," she says. "It's the job."

"Yes," I say. "True. I don't even *own* the damn farm."

"What?" she says.

She is looking at me. I am looking at her.

"I do more of *his* work than mine," I say.

"Yes," she says. "Just so."

"It does have its own rewards," I say.

"I'm not so sure about that," she says.

"Perhaps not," I say. "Compared to the real work."

"Exactly," she says.

We turn our faces away from each other.

We stare into the darkness of our backyard.

It is summer.

It is 1965.

Only now do I realize that the sounds of this summer night have been playing beneath our conversation. Among them, I recognize, are katydids.

So that too found its way into the void, did it?

I do not ask Colleen. She and Hermosa have vanished.

I don't even ask God.

It's a rhetorical question.

I think I'm catching on.

I am also well aware that the thing that energized me for years, more so than my son and my wife, the thing I hankered for after my elevation to editor in chief, was the personal pursuit of each day's fresh news. But after it was captured and wrestled into words and blazoned onto newsprint and into the homes and minds of Chicago, by nightfall that paper was folded and stacked, and by the next night even the previous morning's vaunted front page had vanished into the waste bale of old news. After all, the extensive, assiduously cataloged clipping file of a newspaper's previous stories is called the "morgue." Indeed. Dead indeed.

As I will soon be.

I am sitting in a wheelchair and I'm being rolled along the corridor away from my room, away from the front desk. We are heading for the back patio for my daily sunlight, which is beckoning brightly up ahead.

I am a little bit neither here nor there, as I am able to think, *Daylight means this is a past moment.*

I look up over my shoulder.

Nurse Bocage is pushing the chair. She looks down at me. She smiles. "Fresh air in store for you, Mr. Cunningham. I already took your walker outside. It's waiting for us in the sunshine. You're a wonder, Mr. Cunningham."

Her hair is done in cornrows braided into a bun at the back. From this hairdo, I think, *So this is not so long ago, a week at most.*

I look forward.

Suddenly, up ahead, a wailing begins, a male voice full of dread.

Nurse Bocage slows as we approach the open door of the man's room. She stops.

She says, "Excuse me a moment, Mr. Cunningham." She parks me near the doorway and goes into the room.

I cannot see in. But I hear the man crying, "Is that you? Please now. Please." And her saying, "It's all right, Mr. Martin. It's Nurse Bocage. You're all right."

But Mr. Martin keeps on shouting, and I tune out the words. I've heard voices like this for decades now in this place. I can tune them out. I can turn them into undifferentiated sounds. Thumps of thunder from a summer storm blowing by. A necessary skill I brought with me from long ago. From the trenches.

I focus on the sunlight up ahead. I try to describe the shade of yellow to myself. A headline for the *Cunningham Examiner*, anticipating the story of this day's venture into fresh air. **Sam Walks Awhile in X Yellow Sun.**

The shouting goes on.

What yellow?

Banana Yellow?

Butter Yellow?

Duckling Yellow?

"Sun!" Apt-seeming, Martin's word rings distinctly in my head. And I hear it again, differently: "Your son!" And I cast it out.

Jaundice Yellow.

No.

Yellow-Bellied.

Spike the story. The reporter just can't get the sunlight right.

Mr. Martin stops shouting and mutters himself into silence.

Nurse Bocage emerges from his room.

"Sorry," she says.

She rolls me away.

When we are out of earshot, she says, "They're not all as blessed as you, Mr. Cunningham."

It has been no blessing, my long years of clarity, my consciousness.

I am sitting now beside a hospital bed.

It has come to this.

I am holding Colleen's near hand in both of mine. It is cool to the touch. She is propped up a bit with an extra pillow. Her face is turned to me. She wears a radiotherapy turban. Irish green.

I know, sitting here, that the radiation is over and there is nothing else. Her tumor is on the brainstem. A thing they call a glioblastoma, which can never be fully removed or thoroughly irradiated. She is having trouble swallowing now. A headache has begun that does not cease. The doctors have decided simply to make her as comfortable as possible.

She stretches her free right hand to join our others, inhaling sharply with the effort, the pain.

But she is determined.

All our hands come together.

"My darling," she says.

She is speaking slowly, softly.

"My darling," I say.

"I feel lucid at the moment," she says.

"Good," I say.

"But am I? Have I been so far?"

"More than lucid," I say.

"More? Perhaps even charming?"

"Yes."

"How cruel of me," she says.

I tilt my head very slightly. An unspoken *How so?*

She knows the gesture. She smiles and says, "Don't worry. That was itself a lucid remark. If I am charming, your regret will be intensified."

"I'll take my chances," I say.

"I wish this to be bearable for you."

"I'll deal with that."

She closes her eyes, lifting her shoulders a little. Pain, I infer. "I need to lie back now," she says.

"Of course," I say.

We let our hands go.

Hers settle at her sides and she lays her head in the center of her pillows and she closes her eyes and this vision of her clamps off my breath. The vision of my Colleen in her casket.

Then she breathes abruptly—a breath deep but gratingly ragged—and my own breathlessness persists.

Then her breathing quiets.

She opens her eyes and turns her face to me.

She says, "The doctors have begun to give me something."

"To ease the pain," I say. "They told me."

"It will make me sleep."

"That's best for you."

"They tell me I may not wake again."

"I understand," I say.

"Do you?"

"These may be our last words together."

"Yes."

"Haven't I always given you the last word?" I say.

She smiles. "Don't be cruel. No charm, please."

I reach out and put my hand over hers. "I will be here," I say.

And she says to me, very slowly now, very softly, "Remember our good times. Keep them alive in you. They were real."

Colleen turns her face and closes her eyes.

As if I am seeing what she sees, all goes dark.

I wonder if I too have died.

But I open my eyes and I know this is the dark I have become accustomed to. I am dying but I am not yet dead.

Her voice lingers in me.

And I hear something I missed at her bedside. Loving though those words were in the tone of them—I recognize that in them still—there was also a gravity, a preciseness, even a hint of rigor, all of it saying that this advice she was giving me was, for her, coming from a lesson hard learned. And I think, *It was about our son's death.* Perhaps her last words were not spoken only to me.

Perhaps they were also spoken to herself. I devoutly hope she took her own advice.

And I think, *But did we say the defining words to each other before she began the sleep that would carry her away?*

I did not hear them in the reliving I just went through.

God tells me I'm the one setting the agenda. Why would I have omitted the defining words if that's so?

I wait to return.

I wait.

Nothing.

"Please," I say aloud.

The only way I know to find God is to speak into the dark.

"Please, let me go back," I say. "I apparently can't will it, but I wish for it. I devoutly wish it."

And I am beside her bed again.

She is lying exactly as before, composed as if for funeral-home visitation, having just urged me to remember us.

I worry she has lost consciousness. I worry I've missed my chance to speak the words.

So I say to her, just as I did when I was nineteen years old, on our wedding night, "I love you, Mrs. Cunningham."

She is silent.

I am afraid the pain drugs have prevailed now and she has fallen unwakeably asleep.

Worse. I am afraid she has already died.

Then, though she does not move, does not open her eyes, she replies, just as on our wedding night, "I love you, Mr. Cunningham."

Colleen still got the last word. Mercifully, with no ambiguity of tone. In the dark again, I have a little surge of relieved expectation. I will die now. Like this. My own feature story having a reassuring ending straight from the Sunday supplement.

"I'm ready to go," I say into the dark.

"So I gather," says God.

Another ambiguous tone.

"Not yet?" I ask.

"Not yet," He says.

Of course not. I say, "I never was a Sunday supplement kind of guy." Thinking: *Later that night I missed the moment of my wife's last breath. Even though I was sitting beside her bed and wide awake. She was dead and I did not know.*

Not sappy Sunday reading.

God says, "But you're right, Sam, that we've reached a new phase. Not for you to relinquish your life. You will, however, relinquish the agenda."

"Uh-oh," I say.

"An *uh-oh* is unnecessary. There are indeed the good and the evil on this planet, but there's a third horse in the troika of human life: the oblivious. It's time to help you with that. There are some stories waiting for you, written for the *Cunningham Examiner.* But they never appeared. Never made it as far as your editor in chief's desk."

And the first is before me.

It may never have made it to my desk, but it is ready to print, with headline and byline and dateline.

Ryan & Ben Meet on Shore Leave

By Ryan Cunningham

San Francisco, May 10, 1942—After attacking enemy ports in New Guinea, the *Indianapolis* returned to the States for an overhaul at Mare Island on San Pablo Bay. We were, among other things, to be fitted with naval radar in a cabin just down the corridor from my radio cabin. We were also to be fitted with radar operators.

Including one Benjamin Hubbard, from Philadelphia, as it would shortly turn out.

He and I happened to find each other at the stern of a steam ferry carrying a flock of us sailors in our dress blues to San Francisco for a weekend of liberty.

He and I were both tossing bits of bread to seagulls flying above our wake.

Colliding crusts alerted us to each other.

We turned. We smiled.

He said, "Mr. Audubon, I presume."

I shrugged modestly, as if he were correct but also to buy a few seconds to come up with another ornithologist. Then the choice seemed clear to me. A man of a name to play with and with four dozen species named after him.

"Mr. Nuttall," I said, savoring each syllable.

He smiled, and I sensed he would have laughed except his mind was clearly at work behind his eyes. "You no doubt know me from my namesake woodpecker," he said, savoring the bird name.

We laughed together now, ever so slightly breathless.

How did we know?

I have no idea. But we knew.

I offered my hand to shake. He took it.

"I am also known as Ryan Cunningham," I said, as we shook, firmly.

We kept the shake going as he said, "I am also known as Benjamin Hubbard. Ben."

We shook just a few moments more, studying each other's eyes. His were chestnut, as Mr. Audubon might render the breeding feathers of a Louisiana brown pelican.

We each dispensed all our bread in a single toss, the gulls diving down and away from the ferry in pursuit.

Then it was simply Ben and me, shoulder to shoulder at the railing, leaning out over the water. Flying together.

We knew so much about each other before we knew anything.

So we caught up a bit.

He began it. "I'm twenty-two," he said.

I was tempted to lie. But I didn't. I said, "I'll soon be nineteen."

"You know a lot about birds," he said.

"You do too."

"Audubon was easy," he said.

"The Nuttall's woodpecker," I said.

"I'm from Sonoma County. Just north of here. The oak woodlands up that way are full of those little guys."

"I'm from Chicago."

"Big-city boy," he said. "Not even nineteen and you know so much?"

"I've got a smart dad," I said. "And I've always read a lot."

"Me too."

"He's from Louisiana, my dad. Small-town boy. But now he's the managing editor of the *Chicago Independent*."

"No wonder then," Ben said.

"I had him and the Harvard Five-Foot Shelf."

"Mine's a winemaker. A good one."

"No wonder," I said.

He turned his face to me. He smiled. "That I know so much?"

"In vino veritas," I said.

Ben laughed. "I was more scattered in my reading," he said.

But he had gotten the joke.

We watched our wake for a few moments.

"Mom, dad, one sister," Ben said.

"Mom, dad, only child," I said.

And we both stopped talking. We would learn more of these basic things in the next forty-eight hours, but we'd said enough for now.

Because we were flying together behind a ferry boat, feeding.

"Thank you," I say to the darkness. "To hear his voice again."

And I think, *To hear how he spoke of his dad to his new pal.*

They sounded like real pals.

I'm grateful to know he had a pal on the *Indianapolis*. The two of them realizing how to be that with each other even from their first moments together.

I'm glad. Even as beneath my gladness I think, *In this long moment of my dying, with me setting the agenda, there has been no pal of mine. Maybe there never was a pal in my long life. Something like friends, surely. Workplace, neighborhood, social-circle friends. But no one who has survived into this night, not a real pal, even as a residue. Johnny Moon perhaps? How odd that he's the only one who prompts even a consideration. He wasn't a pal. A battlefield friend, yes. And if he'd survived the war . . . Perhaps.*

But I break from this undercurrent in me and I stroke to the surface of my mind. I rejoice there for my son and his pal Ben.

They have so little time left, these pals.

And another dispatch is before me.

Ryan and Ben, Together on Leave
By Ryan Cunningham

San Francisco, May 11, 1942—It only took a few minutes of our two-hour ferry ride to the Embarcadero for Ben and me to confirm our strategic alliance and take command of our shore leave.

Yes, we stashed our seabags in the navy YMCA across the street from the navy landing. Here we were also expected and strongly encouraged—but not quite commanded—to spend the two nights before us with six hundred other sailors.

Ben and I had no intention of doing that.

We strode away from the YMCA laughing.

Strode and then slowed and then sauntered.

Sauntered and lingered, learning more about the surface of the lives we'd each led prior to this growingly momentous day. Details. The small pleasures and the eccentric connections. L train rides and a beloved katydid. The fleeting floral smell of a vineyard in bloom and Bessie, the neighbor's spooked runaway cow, whom Ben vamped into quiescence. Ben leaned to me and whispered, "She longed for me to her dying day."

Our path led along Market Street and through Union Square and into Chinatown and then to the top of Nob Hill.

Ben had lived his life just across the bay and knew the city. So our sauntering and lingering had reflected that. Chinatown by way of Stockton Street, not Grant Avenue. In a shop window an opium pipe, not a pottery dragon. A market window hung with flattened whole-roast duck glazed in salty wax, not a restaurant facade with a window touting CHOP SUEY in neon.

Now we sat in cushy chairs on the top of Nob Hill at the Top of the Mark bar near the top of the Mark Hopkins Hotel. We were encircled by windows.

Our view was to the northwest: over the roofs of the apartment buildings of the Nob Hill swells, across the bay to the two spindly-legged sentries of the Golden Gate Bridge, and beyond to the undulant headlands of Marin County.

Ben and I spent a few minutes cooing at the view as we waited for our beers—Ben's officially age-legal, mine sanctioned at sight by my uniform—but once the drinks arrived, we turned our faces from San Francisco and leaned into the tête-à-tête table between us.

For all the words that had passed between us in the seven hours we'd known each other, for all our shared skills to shape those words and to appreciate them and to use them to legitimately reveal ourselves to each other, for all of that, there were things we had not yet said.

It was time.

"Authentic," I said, to begin.

"Yes?" Ben said.

"Yes."

"You do that," he said.

"What?"

"Make a leap after a little silence between us. A few times it's happened."

"Sorry."

"No. Please. It's intriguing. So far I've always traced it back. Always to something working in you from before."

I leaned a little toward him. The table was very small, really. "So where do you trace it this time?"

He pondered a moment, his eyes fixed on mine. "Stockton Street."

I smiled. "Yes," I said.

"Our lunch there," he said.

"The whole street," I said. "But Chinatown isn't the leap. It's the step before."

"So do you want to talk about Chinatown first?"

"Not necessary, really. The leap is to a new thing."

"You're speaking low," he said, softly.

"Yes."

He shifted forward the final few inches to be as close to the table as he could.

So did I.

Beneath, our knees touched.

Ben said, "So you planted your step. Please take it from there. Authentic, you said."

"We're striving for that with each other," I said.

"We are."

I softened my voice even further. "Still, there's one thing we haven't spoken of. Till that's in the open between us, we're not fully authentic."

Ben slowly, quite casually, looked over my shoulder and then scanned toward the oval bar in the center of the room.

I did the same in his direction.

"No one within earshot," I whispered.

"No one," he whispered.

Our eyes met.

He waited.

I waited.

"Yes?" he said. He gave me a little nod.

It was time. He wished for me to say this. Only fair, since I'd initiated it.

And I said, "I'm actually slightly taller than you."

His eyes went wide. He fell back in his chair and laughed, the first bark of which was sharp and loud. He slapped a hand over his mouth and gurgled on for a few more moments.

Then he leaned forward, pressed as close to me as the table would allow, and he said in a dulcet tone befitting a declaration of love: "And *I'm* slightly taller than *you*."

Our window-side hands slipped beneath the table and found each other, clung to each other, for a long, silent while.

There is a stopping in me. If I were not already dying I would think this feeling in my chest was simple to understand: it's my heart that has just now stopped and I will be dead momentarily, dead before this thought is even finished. And that will obliteratively be that.

But I know. I know. I'm not dead yet.

I'm deadened.

I've just slammed into the wall of my obliviousness.

I say into the dark, "Didn't you say you were going to give me some help with that?"

"I did," He says.

"Then am I lost? The stopping in me is just that. Behind the wall must be something. But on this side I've got nothing."

"That's so you can take it all in first," God says.

And I hear my son's voice. From within. As it once might have spoken the way my voice is speaking now, in the presence of God. As if the Pacific Ocean has overwhelmed him in his radio cabin and his dying has begun.

On this night of our first meeting, after the sweet and trembling few hours of our first touching, I stand smoking at the bay window of our room in a small hotel in North Beach. Ben sleeps nearby on our cast-iron bed.

I think how my mother would love Ben.

I think how my father would not.

How my father would not love me*, if he knew who I am.*

At this thought, something falters in me. I know it to be true. No matter what my mother has always said, from the time she and I first fully understood about me. When I was eleven. She said Papa would love me anyway, but there was something from the war he fought that would make this difficult for him. Difficult enough that she has encouraged—she has constructed—this profound secret around the two of us. Whatever the cause, she does not trust him ever to understand what has happened in this room tonight.

My father would stop loving me.

Even though I have gone to war. Even though my beloved has gone to war. My beloved Ben, whose own father beat him for who he is.

So in this moment—with Ben sleeping nearby after the two of us have fully become who we are—the cigarette in my right hand pauses in its path to my lips. Pauses and can go no farther. Only my love for Benjamin Hubbard and his for me will let this night—will let the rest of my life—go on.

But for now I stop.

And I see my son. He is bent to his wireless key. In the radio room. Headset on. The klaxons are howling to abandon ship. The *Indianapolis* is sinking.

I howl.

At God.

I try to cut off what I'm seeing. But my eyes can't close.

I plead with God: *Stop this.*

I know He won't stop it, He can't stop it. Not from happening. I even know He won't stop its visitation upon me now. *But just pause it. Please. Let me deal with the other first. At least that. Please.*

My son is about to die with the belief that I will hate him for who he is.

And maybe he was right to distrust my feelings from more than seven decades ago. Because of who *I* was then. Maybe so. Close to right. But not *hatred.* Three-quarters of a century ago perhaps a deep-muscle reflex of aversion. Bad enough. But surely not hatred.

And I ache to give him better than that, far better than that in this moment, before I have to witness this, before he has to die again as I die.

But no.

God will not grant me that.

I have not earned that.

My son remains before me, keying in his ship's cry for help. The tones short and long, short and long, unwavering, absolutely regular, my son's hand steady even as he expects to die doing this. My brave son. This brave man.

Please! I cry to God. Perhaps aloud. *Just pause. Let me be this other man.*

But the vision goes on.

My son keying and keying while his face remains implacably, transcendently calm.

And now there is a movement. From behind him.

A hand falls upon my son's shoulder.

Ryan flicks his face to see that hand, even as his own hand keys on.

Ryan glances upward.

It is Ben.

My son pauses, puts his hand on Ben's. "Go," Ryan says. "Please save yourself. I have to try till I hear a response."

And Ben says, loud enough to get through Ryan's headset, "No. I will not leave you."

Ryan returns to his keying, and when he finishes the last word of this iteration of the distress message, he immediately pushes back his chair, pulls off the headset, stands and turns to face Ben.

And these two men embrace. These two brave men.

They press each other close, and Ben whispers, "Till death do us part," and my son whispers, "Till death do us part."

And they kiss.

And my eyes fill.

My son turns back to his operator table and sits.

Ben puts his hand on Ryan's shoulder once more as my son keys on.

Now at last I am in darkness.

I have a brief moment of hope. Maybe we can slow down now for a little while, God and I. To let my tears go on. To show my tears to Him, for they are real, they are felt. Yes. Felt. From beyond the wall.

But instead I hear Colleen's voice:

I touch Hettie on the arm.

She is already beginning to tremble, tough girl though she be.

But I need to go back and assure Sam. He's so keen. I'm certain he knew he was on display, was being judged.

"Only a moment," I say to her.

I push through the bustle of the lunch crowd starting to disperse and his face lifts to me and I love his eyes, they help make this possible, these eyes that are the blue of a twilight sky.

He smiles at me. I lean near him and say, "I knew you two would get along."

Those eyes widen a little. He is surprised. Which does not surprise me. That's Hettie. There are times when I think I am the only person in the world who knows how to read her. Which is a thought that slips into me and threatens to make me cry. But I am a tough girl too.

"Did we?" Sam asks. Hopeful.

"Yes," I say.

Then Hettie and I spend a few hours together in her tenement flat on West Madison, knowing they will be our last few hours, not just for this day but for any foreseeable future. Probably forever. That much we have come to understand.

But for now we sit together on her bed, side by side, propped against the headboard, all clothed except for our stockings, our feet bare, our twenty toes lined up before us.

We don't say anything for a long while.

We stare at our toes. Me, mostly at hers. Very slender, very dainty, in spite of her trimming their nails severely to fit her Hettie Harper–ness.

She and I have played this scene once before. When I knew it was time for Paul and me to begin to woo.

She says, gently, not argumentatively, not scornfully, though perhaps with a bit of lingering puzzlement along with the gentleness: "I still don't quite understand, Shamrock. The either-or."

I say, "I understand how you don't understand, my sweet Harpy. You know how I love you being so single-mindedly you. But there's something in this man . . ."

"This boy?"

"A boy and a man. Didn't he—"

"Kill a hundred?" Hettie shrugs. "Yes. Boy and man."

"He's like me then, isn't he? Two things at once?"

She humphs. It is a concept she refuses to accept.

I lean my shoulder against hers. "My darling," I say, "the ilk of you and me have been on this earth for at least three millennia, but we still could not show our Sapphic selves on the streets of Chicago—not as who we truly are—without being arrested or worse. If I did not have this other *self inside me, I would be content to live in the shadows with you, my precious, but I know I can fall in love with this man. I want to fall in love with him. I have already begun."*

We are silent for a moment.

Hettie takes up my hand.

We look each other in the eyes.

She says, "And he can give you a child."

"Yes," I say, though I can manage only a very small voice. She knows how much I want that as well. Need that. A child by way of my own body.

She bends to my hand. Kisses it. "I like this one," she says. "This boy-man of yours."

"I'm glad."

"I don't say that lightly."

"I know."

"But still, he can never know."

"Of course not," I say. "Three thousand years."

We understand what all this means for the two of us. Hettie says, in a composed voice, "I'm going west."

I cannot speak for a long moment so I can be as strong as she. Then I say, "You always wanted to be a cowboy."

She laughs softly.

And we slide down together from the headboard and begin to hold each other close for the last time.

I am empty.

I have no words to say. Not even to the dark.

God says, "You've spent too much of your life dwelling in words. Just abide with this for a time."

"I loved them both," I say. "Wife and son."

"As best you could," God says.

"I let them down," I say.

"There's quite a bit of that going around on your planet," God says.

I feel the need to say more. I feel myself trying to find words, as if I were sitting before my Oliver Model 9 on deadline.

"Stop," God says. "Just be still."

"Is that a commandment?"

"If need be."

So I heed Him.

I expect it to be difficult, but it's not.

I am still.

The room is still.

And then a voice.

Crying out.

Not carrying me to a memory. A cry present in the darkness but from beyond it.

And again, the cry. A man's voice.

Full of dread.

I know the voice.

Mr. Martin down the hall.

And I know what to do.

I sit up. I turn my body. I swing my legs off the side of the bed and ease myself down.

I have not done this by myself for a long while. They won't let me. But I can. *You're a wonder, Mr. Cunningham.* I am. Whenever Nurse Bocage rolls me out into the sunlight, she assists me to my feet and then I am fine with my two-wheel walker, just fine.

I grope for my walker now in the darkness.

I find it quickly, where it leans against the wall near the head of my bed.

I unfold it, lock it, set it before me.

And I go out into the hallway, lit for night in dim orange.

I look toward the front desk.

That scene is finished. The nurses are off to other wings, no doubt. The handyman has gone off duty. Bocage likely is in her office. Napping, I assume, after her wearying political debate.

From the other end of the hallway Mr. Martin is still audible. No more outcries. From this distance, just a muddle of anxious sounds.

I point the walker in his direction and I ply my way to his door.

A baseboard night-light strip is on and I can make out Mr. Martin in his bed, his torso slightly elevated.

He's talking about a fire engine. Talking to a spot high on the wall opposite his bed. He says, "It's stopped just up the street. Not even a block. Can't I go? Can't I see? Please. I'll keep back. What is it you think? That I'm going to run into the flames?"

Before I step in, I look at the identifier card by the door. EDWARD MARTIN.

I move into the room.

He knows.

He turns his face.

He shuts up about the fire engine.

I approach his bed.

"You," he says. "I thought you were up *there*." He turns his head a little, lifting his chin toward the spot on the wall he was talking to.

I sit down sideways on the edge of the bed, facing him the best I can.

He's focused intently now on my face. "But you're *here*," he says. "I'm glad. I'm so glad you're here. It's time. It's getting dark now, around the edges. It won't go away, the darkness."

"It's all right," I say. "It's night. This is your room at the nursing home. There's going to be some darkness."

And he says, "Please, Mama." Looking directly at me. Talking directly to me. He says it again, "Mama."

I say, "You're going to be all right. You should sleep now, Edward."

He draws a sharp breath. His eyes narrow at me.

I start to thrash around in my head. *What's the matter with him? Didn't I give him what he wants? Why am I here anyway? This isn't the first night he's had the dreads. Bocage or whoever has dealt with this before. Let* them *handle this.*

I'm backsliding. *Help me.* I think this to God, but I feel like I've left Him down the hallway.

And in a small, miserable voice, Mr. Martin says to me, "Have I been bad, Mama?"

I try to struggle back into the moment.

"Am I bad?" he cries.

I realize what's happened. I called him *Edward*. His mother formalized his name whenever he was in trouble.

I feel a surge of why I'm here.

I know what to do.

I say, "It's okay, Eddie. You're a good boy, Eddie."

He whimpers for a few moments in relief. But then he shifts. "Mama," he says, low, intense. "Help me. I'm dying."

Edward Martin is nearly ninety years old. He might be right about this.

"You're not going to die tonight," I say. "You've just had a bad dream."

His hand flails toward me.

I catch it.

"Help me," he cries. Seeing me, but pitching his voice as if I'm far off, down the street.

I hold his hand with both of mine.

"Mama," he says. Softly this time. "I'm afraid."

"I'm here beside you, Eddie," I say.

"I'm sorry I have to go away," he says.

"You've been a good boy," I say. "All your life. The best."

And he says, "I'm afraid."

I know what he needs now.

It's time for this.

For him.

For me.

I say, "I love you, my son."

I lean down.

I put my lips against his forehead.

And I kiss him.

I pull back just a little.

He closes his eyes.

I put my arms around him and pull him to me.

I sit there, holding him close.

He is calm now. He is breathing.

I hold him.

And then I cup the back of his head with my hand, and I whisper to him, "Sleep now, Eddie. You will wake in the morning. I promise."

I lay him back against the bed.

He does not open his eyes.

But he breathes on.

I gently disengage and pull away from Eddie Martin's bedside.

I go out of his room, and I start down the hallway with my walker.

I think that on this night *I* will have no one I can mistake for my mother.

But I am glad for Eddie.

As I draw within a few steps of the door to my room, I feel for the first time since I began to die that I am actually existing in real time: the emptied front desk ahead; Mr. Martin, who needed for me to make my own way to visit him tonight; his night-light, which reminds me now that mine would have been on for all this time if I'd been dying in something like a present moment.

So I arrive at my door expecting to actually see into a dimly night-lit room.

But the room is impenetrably dark.

Of course.

"So you're still there," I say.

"Yes," God says from within.

I wait.

He says, "You got your walker and went out on your own. Good for you. Come lie down now."

So I go in and feel my way to the bed and along it to its head, where I refold my walker and lean it against the wall. Of all things to scrupulously do under the circumstances.

"Indeed," God whispers in reply to my thought. "Climb on into bed," He says.

Which I do.

I start to thrash in my head again. Looking for words. More memories. More explanations.

I think, *I reported but I did not see. I cared but I did not do. I loved but I did not comprehend. I'm sorry for all of this, deeply, but I don't even know how to properly be sorry.*

God says, "Hush now. You found your way down the hall."

I feel Him draw near.

I suddenly understand: it's time to die.

I should be at peace. But I've lately had words in my head. Just words. Summarizing and abstracting words. And so I find myself unsettled.

And I hear myself say, "Mama."

And God says, "I'm here." In His own voice. What I've been hearing as a man's voice.

Who's He trying to kid?

"I know who you are," I say.

"Do you?"

"God. Not my mother. Though don't get me wrong. I loved her dearly. And thanks for trying to stand in. That was Loving God of you."

"It's a little more complex than that," God says.

"Then let's not pretend," I say. Sharply.

I suddenly hear myself. "I sound like I'm finally terrified, don't I?"

I do. I am.

"Yes," He says. "You do. You are."

"Me terrified," I say. "A fucking teenage killer." As if that were a refutation.

But my lying here plausibly talking to God would suggest that there's something yet to come after earthly death. Something for a teenage killer of a hundred men who after that became a profoundly oblivious man. Of course all that terrifies me.

Which God knows. He says, "I already told you we're square on that. No more words now. No more trying to figure it out."

There is movement.

A press of air.

And then I feel hands slide in behind me on the bed and I am lifted a little, one hand moving up to cup the back of my head.

And then, against my forehead, comes a touch.

A soft touch.

Lips.

And now a kiss. A lingering kiss.

Then a lifting away of that mouth.

The voice that has been near me all through my dying is suddenly much nearer, as near as those lips were a moment ago, and the voice says, "I'm your God. We love you."

And a faint brightening begins in the room. Slowly. Minutely. As if each molecule of air has its own latent luminosity and has now commenced to find its light.

And a face comes into focus hovering before me.

God's face.

It is the face of the multitudinous nurse from the outer lobby, with the dark eyes and the bun of hair.

But not for a nanosecond do I think I've been mistaken.

I know this is God.

"I know you for who you are," I say.

"That's a good sign," He says. "It's what I've lately come to expect from you."

And He bends near me once more and He kisses me on the forehead once more, and I close my eyes to the kiss in reciprocated love, as if it is Mama kissing me to sleep.